STABBING IN THE SENATE

STABBING IN THE SENATE

COLLEEN J. SHOGAN

A Worldwide Mystery®/April 2018

First published by Camel Press, an imprint of Coffeetown Enterprises, Inc.

ISBN-13: 978-1-335-45276-2

Copyright © 2015 by Colleen J. Shogan

All rights reserved. No part of this book may be used or reproduced in any manner whatsoever without the written permission of the publisher, except in the case of brief quotations embodied in critical articles and reviews. For permission please contact Coffeetown Enterprises, Inc., PO Box 70515, Seattle, WA 98127.

This is a work of fiction. Names, characters, places and incidents are either the product of the author's imagination or are used fictitiously, and any resemblance to actual persons, living or dead, business establishments, events or locales is entirely coincidental.

W❂RLDWIDE®

TORONTO • NEW YORK • LONDON
AMSTERDAM • PARIS • SYDNEY • HAMBURG
STOCKHOLM • ATHENS • TOKYO • MILAN
MADRID • WARSAW • BUDAPEST • AUCKLAND

Recycling programs
for this product may
not exist in your area.

Stabbing in the Senate

A Worldwide Mystery/April 2018

First published by Camel Press, an imprint of Coffeetown Enterprises, Inc.

ISBN-13: 978-1-335-50654-2

Acknowledgments

It's never easy to write a book. First and foremost, I would like to recognize publicly the role of my husband, Rob Raffety. I never thought I would or could write or publish a work of fiction. He encouraged me to finish the novel and persevere. My agent, Dawn Dowdle, believed in the concept of the book and writing a mystery series set in Washington, D.C. Her enthusiasm and optimism were instrumental.

My mother, Patricia "Joy" Shogan, loved mysteries and encouraged me to read them. I started with Encyclopedia Brown, the Hardy Boys, Nancy Drew, and Trixie Belden. She read Agatha Christie and *Ellery Queen Mystery Magazine*. I signed the contract for this book a few days before she passed away. I hope she's reading *Stabbing in the Senate* and enjoying it. Additionally, my father, brother, sister-in-law, in-laws, aunts, uncles, nieces, cousins, and co-workers listened to numerous updates on the manuscript and the publishing process. Thank you for your patience.

Marcy Gallo and Eileen Hunt Botting read an early draft of the manuscript and encouraged me to keep writing. A Sisters in Crime peer review group read portions of the book and offered insightful comments. Michael Garrett provided a crucial edit and helped a political scientist become a fiction writer. Susan Froetschel shared much-needed feedback at a pivotal point of the manuscript's development. Catherine Treadgold and Jennifer McCord at Camel Press were terrific editorial partners, patient and thorough. The Washington Independent Review of Books conference provided me with sage advice about the business of writing. Finally, I benefited from valuable tips and constant encouragement courtesy of the authors who attend the semi-annual Washington, D.C., writers' dinner held at Georgetown's Old Europe restaurant.

I especially want to acknowledge all the people I've worked with on Capitol Hill. Congressional staffers labor countless hours not to accumulate personal fame and fortune, but because they truly believe in their bosses, the promise of better public policy, and the fulfillment of representative government. Thanks for providing me with great memories and terrific stories to tell.

ONE

ASCENDING FROM THE underground depths of the Metro, I confronted the alabaster dome in the distance. The sight never failed to leave me awestruck. It was an imposing reminder of the city's fundamental purpose. New York City has the Empire State Building, Paris the Eiffel Tower, and Washington, D.C., the Capitol Rotunda. The stillness of morning on the Hill was a rare gift. Only a few ambitious politicos beat the nine o'clock cattle call summoning over 10,000 congressional staffers to their lairs.

A gentle breeze blew mist from Columbus Fountain across my face as I strode toward the landmark. Debilitating heat would descend in a few hours. People forget that our nation's capital was built on a swamp. Stately monuments sit where the marshes once stood, yet the climate in July is reminiscent of the original ecosystem that thrived for thousands of years prior to the ascendancy of the political muck.

I silently congratulated myself for being early to work, atypical for me. After crossing Upper Senate Park, I arrived at the Hart Senate Office Building. The police at the staff entrance glanced at my official identification badge, and I hustled toward the elevator. I was alone in Hart's vast marble atrium. The only other obstacle was Alexander Calder's massive industrial fifty-foot statue of steel mountains and clouds. Unlike law firms and the military, Congress didn't subscribe to the "early to bed, early to rise" axiom.

I exited the elevator on the sixth floor and mechanically made the left turn down the hallway. My destination was the office of Senator Lyndon Langsford, a prominent New England legislator with a recent penchant for ignoring his fellow Democratic partisans and voting his conscience. His newfound independence had staffers like me scrambling to explain his complicated politics. Reaching for the glass door, decorated with Langsford's nameplate and the requisite state and American flags, I discovered it was locked. Muttering a few choice four-letter words, I rummaged through my purse for the office key. I couldn't remember the last time I'd used it. I found it in a zippered pocket, stuck to an unwrapped piece of chewing gum.

It was eerie entering the suite in silence. Our office was normally a constant buzz of activity and noise. After locating the light switch, I headed to my cubicle. Private offices were reserved for senior staffers who had toiled for countless years on Capitol Hill. My "office" was a small, semi-walled compartment with little privacy. Since I considered myself a person with few secrets, working in the open wasn't much of a sacrifice.

Senator Langsford needed a memorandum I was supposed to have written yesterday about an Appropriations Committee hearing later in the week on the renewal of a mega defense contract. It was my job to make sure he was prepared for that hearing. Langsford was the only senator on the committee who hadn't announced his position. So far he had refrained from public comment. He needed to read the background memo this morning so we could talk about it later in the day. I had printed it out the night before and my immediate supervisor signed off on it, but I missed the early evening deadline for getting memos to the senator prior to his departure. Most senators, Langsford included, didn't read memos via email. The only option had been to get him the memo as early as possible this morning.

I unlocked my file cabinet drawer, deposited my purse inside, grabbed the memo from underneath a stack of papers, and headed toward his private office. I zipped by the desk of the senator's personal assistant, situated right outside his sanctum. Even Kara, right-hand keeper of the inviolable senatorial schedule, still hadn't made an appearance.

The senator's office door was ajar, and I barreled forward to position my memo on the top of his "to read" pile of papers. Staffers weren't supposed to enter the senator's office without a reason. Kara might turn the corner any moment. If I could just slip in and out unnoticed, this memo would be the first document he read when he arrived for work.

I glanced toward the sitting area. A hand rested on the arm of a regal chair. The chair, turned away from me, faced the windows and a beautiful view of the Capitol grounds. Royal screw up. I wasn't the only person in the office. Senator Langsford was already here! He always arrived through a private entrance, not the main door. I had infiltrated his office unannounced. There was no way I could back out of the office gracefully.

I cleared my throat and stammered awkwardly, "Senator Langsford, I'm sorry, sir. It's Kit Marshall, Senator. I didn't quite finish up the Appropriations hearing memo before you left last night. I wanted to put it in your inbox this morning so you could read it, and if you'd like, we could discuss it later today or whenever."

No response. After a minute, I asked, "Would you like me to put it on your desk?" I waved the memo back and forth.

Lyndon Langsford was a suave politician who rarely missed a beat. That was why I enjoyed working for him. Nothing fazed him. Persistent protesters, disgruntled constituents, slimy lobbyists, and aggressive political reporters—he handled all with ease. In my thirty years on the planet, I wondered if I would ever manage to exude a fraction of his panache. Yet I never felt self-conscious around him. I waited for him to say something polite to let me off the hook for my transgression.

Utter silence. Was he asleep? It was an odd time for a power nap. Beads of sweat trickled down my neck, saturating the collar of my blouse. Senator Langsford was well-mannered, often to the extreme. Had he decided to give me the cold shoulder this morning? The stillness was stifling.

I could just put the memo on his desk, sidle out the door, and pretend I had never spoken. But I would not be able to work at my desk for the rest of the day, thinking Langsford was upset with me.

"Senator, I'm sorry," I repeated. "I feel terrible for interrupting you. Should I leave the memo on your desk so you can read it?"

I'm not sure how long I stood there. A few seconds seemed like an eternity. I noticed there was *no physical reaction at all* to my question. That was weird. If he was irritated, his body language should have indicated annoyance. He had to be asleep.

As I approached tentatively, I noticed crimson drops

of blood on the thick carpeting of his office. His head was thrown back, and two vacant eyes stared at me. Lyndon Langsford wasn't giving me the cold shoulder. He was dead.

TWO

I STUMBLED AROUND the armchair to look at Langsford straight on. A stainless steel replica of an Army attack helicopter protruded out of his chest. Dribbles of blood were oozing onto the propeller blades. It was a ghastly sight—a senior senator stabbed with a miniature prototype of a helicopter he had proudly helped fund for years with federal dollars. I wanted to run, but every muscle in my body was tense.

My next move was stupid. The only defense for my actions was a desperate belief that Senator Langsford had survived. I had watched too many *Matlock* reruns.

A burst of adrenaline propelled me into action. I grabbed the Apache model with my right hand. Pulling with all my strength, the helicopter came out of his chest more easily than I anticipated. I fell backward to the floor.

At this precise moment, Kara appeared. She saw me on the floor with a bloody model helicopter in my hands and looked puzzled. When she moved closer and spotted Senator Langsford dead in his chair, she screamed.

After a few high-pitched squeals, I realized she wasn't screaming for medical help. She was shrieking because she thought I was the killer. "Help me, there's a murderer in here, and she's killed the senator! Somebody help me!" Before I could explain to her what had happened, she ran out of the office.

I picked myself up off the ground and followed, still carrying the helicopter. The senator's press secretary and a few other people were gathering outside the office. The group stepped back once they spotted the bloodstained Apache in my hand.

Kara backed herself into the corner of her workspace, her fingers furiously punching the phone number for the Capitol Hill Police. She squawked into the phone and stared at me defiantly. The senator had been murdered, and the woman who killed him was still in the office.

Kara was the glue that held our office together. If a congressional office was dysfunctional, the source of woe was often situated in one of two places—with the member of Congress or the scheduler. The best staff could do little to mask an inept, frantic member of Congress. The most intelligent, dedicated member of Congress could accomplish little with an unhinged, disorganized scheduling assistant.

Kara was a terrific employee, though known for her dramatic flair in the office and her tendency to rule with an iron fist. New staffers feared her. She guarded Senator Langsford's appointments with extreme care. She was his lifeline, and that explained her meltdown. Each staffer in the office had a personal connection with Senator Langsford, but Kara knew as much as could be known without sharing physical intimacy. She had internalized every one of his preferences, from the type of breakfast bar he ate in the morning to his policy positions. Seeing his body had sent her over the edge.

As I took a few steps toward Kara, she yelled to a young male intern across the room, "Tackle her now! She killed the senator with that helicopter!"

Sam, barely out of college, had earbuds firmly in

place and didn't hear Kara's order. His bewilderment gave me a chance to get a word in edgewise.

"Kara, I didn't kill him. I found Langsford in his office right before you walked in. I tried to save him!"

But Kara didn't wait for me to move closer. Lunging, she knocked the murder weapon out of my hand. It fell to the ground, breaking in half.

Two Capitol Hill Police officers stormed the office suite with guns drawn and commanded, "Put your hands where we can see them, and step out of the office immediately." Kara and I obliged, walking slowly out of the office. With blood on my hands, I was obviously the more likely culprit, and the officer immediately slapped handcuffs on me and pulled me into the hallway.

Out of the corner of my eye, I saw my best friend and office mate arrive for the day, clutching her Kate Spade bag, her blond bob perfect and her makeup flawless as ever. Meg's mouth hung open, as though gaping in shock but also forming a question. I just grimaced weakly, cutting her off before she could say a word.

"Meg, Senator Langsford is dead. I found him in his office. Call Doug and tell him I need one of his family's lawyers to sort this all out."

She couldn't quite process the news, but her hands obeyed. She grabbed her BlackBerry from her purse and typed furiously. Doug was my main squeeze. For many years we had an on-again/off-again relationship. Right now we were in the "on" phase and lived together. His family had considerable connections, and he could find a good criminal attorney if necessary.

Before anyone could ask what had happened, my immediate boss, Matt Rocker, arrived on the scene. With one of his legislative assistants crying and another in handcuffs, he probably thought he was in D.C. district court instead of the Senate office where he had worked for the past ten years.

I couldn't look Matt in the eyes. Although the senator's legislative staff argued incessantly about policy priorities and who got more precious time and resources for their assigned initiatives, we universally admired Matt and enjoyed working for him. Our chief of staff wasn't so certain about hiring me, but Matt had stood up for me. Standing in front of him in handcuffs compounded the misery of the current situation.

Matt was a slight guy in his late forties. His hair was sort of bushy, and he constantly tried to push it out of his eyes. It was a nervous habit. If Matt thought the senator was about to make the wrong decision on a vote or undertake a politically dangerous line of questioning at a hearing, he would tug at his hair, trying to get it to lie flat on his head. Now he was almost pulling it out of his scalp.

Matt gestured toward my handcuffs. "Are those absolutely necessary? Kit Marshall is a valued staffer in this office, and I doubt, with the police presence, she's a flight risk."

"Sorry, sir." The police officer shook his head. "This is a murder investigation. This woman was found at the scene holding what could be the murder weapon."

I tried to protest, but Matt cut me off. "Kit, stay quiet for now. This will be sorted out quickly. I have no idea what happened here, but I need to find Lucinda and Mandy." Matt was referring to our chief of staff, Lucinda Porter, and our press secretary, Mandy Lippman.

Lucinda was his boss and had been friends with the
senator for almost twenty years.

Above all else, Lyndon Langsford was a politician
and therefore was often guided by mutually beneficial
relationships. Lucinda knew the right people and had
good connections. Every chief of staff on the Hill recognized Lucinda, and she received invitations to A-
list Beltway soirees without fail. Furthermore, she had
a Rolodex full of donors with big pockets. Profound
policy ideas could come from people like Matt, Meg,
and me, but politics is about "who you know," and everyone knew Lucinda.

Staff understood why the senator kept Lucinda
around, yet the same couldn't be said for Mandy. Press
secretaries often cultivated tenuous relationships with
the policy gurus in a congressional office. Policy people cared about passing legislation and press folks cared
about selling their boss's persona to voters, and rarely
the twain shall meet. That said, Mandy was beyond
unpopular in our office. In a nutshell, she was a typical Washington cliché, hunting to work for anyone she
thought potentially powerful. If Langsford didn't meet
her standards, she would switch jobs in a heartbeat.

Langsford had recently fostered a reputation as a
political maverick. Nearing the twilight of his career,
he had begun to buck the party leaders in the Senate,
taking several controversial stances. Due to his unpredictable behavior, he had become a media darling and
a favorite on the Sunday morning talk shows. Mandy
showed up soon after Langsford's political stock had
started to rise. She was more than an opportunist. The
whole city was full of opportunists. Distaste for Mandy

proliferated because she didn't bother to mask her un-principled ambitions.

Not that I wasn't ambitious, too. Besides possessing raw political intuition that in my line of work passed for street smarts, the primary reason for my success on Capitol Hill was that I implicitly understood one basic fact. I worked for a senator, but I wasn't a senator. It seemed like an obvious concept, one too many people on the Hill failed to grasp. The problem with thinking of yourself as a quasi-member of Congress is that from time to time, your boss is going to take your advice and essentially flush it down the toilet. I understood that Senator Langsford made the final decision. The sooner a staffer realized how it works, the better.

That's what bugged me about Mandy. Pretty much everyone else who worked for Langsford had a "do-good" look in his or her eyes. He was famous for hiring people with small egos and a strong work ethic. I never figured out how Mandy had slipped through the cracks. Somehow she had managed to pull the wool over the senator's eyes. Unless...perhaps Langsford could see perfectly well, given she was a silhouette size-four red-head who sauntered around the office in stiletto heels and skirts stretched tautly over her toned behind.

A moment later a chunky, middle-aged guy with a bald spot entered the hallway and checked in with the uniformed officers. They nodded and pointed in my direction. As the only person standing around in hand-cuffs, I was hard to miss.

The man walked over and introduced himself. "Hello, Kit. My name is Detective O'Halloran. I understand you have some information about what happened here. I need to get a statement from you, and the sooner, the better. In about ten minutes this story is going to leak. So how about we sit in a conference room here, and you tell me what you know?"

I hesitated. I wasn't a lawyer, but on television shows, the dumb suspects never ask for legal counsel and usually end up saying something incriminating. But I was innocent and had nothing to hide. One side of my brain said to take him up on his offer so I could clear my name. The other side said I needed to wait to hear from my boyfriend and the lawyer he would soon be dispatching.

If I could just get someone to listen to me for more than two seconds, I could probably clear up the confusion on my own. I needed a moment to collect my thoughts. That was impossible with crime scene investigators rapidly arriving, along with every other uniformed cop who could possibly fit into our office suite.

"Detective, I'd like to tell you what happened," I told O'Halloran. "But first, I need to use the ladies room."

O'Halloran sighed and fixed a steely stare on me. "Rodriguez, come over here," he called out. "Escort Ms. Marshall to the nearest women's facilities on this corridor. Do not, I repeat, do not let her out of your sight." He pointed at two male cops. "Randolph and Jenkins, secure the perimeter of the restroom while Rodriguez enters with Ms. Marshall." Never had going to the bathroom been such a production.

Officer Rodriguez placed her hand on my arm to guide me out of the foyer toward the office exit. As we headed down the hall, Meg walked toward us, still intent on her BlackBerry. As she passed, she whispered, "Doug's on it. Don't worry." She kept walking without looking up from her phone. Damn, she was good.

I sure hoped Meg was right. The enormity of the events of this morning was beginning to sink in. Senator Langsford was dead. The world I had known for the past four years had vanished.

The only thing worse than having a murdered boss was being named the prime suspect.

THREE

I GLANCED QUICKLY in the restroom mirror. My hair was a mess and perspiration had ruined the makeup I had hastily applied earlier this morning. I saw no way to fix my coiffure with hands in cuffs.

Instead, I took several deep yoga breaths to restore a modicum of calm to my brain. The fog started to lift, and an immediate plan of action materialized. My answers to the police would be brief and honest. This was a clear instance of the less said, the better.

I had followed the police officer out of the bathroom and was headed toward the office when a swarm descended on me. Flashes of light blazed across the dimly lit hallway, and someone shoved a microphone close to my mouth. Frowning, I blinked to avoid the bright flickers. When my eyes adjusted, I found myself in the middle of an old-fashioned Washington, D.C., press assault. Questions flew in staccato rapid fire:

"What's your name?"

"Why did you murder Senator Langsford?"

"Are you having an affair with the senator?"

"How many years have you worked for him?"

"What weapon did you use?"

How did the press learn so quickly a salacious story was brewing? I might have been delusional, because I thought I caught a glimpse of Matt Drudge in the crowd that assaulted me.

My police escort whisked me away quickly, but not before the damage had been done. Maybe if I could clear up what happened with the police, no one would run with the story. That hope was delusional, too.

Back in the safety of the office, Vivian, the senator's wife—now his widow—had arrived. Her gray hair was perfectly styled and she was dressed in an impeccably tailored suit, matching handbag in tow. Vivian was a hard woman to understand. Always polite with the senator's staff, she had given us no obvious reason to dislike her, but we still did. She wasn't overtly interested in legislation or policy, but was invested, literally and figuratively, in her husband's political career. For more than twenty years she had been the wife of a senator. Independently wealthy, she had funded Langsford's initial run for elected office and had kept the money flowing ever since.

The rumor around the office was she wanted Langsford to finish his current term in office, retire, and then accept a lucrative job with a lobbying firm on K Street. Vivian had played her part well during the many years of public service. Now, she wanted a big payout.

Langsford had given no indication he was willing to grant Vivian her wish. All senators possessed a healthy ego, and Langsford was no exception. The prospect of growing the family fortune did not motivate him. In fact, he relished his new role as a political maverick. He also liked the attention it attracted. Sources within the office reported that if he thought he could win reelection, then he would run for office again, whether Vivian liked it or not.

I took a long look at Vivian. Never rumpled, she always looked as if she'd just stepped off the cover of

Vogue. Now was no exception. It took a moment to register what was bothering me. Her face showed expected signs of strain; her brow was appropriately furrowed. Sniffling, she used a monogrammed "V" handkerchief to dab at her eyes and nose. The slight tearing and congestion might be attributed just as well to summer allergy season as to the unexpected death of her husband. Studying her closely, I decided Vivian was trying to muster up a façade of sadness.

Nobody else was looking at her. Instead, everyone was looking my way as O'Halloran led me into one of our conference rooms. The place had quickly morphed into a communications and operations center to handle the crisis. The Capitol Hill police captain on duty joined O'Halloran for the interview. Before I had much time to consider Vivian's apparent charade, Detective O'Halloran began hitting me with questions. My head was pounding. I pleaded for coffee.

O'Halloran sighed and narrowed his eyes as if to express his disapproval of spoiled Capitol Hill staffers. First I had asked to go to the bathroom. Now I wanted coffee. To put the situation into perspective, I reminded him I was talking without the benefit of a lawyer.

The captain nodded. Before long, a "Lovin' Lyndon" campaign mug was placed in front of me, and another officer removed my handcuffs. I massaged my wrists, eagerly picked up my coffee, and took a long sip. O'Halloran waited politely, then read me my rights and asked me to recount exactly what happened, for the record this time. Despite my earlier resolve, I'd never considered brevity my strong suit. I explained in detail the events of the morning. Both O'Halloran and the captain wrote in their notebooks.

O'Halloran asked the inevitable question: "What possessed you to remove the murder weapon from the senator's body?"

Having been a mystery reader since the second grade, I felt like a fool. My answer was simple. A tear running down my face, I said, "I thought maybe I could save him. I'm sorry."

O'Halloran asked me to stay put while he talked to his boss. As the minutes dragged on, I noticed I was the only staffer inside the conference room, now filled with uniformed police officers and law enforcement types in business suits, likely from the FBI or some other federal law enforcement agency. There were so many conflicting law enforcement jurisdictions in Washington, D.C., that it was hard to keep them all straight.

A few minutes later, O'Halloran returned without the captain and said I was free to leave the conference room as soon as I wrote out my statement and signed it. My story had apparently checked out, since the Senate's public corridors were recorded on video cameras. Video recorded my entry into the office building less than ten minutes before Kara had called the police.

"The timeline is problematic," admitted the detective. "If you were our perp, this would be a slam dunk, and I could plan on having the semblance of a normal life in the foreseeable future, but the medical examiner says the temperature of the body tells us the senator died at least an hour before you arrived. So you're free to go." I breathed a sigh of relief. O'Halloran must have heard my sigh. He added quickly, "For now."

I stood and turned toward the door, but O'Halloran wasn't finished. "Ms. Marshall, do you have any plans to leave the D.C. area in the next several days?"

I shook my head and answered automatically, "The Senate is in session, and staff must stay in town when the Senate is legislating."

"Don't leave town until we get to the bottom of this. Do you understand?" I nodded and walked out the door.

After the session with O'Halloran, I had a new worry. I was effectively unemployed and my days in the Senate were numbered. Capitol Hill jobs had coveted perks, yet one of the biggest downsides was a complete lack of job security. I served at the pleasure of Senator Lyndon Langsford. Most staff terminations followed after a failed reelection bid. Murder, while outside the norm, also killed the job.

I returned to an office suite in chaos. Some people were crying; others were stoic. No one sat at desks or cubicles, and the staff was not alone. Police filled the office, conducting interviews or chatting with one another. Controlled pandemonium was one way to describe it. I moved through the din to reach my cubicle.

On my way I found my pal Meg, who grabbed me by the arm.

"Kit, I've been trying to get confirmation from Doug that one of his family's lawyers can come and help. But he's at the vet with Clarence, and he can't access the phone numbers he needs. Are you okay? What happened?"

I heaved myself into my ergonomically approved chair and put my head in my hands. Thank goodness Clarence, our considerably overweight beagle, had distracted Doug. If Doug had sent a lawyer immediately, I might not have been able to get away with just an interview in our conference room. Instead, my next stop would have been downtown for a full-scale interrogation.

I recounted the story, and my best friend listened intently. One of Meg's finest virtues, besides her impeccable taste in fashion, was her ability to remain unruffled under pressure. I finished my tale, and she whistled softly. "Do you think they believed it? Or are you still a suspect?"

There were some obvious problems with my status as a suspect. First, I had no discernible motive. Second, as the detective had said, the timing was off. Nonetheless, I had emerged from his private office with the murder weapon in my hand. That might be hard for the police to forget.

I shrugged. "They can't believe I did it; the evidence doesn't support it. But they may think I'm involved somehow. Let's face it. None of us is going to rest easy until they find the person who did this. What if it's someone we know?"

Meg nodded. I dug in my purse and found my hand mirror. "Here," I said, holding it out to her. Her makeup was streaked from the tears she shed after learning about the murder. "Friends don't let friends look smudged."

"Oh no," she said, using a tissue and a cup of water to repair the damage.

We had met four years ago when Langsford had been in a tough reelection fight. We both worked on the campaign and had spent a lot of time together marching in parades, visiting senior centers, knocking on doors, dialing for dollars, sharing crappy motel rooms, and indulging in unhealthy fast food. Since then we had worked together in the Senate office. We both knew this was the end of an era.

"Excuse me, I'm trying to work," said a whiny male voice. We instinctively recoiled. The interruption came from the staffer who sat directly next to my cubicle in the rear of the office, Trevor.

In many ways, working in a congressional office was like returning to high school, or even kindergarten. There were popular people and not-so-popular people, and Trevor fit into the latter category.

He was a skinny, short guy with mousy brown hair who looked more like he should be learning to drive rather than working in a Senate office. As far as we knew, Trevor had no life outside work. He was extremely smart, and the long hours he put in had won him favor with the senator and our boss, Matt.

Meg was the self-appointed social organizer of the office, coordinating happy hour sessions and other events. Much to her surprise, Trevor always rebuffed her invitations. Her numerous attempts to lure him out of the office had consistently failed and his lack of interest in her escapades aggravated her. Meg was the office social butterfly, and Trevor was her lost cause.

She turned toward him. "Trevor, our boss was murdered today and we'll be out of work in a few weeks. What could you possibly be working on?"

Trevor wrinkled his nose in distaste. "You may not know that even with our boss deceased, *Megan*, our work continues until the governor selects a replacement. Our constituents deserve our undivided attention." He looked curtly at her from behind horn-rimmed glasses with superior disdain. His use of her full name made the insult worse. "If you can move your chair, I need to get to the printer to retrieve the document I have been working on." He gave us a curt nod. Meg rolled her eyes and squeezed in closer to me to clear the aisle.

Meg turned toward me, lowered her voice, and jerked her thumb in Trevor's direction. "If you ask me, the police should take a hard look at that one."

"He's a nutcase," I murmured.

"Our boss was murdered today, and all he cares about is a memo. Who is he writing a memo for, anyway? The senator isn't even alive!"

Trevor was a nuisance, and I despised sitting next to him. Meg had asked for the cubicle next to me a long time ago and Matt had refused. I couldn't blame him. Sitting next to each other, we would have accomplished little. As a result I got stuck with Trevor, who had all the personality of an Elmer's Glue Stick. "Do you really think Trevor could kill anyone?" I asked. "Besides, why would he do it?"

Meg narrowed her eyes and whispered, "I heard Langsford hasn't been interested in Trevor's ideas lately. Trevor wanted Langsford to wage a coup within the party. Langsford felt he could do more by pushing the envelope but staying within the fold."

The rumor was in line with Trevor's character. Besides shunning all social advances, Trevor drifted outside of the office's political mainstream. Sitting next to him, I had overheard his frustration over disagreements with the senator. But could Trevor get angry enough to kill?

I glanced at his empty cubicle. Nothing was on his desk except a few neatly stacked folders, two pens placed side by side, and exactly five paperclips.

I wondered if I had been sharing office space with a killer. But if not Trevor, then who did kill Lyndon Langsford, and why?

FOUR

MY PHONE STARTED RINGING, shaking me from my thoughts. I checked the caller ID. It was Doug, who must be wondering if I had been arrested. In the midst of the pandemonium, I had forgotten to let him know the lawyer wasn't necessary, at least right now. I picked up the phone.

"Kit, are you okay? What's going on? CNN is reporting Senator Langsford was murdered this morning. While Clarence and I were at the vet I got messages from Meg saying you might need a lawyer." Doug's voice sounded frantic. My brilliant boyfriend, extremely accomplished for someone in his early thirties, had recently received tenure from the history department at Georgetown. His first book on early American presidents had earned favorable reviews in top scholarly journals. Academia was the perfect fit for Doug. He didn't like the unpredictable and appreciated routine more than anything. Something like this was bound to throw him for a loop. If I didn't calm him down, he'd need a stiff shot of whisky and a Xanax.

"Everything's fine. Don't worry. But that's right. The senator is dead." Saying those words out loud made me choke back a sob. "He was murdered. But I talked to the police and I've been released, at least for the time being."

"Why would the police consider you a suspect?" Anxiety escalated in his voice.

There was no way around it; I had to tell Doug I'd been the one to find the senator. I braced myself for his reaction. "Well, I walked into his office this morning and discovered his body."

His voice roared. "You what?"

"It gets worse. I also pulled the murder weapon out of him." Better he heard it from me than read about it later in the *Washington Post*.

He was silent, which wasn't exactly what I expected. It was too much for Doug to process at once. "Doug, are you still on the line?"

Finally, he said quietly, "Yes, I'm here. Are you sure I shouldn't call my father and have a lawyer come to the office to meet you?"

I paused. Doug came from a wealthy New England family with deep roots and strong political ties. I already had a complex that his connections had helped me get the job with Langsford. It was inevitable his family would find out I had stumbled across the body. Hopefully, that revelation could be delayed as long as possible, and in the meantime, the police would find the real killer.

"No, I'm sure the police will find who did this quickly. I mean, you can't just murder a United States Senator in a congressional office building and get away with it, right?"

The line went silent again for a moment. Doug finally said, "I guess you're right. It's not like you can just carry a knife or gun into the building."

He had a good point. Since the era of terrorist threats and mass shootings, the United States Capitol had been on lockdown. Everyone who entered the Senate office buildings had to go through a security scanner. The police officers operating the scanners were vigilant. A few months ago, Kara had attempted to bring in a knife to cut the huge cake the office had bought for Langsford's birthday. She was stopped at the entrance and detained until Lucinda came to her rescue. The police kept the utensil, and we had to cut the cake with a plastic knife instead.

Carrying out a premeditated murder was complicated. A weapon or firearm was out of the question. Senators could sometimes bypass security when they arrived from the parking garage, but anyone accompanying senators, including staff and spouses, had to pass through the scanner.

Maybe someone had argued with Senator Langsford, and seeing a sharp object handy, had stabbed him in the heat of the moment.

Kara interrupted, leaning over my desk. She whispered, "Matt wants to see you, pronto."

I nodded. "Listen, I have to go, Doug. My boss needs to talk to me. I'll call you when I find out anything more. In the meantime, don't worry. I have everything under control."

I could sense Doug's furrowed brows over the phone. "I was afraid you were going to say that. Please, Kit, don't do anything stupid. Let the police do their job so they can find the person who did this. Remember, chances are if Senator Langsford knew the person who killed him and the murder took place in his Senate office, it's likely someone you knew too."

I shuddered as I hung up the phone. He was right. I had worked for Langsford for four years and knew most of the major players in his political world. Had an insider ended the senator's life?

Walking down the hall, I glanced inside Lucinda's office. Her face was red and puffy, and tears streamed down her mature face. If Vivian wasn't bawling, Lucinda was certainly making up for her lack of waterworks. Her phone headset was on and her Rolodex in front of her. As the chief of staff, Lucinda had the unenviable task of calling the senator's closest associates to let them know personally about his death. She wouldn't beat the cable news reporting the murder, but the senator's long-term friends and donors deserved to be personally notified.

I knocked, then cracked open Matt's office door. "You wanted to see me?"

Matt seemed to have aged about a decade since this morning. Judging from the dishevelment of his mane, a record-breaking amount of hair tugging had taken place in the past hour. Matt had known the senator since his first campaign for office. This was an emotional blow. Also, if Trevor was right, Matt had to figure out how the senator's office would continue to function until the governor appointed a replacement.

Matt motioned for me to sit. "I hear that despite emerging from the senator's office with the murder weapon in your hand, you're no longer being detained." He managed a small, wry smile.

"According to Detective O'Halloran, I'm not supposed to leave town," I said. "I'm sorry. I probably caused you even more trouble this morning than you were already handling."

He waved his hands in earnest denial. "I'm glad you're okay and you weren't the second victim."

The possibility hadn't occurred to me. If I had arrived earlier, I might have stumbled across the perpetrator. The detective said the senator was probably killed about an hour before my discovery of the body. I racked my brain to access knowledge of forensics from television shows. That timeline was a crude crime-scene estimate. The coroner would confirm the time of death within an hour, give or take. I could have come close to spotting the killer, especially if the person had stayed in the office for any length of time after the murder. But I had passed no one in the hallway or the building before entering the office. Nothing stuck out. With security cameras monitoring the entrance to the building, I wondered, how had the killer escaped detection this morning?

Matt seemed to have something else on his mind besides celebrating the fact I hadn't been killed. I waited.

He shifted uncomfortably in his seat. "Kit, there's something you should know. You probably haven't had a chance to turn on your computer." I had printed the memo for the senator the night before. All I had done this morning was unlock my file cabinet drawer underneath my desk and head toward the senator's office.

"No, I haven't even logged on."

He hesitated and gave his hair another tug. "Pull your chair up and take a look at the news reports." Matt turned his computer monitor around so I could read it. My jaw dropped. A color photograph of me in handcuffs appeared, with the headline STAFFER LEAD SUSPECT IN SENATOR'S DEATH.

FIVE

ONCE I COULD SPEAK, I asked Matt which news outlets had reported the story.

He sighed. "Which hasn't?"

The Capitol Hill newspaper, infamously known as *Roll Call*, had probably started the stampede. I had seen their lead photographer among the crowd of reporters surrounding me earlier. The *Drudge Report* had picked it up, which meant the story had gone viral in less than five minutes. It didn't matter what the police had said in the brief statement released thirty minutes later. *Politico, The Hill, The Washington Post, The Daily Caller*—you name it. Every media outlet led with the photo of me in cuffs. There was no escape. The entire Washington press corps viewed me as the lead suspect in the murder of a powerful United States Senator. My stomach lurched.

Matt poured me a cup of water and sat next to me. "Listen, it could be worse. Everyone here knows you didn't kill Langsford. This will get cleared up. As soon as the police find the real murderer, you'll have had your fifteen minutes of fame and that's it." He smacked his hands together. "And then, presto, you're back to being another faceless staffer on Capitol Hill." He chuckled. Matt was right about the brief interlude with notoriety, but anxiety over future job prospects on Capitol Hill fluttered in my stomach. Avoiding arrest was the top priority, but the prospect of months of unemployment terrified me.

"Thanks, Matt. You really know how to cheer a girl up."

He put his arm around me and gave a little squeeze. "I've got your back."

Just when I'd started to feel a little better about my predicament, the press secretary Mandy barged into Matt's office. She looked like hell. Her shoulder-length auburn hair was tangled, and her blouse, instead of being neatly tucked in, was half pulled out, wrinkles spilling over her pencil-straight skirt. The press had endless questions about Langsford's murder and office politics. From her perspective, it was the equivalent of a press tsunami.

Mandy peered at me with pure revulsion. "Just the person I'm looking for. Not only do I have to deal with the fact that the senator was murdered, but I also have to explain why his legislative assistant couldn't have murdered him."

I stayed silent. Great. Obviously Mandy would not be jumping to my defense against the media.

Her rage intensified. "I mean, did you have to pull the helicopter out of his chest? Do you know what a nightmare that is to explain?"

"I was trying to save him. That's what you should tell people. I thought he might still be alive."

Mandy held up her hands as if balancing a scale. One side tipped heavily and she scoffed, "Let me think. Is that little detail going to compete with a photo of you in handcuffs?"

She faced Matt. "I can't answer questions about our

office paramedic. Until you come up with a statement, I'm saying we have no comment."

She turned back to me. "I work for the senator and not you. Get your boyfriend and his family to do your PR."

Mandy wasn't my friend, yet her scathing words hit me hard. She was throwing me to the Washington wolves. I looked at Matt, who had listened to the exchange with a raised eyebrow.

Matt stood and faced her. "You don't have the authority to make a decision like that, Mandy. We won't abandon our colleague at a time like this. We both know Kit is innocent."

Mandy cleared her throat and pointed at me for emphasis. "I know no such thing. As I said, I don't work for her. I work for the senator, and that's my priority."

Matt looked puzzled. "I'm sorry to break this to you, but none of us work for Lyndon Langsford anymore. He's dead. Officially, we're United States Senate employees waiting for the governor to appoint a successor. Your diatribe about working for the senator might have worked, but only when he was alive."

As Mandy huffed and headed for the door, Matt called for her to stop. "Your immediate supervisors, until further notice, are Lucinda and me. If press calls come in about Kit, you set the record straight. We're fully supportive of our staff at this difficult time. Do you understand?"

Mandy straightened her skirt and managed a fake, weak smile. "Yes, sir. I'll give those calls my absolute attention." She left the office.

Matt glanced at me. "Well, that settles that. Go back to your desk, Kit. It's a media circus outside. Stay here for a while. We'll figure out a way to get you home later on. For now, I think it's best if we all lie low."

I thanked him. "I'm lucky to have you as a boss." On my way back to my desk, I passed the recycling bin. Our office had "gone green" recently. Senator Langsford had been a strong supporter of the environment and eagerly signed his staff up for every recycling and eco-friendly project run on the Capitol grounds. Our lights were motion sensitive and we relied on filtered tap water instead of bottles. Automatic thermostats controlled office heat and air conditioning.

The lid of the recycling bin was off-kilter. I stopped to straighten the lid and refasten it to the bin. But a piece of paper was stuck, preventing the lid from attaching to the bin. I pulled the paper and was surprised to see my memo, the one I had carried into Langsford's office earlier today.

The police would not have allowed anyone to clean up Senator Langsford's office already. Then why was it in the recycling bin? I closed my eyes as I forced myself to visualize the details of this morning. When I walked into his office, the memo was in my hands. I hadn't placed it on his desk. I pulled the model helicopter out of his chest with my right hand. At that point, the memo was in my left hand. After falling backward, I encountered Kara. Then I stumbled out of the senator's office and into Kara's adjacent office area.

Somewhere along the way, I'd dropped the memo.

Maybe Kara recycled it, thinking it was trash that had fallen in her office. But she was meticulous and wouldn't discard any paper that had the remote chance of being important. Also, the senator archived all his official paperwork, including policy memos written by staff. As his personal assistant, Kara certainly would have wanted to preserve what might have been the last memo for Senator Langsford.

I decided to take a detour to find Kara and ask her myself. I glanced out a window. It was beautiful, without a cloud in the sky, a typical summer day in Washington. The city was past the rainstorm season and in the "hot and humid" phase that could last several months. It looked like ideal weather for a run, but any jogger setting foot on the Mall at this hour would suffer a heatstroke. I wished with all my heart that I could be outside, running free toward the Lincoln Memorial, far from Capitol Hill, the murder, and all my problems.

Instead, I entered Kara's office. Her workspace was usually the model for serenity and order, every paper and folder in its proper place. Now, everything was strewn about on her desk as if a tornado had touched down.

Kara still looked professional, despite the disruptions. She always dressed in a slightly offbeat manner, without pushing the hipster attire too far. Today, she had on a stylish purple suit with a pleated skirt. A small bow in her black pixie hair completed the ensemble. Dark tights, Mary Janes, and carefully accented makeup gave her a funky, career-chic look.

Her desk phone rang, and she ignored it. Instead, she focused on a cellphone call. She politely explained that funeral arrangements hadn't been finalized, clicked the phone shut, and turned to me.

"Well, you certainly look less menacing than earlier this morning. You know, when you had a murder weapon in your hand and waved it at me?"

I was relieved. Unlike Mandy, Kara was trying to

bring a little levity to the stressful situation. "Yeah, I know. It was dumb, and we were both scared. And sharp, bloody objects aren't good accessories this season."

"Touché. What can I do for you?"

"I noticed this memo in the recycling bin." I showed her the memo to Senator Langsford on the upcoming defense contract renewal. "I was about to give it to Senator Langsford when...um...well, you know."

I didn't want to say "I found him murdered" to Kara. She was upset about losing the senator. She had worked as his assistant for over five years.

"Is that why you were in his office?" Kara asked. "I wondered why. You never get here early. So you wanted to give him this memo, huh?"

"Right. I must have dropped it in his office. I just don't understand how it got into the recycling bin."

She had bigger problems and shook her head. "Beats me. This place is complete chaos. I've had everyone in here, from the police to the FBI. Even Senator Regan was here earlier. And that annoying Carter Power lobbyist, Jeff Prentice. I admit, I won't miss him much..." her voice trailed off.

My mind raced. I wanted to make sure Kara hadn't thrown away the memo by accident. "So, maybe you put the memo into the recycling bin? To tidy up the place before Mrs. Langsford arrived?"

She frowned. "Listen, you know I would never put a memo into the garbage. That's against office protocol. Besides, I have other worries this morning besides cleaning up this place."

I offered her the paper. "Do you want the memo for the archives?"

Kara tapped her fingers on the desk and considered my question. "No, I don't think so. Not if Senator Langsford never received it. It's not part of his legislative history. If he had received it last night and read it, I would take it for the archive. But since he was…" she paused a second to clear her throat, "deceased before you could give it to him, it's not really his memo, is it?"

I wasn't certain about her logic, but a voice in my head told me to hold on to the memo. Matt's handwritten initials were on the hard copy. It was proof he'd cleared it for the senator and we'd agreed on the suggested course of action.

The atmosphere in the office was still hectic. I looked across the hallway and into our office's large conference room, where at least ten police officers huddled. A few examined file folders, others talked back and forth, and several looked downright bored. I thought about my picture online, the image being disseminated exponentially at this very moment.

I needed to be alone and think. A lot was at stake. I might have a few more days working in the Senate office, at least until the governor appointed a successor. New senators, even a temporary appointment, would want to bring in their own staff. In other words, I would be out of a job soon. The most valuable commodity on the Washington, D.C., job market was a professional reputation. I had worked hard for Senator Langsford and had my share of contacts on Capitol Hill. Nonetheless, even a hint that I was a suspect in the murder of my boss, however wrongheaded the notion, wouldn't enhance my job prospects.

To make matters worse, my brief foray into the limelight would embarrass Doug. He was a prominent professor at Georgetown and had just started going on television as a historical commentator for the multitude of talk shows. He was young, photogenic, newly tenured, and an expert on American history, which made him the ideal news show guest. My status as a murder suspect would not help him, and it could be devastating, both to him and our relationship. We had been through our share of challenges—finding jobs in the same city, learning to share an apartment, compromising on our priorities. Dealing with infamy would be the ultimate test.

On top of it all, there was the delicate subject of Doug's family. They traced their history back to the Massachusetts Bay Colony. His great-grandfather, a proud Winthrop Society member, started a prominent law firm in Boston, still employing many of his male descendants, along with the women in the current generation. Doug inherited the smarts, but not the desire to become a lawyer. Even though he was a wildly successful historian by any academic standards, his father had never accepted his son's career choice. He was devastated Doug didn't study law and wouldn't join the firm. Doug was close to "black sheep" status. The worst thing I could do was to bring dishonor upon his family. Those ski trips to Killington over the holidays would be torture if my name wasn't cleared quickly.

The easiest and most obvious move on my part would be to step back and allow the police to solve the crime. The Capitol Hill cops would spare no expense on this investigation, and other law enforcement agencies would help. The big problem with this option was it would take the police several days to figure out the likely suspects. They didn't know Senator Langsford, they didn't know his staff, and they certainly didn't know much about his contacts and inner circle. I had worked for him long enough to know all these people.

I kept coming back to my memo. It wouldn't have been difficult for someone to snatch it out of the office in the midst of the confusion and slide it right into the recycling bin across the hallway, but why would he or she want to do that? Was it a pure coincidence, or was it related to Senator Langsford's demise?

It made sense to keep my recovery of the memo a secret. Let the person who trashed it think he, or she, had gotten away with it. I doubted any innocent office staffer or the police had put my memo in the trash deliberately. That meant it either landed there by accident, or its timely disposal had something to do with Senator Langsford's murder.

I could put my fate into the hands of the cops, or I could try to figure out who killed Langsford and clear my name. The quicker this mystery was wrapped up, the better—for me, Doug, and everyone who had worked for Langsford.

SIX

I TUCKED THE memo under my suit coat sleeve and walked quietly back to my desk. Opening the file cabinet drawer, I slipped it inside a side pocket of my oversized handbag. I zipped my purse and locked the drawer. Only Kara knew about the memo, but she was busy. No one else had seen me with it. For now, it would be safe in my cabinet.

I turned on my computer to see if anything pressing required my attention. Since my job was to make sure the senator was prepared at hearings and for votes on legislation, I didn't expect much. My email inbox was flooded. Besides a ton of messages from other Hill staffers offering their condolences, there were several emails from enterprising Washington reporters trying to get the scoop from the one person who knew something about the crime.

Mandy's voice startled me as her face appeared on my screen. Most days when the Senate was in session, Mandy did a live video blog first thing in the morning about the weekly legislative calendar, the senator's schedule, and press opportunities that day. A link to the blog was delivered automatically to our computers to keep us informed. Her annoying voice rambled on and on, "Senator Langsford will attend the bipartisan senators' luncheon today, 11:45 to 12:50. He'll meet with constituents in his office to talk about preserving green space in western Massachusetts, 1 to 1:30. Also this afternoon, Senator Langsford plans to ask questions at an Appropriations Committee hearing about subsidies for ethanol, 2 to 4. He will be available for press comment afterward, 4 to 4:15."

I clicked to close the video so I wouldn't have to hear more details of what my deceased boss was *not* going to do today.

I was wondering where Meg had gone when an IM from her popped up on my computer screen. Instant Message was the preferred method of interoffice communication. On our closed communication network, staffers could send an "instant message" to another Langsford coworker. The message appeared immediately on the screen, enabling a virtual chat. Although we liked to think IM made us more efficient, it was usually used to transmit office gossip.

Meg's message blinked at me. "Come over here!"

I typed back, "What's up?"

She immediately responded, "Regan is here. Mandy has her claws in him."

I sighed and keyed, "Job hunting."

It didn't take Mandy too long to work her magic. Senator Jonas Regan, Democrat from California, was a close acquaintance of Langsford's. He might be inclined to hire some of Langsford's staff as a favor to Lucinda and Matt. He could also benefit from the experience and seniority of Langsford's staffers. Mandy wasted no time sidling up to him.

I was the Langsford staffer who knew Senator Regan best. Langsford and Regan were buddies because they served on the powerful Appropriations Committee together in the Senate, and I staffed Langsford for that committee. In the past, there had been numerous pictures in newspapers across the country of the two sitting next to each other at hearings, fundraisers, and rallies, usually deep in discussion and sometimes even laughing. More recently, the relationship had become strained due to Langford's new independent streak, which involved asking tough questions about the federal budget and occasionally voting differently from Regan and other members of his party.

More than anything, the controversy over Carter Power had driven a wedge between the two senators. In fact, the memo I'd tried to deliver to Senator Langsford earlier this morning was about the Carter Power decision. Carter Power was a big defense company in Senator Regan's home state that had supplied batteries, generators, and power supplies to the military for decades. Most people assume the companies who supply planes, fighter jets, and tanks are the big defense contractors. Yes, they're major players, but almost everything the modern military consumes runs on batteries or some other power source. Carter Power was a multi-billion-dollar company and employed thousands of people, mostly in Senator Regan's state.

The problem? Carter Power had rested on its laurels while other companies had developed more energy-efficient batteries and power supplies, incorporating solar and other renewable energy sources. Carter hadn't kept up with the innovations. I wasn't a scientist and neither was Senator Langsford, yet we had done our homework and concluded that Carter Power, with its antiquated technology, was living on borrowed time. More efficient batteries that reduced the military's carbon footprint were needed. Better performing batteries meant soldiers could carry fewer power supplies with them, lightening their load. It wasn't only about saving money. The lives of our soldiers depended on the military acquiring state of the art technology.

The Pentagon wanted to switch contractors, but Congress wrote the appropriations bills. The jury was still out in the Senate about the future of Carter Power. From a policy perspective, it was time to explore other power supply options. From a political perspective, Carter Power still had die-hard supporters in the Senate who wanted to protect lucrative jobs in their states.

The troubled economy and budget stresses made the job of the Appropriations Committee difficult. Instead of awarding Carter Power another long contract with the military, several senators on the committee wanted to diversify and fund other suppliers that offered less expensive and better power sources. There had been several high profile hearings, and the debate had been contentious. Senator Regan supported full renewal of the contract for Carter Power and had asked Senator Langsford to support him. Regan was up for reelection soon. If the Carter Power contract failed, he would be saying *sayonara* to his political career.

Much to Regan's chagrin, Senator Langsford did not jump to support Carter Power. In a time of considerable economic troubles complicated by a ballooning national debt, Langsford couldn't rush to support a contract that might waste taxpayer money. Spending over $20 billion a year on power, the Pentagon was the largest single consumer of energy in the world. My boss believed those costs could be reduced. Langsford had participated in hush-hush discussions over the controversy, and Matt and I had met several times with Jeff Prentice, a lobbyist representing Carter Power.

The committee was moving toward a vote on Carter Power later this week. My final memo to Senator Langsford, the one in the recycling bin, outlined the competing arguments and offered a comprehensive set of facts and figures. Matt and I felt comfortable recommending a vote against contract renewal. In our private conversations, Senator Langsford agreed with our recommendation. And with the committee deadlocked on the matter, his vote would have tipped the scales against Carter.

Matt and I had been careful to keep his decision quiet. We didn't need an enterprising reporter finding out which way Senator Langsford was leaning. Also, Langsford had told us he wanted to tell Senator Regan privately about his decision not to support Carter Power before the public vote in committee. We didn't want Regan reading about Langsford's decision in the *National Journal*.

I had kept my lips sealed, even with Meg and Doug. It was easy to keep Doug in the dark. He barely followed Capitol Hill news; he was more concerned about what happened three hundred years ago. Meg had been hurt by my unwillingness to dish.

Matt and I did inform Lucinda. She usually stayed out of Langsford's policy decisions, but at a certain point, as his top aide, she needed to know. Matt and I had briefed her last week and informed her about Senator Langsford's strong leanings. To put it mildly, Lucinda wasn't thrilled with the decision.

As chief of staff, Lucinda managed most of Langsford's political relationships. She met with lobbyists, helped the senator with contacts to raise campaign money, and tried to cultivate friendships within the Senate among senior staff. Voting against Carter Power and Senator Regan was going to cause her a lot of problems. Carter Power had been a generous donor to Senator Langsford during his last election cycle. If he voted against the contract renewal, that money would dry up.

Lucinda also counted on Langsford's good relationship with Regan. The population of California was six times that of Massachusetts. A solid friendship with a senator from a big state meant increased opportunities for political networking and fundraising. The alliance with Regan was beneficial for Langsford. If he voted against Carter Power, that relationship would suffer.

In the end, Lucinda accepted our recommendation and allowed the memo to move forward. She had no choice. The chief of staff worked for Langsford like the rest of us and knew that when he made a decision about an issue, it was a done deal.

I walked over to Meg's cubicle on the other side of the office. My neighbor Trevor appeared to be hard at work on something, his hands furiously typing away on his keyboard. What could possibly have him so occupied when our boss was dead? A cover letter for his next job?

Normally, we would all be working on the background information and support materials needed for Langsford to attend the events Mandy had outlined for the week. None of that mattered now. Maybe Meg was right and Trevor had some less than admirable explanation for his strange behavior.

Meg was sitting at her desk, shooting daggers with her eyes in the direction of Mandy and Senator Regan. Unlike Senator Langsford, Regan was a slimy politician.

He kept a fake smile plastered on his face. His teeth were brilliant, several shades too white to occur in nature. He was a good actor, intensely interested in what his interlocutor had to say. You might well be taken in, unless you followed his eyes closely. I had picked up on his annoying trick of casting furtive glances, checking out the room for anyone more important to meet. Like many politicians, he was a predatory shark personified, and the resemblance grew more striking as his reelection date loomed.

I followed Meg's gaze. Mandy, as usual, was hamming it up. Batting her long eyelashes and twirling a finger around a strand of her luxurious locks, she stared adoringly at Regan. Mandy was no dummy. Her job for Langsford had a short shelf life. Although I disdained her tactics, I admired the strategy. She let nothing, including a murder, get in her way.

Meg nudged me. "Come on, Kit. Interrupt her and say something to Regan. You're not just going to let her monopolize him, are you?"

Meg was right. I had the closer relationship with Regan. If anyone was going to get a job with him after this horrible tragedy, it should be me. Sometimes I thought I just wasn't cut out for Washington. My boss had been dead for less than five hours and I already had to jockey for position. I didn't relish the idea of working for Regan, but a paying job was better than the unemployment line.

I strode over to Regan and Mandy, who shot me a glance as if I were a cockroach she wanted to squash.

Senator Regan made it easy for me. "Kit, I'm so glad to see you. How are you holding up? I heard from

Lucinda and Kara you were unfortunate enough to..."
he trailed off.

I saved Senator Regan from having to say the uncomfortable words. "I'm afraid so, sir. Yes."

Senator Regan reached out and gave me a polite hug before I could finish my sentence. Mandy could see where this was headed. The conversation had nothing to do with her, and her time could be spent elsewhere. She said, "Senator Regan, it was so nice speaking with you. You truly provided me with the most comforting words at exactly the right time. I must get back to answering the thousands of press inquiries flooding in."

She batted her eyelashes one last time, and Senator Regan took her outstretched hand and gave it a polite shake. "Mandy, do take care. We'll pick up our discussion in the next several days." He bowed his head politely and gave Mandy a restrained smile.

She nodded, took his hand, and gave him one more seductive look before tossing her red hair and walking away.

Regan returned his gaze to me. He was grave. "Kit, thank goodness you didn't come upon the killer. You must be thankful you're safe."

I couldn't tell if Regan was dramatizing or if he was truly concerned about me. I had lost my appetite for politics this morning. I was upset, and I wasn't going to hide it. "I never really thought about that, Senator Regan. I can't believe he's gone." I wiped a tear from my cheek.

He nodded in agreement. "I understand. You were such a valuable asset to Lyndon. I know he appreciated all the work you did. Try to remember him in life and not death."

He took a sip from a red plastic cup he was holding. I wondered what was in it. Water? Doubtful. I bet he and Lucinda had raided the stash of scotch in Langsford's office. Nothing gets you through tough times better than alcohol. That was especially true in our nation's capital.

I mechanically nodded in polite agreement. What should I say? When I didn't reply, Regan, like most politicians, couldn't stand the uncomfortable silence and filled the void.

"I imagine, Kit, now that Senator Langsford is gone, we will proceed to our work as he wanted, funding the Defense Department and giving our soldiers the finest products and support possible. Senator Langsford was a big fan of Carter Power, and I'm sure he would have been happy to see a continuation of Carter's relationship with the military."

I studied Regan's face. Was this guy for real? In every meeting we'd had about Carter Power, Senator Langsford had voiced his doubts, never support.

I should have just agreed politely, but I couldn't. The last thing I had done for my boss was draft the decision memo to defund Carter Power, not serve as the lifeguard for big business. It seemed wrong, almost unethical, to allow Regan's words to stand without repudiation. A wave of anger erupted within my body, and self-interested concerns about finding my next job disappeared. After all, Senator Langsford couldn't speak for himself anymore. It was up to me to set the record straight.

Either Regan really counted on Langsford to have an abrupt change of heart, or he was a darn good bluffer. It was impossible to tell. Impressive politicians had the ability to make their followers believe what they wanted them to believe. His expression was inscrutable.

I cleared my throat and stood tall, glad I had worn heels so I could almost look him in the eyes. "Well, eh... Senator Regan..." I stumbled, my mouth giving my brain one last chance to let sleeping dogs lie. Frustration at his blatantly ridiculous statement overcame my hesitancy.

He looked at me expectantly. He had made the statement about Carter Power to rewrite history and provide me with the opportunity to do the same. He wanted me to "play ball" and probably work with Mandy to write some hokey press release that stated how much Senator Langsford had loved Carter Power. If we did that, Langsford's temporary replacement would have little choice but to follow in step and vote with Regan. A senator who succeeded deceased or vacating senators usually received the same committee assignments as his or her predecessor. Out of respect, they didn't deviate much from stated positions. Langsford was dead. That meant Mandy and I could help him out with the vote he needed in committee.

This revelation made me more irate and a little confused. I had always thought of Senator Regan, despite the Carter Power imbroglio, as a close ally and friend of my former boss. Now, he seemed more like a desperate politician, clinging to the hope his meal ticket to reelection wouldn't evaporate at the hands of a lowly Senate aide. If he had truly been Senator Langsford's friend, he wouldn't be so worried about self-preservation.

I looked directly into Senator Regan's eyes. I wanted to see his reaction. My voice quavered at first, then grew stronger. "Senator, with all due respect to Senator Langsford's memory, you and I both know he wasn't going to support the decision to continue to fund Carter Power in the committee hearing this week."

A dark cloud came over his face. He frowned. "Kit, I'm not sure you knew the full extent of Senator Langsford's opinion on this matter. There were conversations about Carter Power that did not include you."

That was a load of bull. Senator Langsford held his cards close to his vest, but he would never tell me to prepare a lengthy memo to support his decision not to fund Carter Power if he had decided to support the company. He wasn't the kind of senator who kept his staff second-guessing or chasing down fruitless leads. He valued our time almost as much as he valued his own. Now that his life had been cut short, it was up to me to make sure his last wishes were honored.

"You should know that Senator Langsford already had me prepare a decision memo on the matter."

Regan's eyebrows shot up in surprise, but he recovered immediately. "Kit, that's certainly water under the bridge now. We will never know how Lyndon would have voted."

His last comment caught me off guard. What was he implying? It seemed Regan was happy Langsford wouldn't be around for the committee vote this week. No doubt Carter Power would be overjoyed, too. Could that be the reason for Langsford's death? Silencing him before he had a chance to cast the definitive vote against Carter Power? Senator Regan's demeanor didn't seem like that of a grieving friend.

Time to end an uncomfortable conversation. I had clearly maneuvered myself out of a job with Senator Regan. "Senator Regan, I need to get back to my desk.

I'll see you in the coming days, I'm sure." He gave a curt nod, and I retreated to my carrel.

I wasn't back at my desk for thirty seconds before Meg raced over. "What happened with Senator Regan? That didn't look like your usual chummy chat."

Meg always told me I lacked political savvy. I could have played the conversation better with Senator Regan, keeping Langsford's decision a secret. I could have tried to pump more information out of him and find out if he had any suspects in mind.

"He was under the false impression that Senator Langsford was going to support Carter Power fully in this week's hearing. I had to set the record straight."

Meg's eyes widened. I had never told her about Langsford's decision to put national security and the growing deficit ahead of the wishes of his friend from California. Most of the Senate worked on the premise of "I scratch your back; you scratch mine." Langsford's choice to ditch Regan in the name of the country's best interests was a shock.

"How many people knew Senator Langsford planned to vote that way?" Meg asked.

I shrugged. "Not many. He wanted to keep it quiet. He'd already had his share of grief from lobbyists, mostly Jeff Prentice, and he didn't want his phone ringing before the vote, trying to change his mind."

I thought a second. "I think the only people who knew were me, Matt, and Lucinda. But Senator Regan had to be aware that it was unlikely to go his way. The last meeting we had with him, it was clear Senator Langsford wasn't going to support more funding for Carter Power. And then, of course, Jeff Prentice probably knew, since Senator Regan had to have kept him informed about how the votes were shaping up for the big committee hearing later this week."

Meg hovered over my desk. "Are you sure no one else knew which way Senator Langsford was leaning? Is that the complete list?"

"I don't see how anyone else could have known. It's possible Senator Langsford told someone else, like Kara. But in this case, I doubt it. He asked us to keep his decision quiet. We only told Lucinda a week ago."

I heard someone clear his throat in an obvious manner. Both Meg and I looked over at Trevor. It was easy to forget he was even there.

With a snide tone, Meg asked, "Trevor, would you like to say something?" She faced him, hands on her hips.

Trevor straightened up in his chair and fixed an annoyed gaze on Meg. "You just stated no one knew about the Carter Power decision. Is that correct, Kit?"

What was the point of keeping the secret anymore with Langsford dead? "Yes, although I guess that means you were eavesdropping on our conversation. Is that correct, Trevor?"

Trevor chuckled in a stifled way. I couldn't remember him laughing in the four years he sat next to me. He wasn't a fun-loving person, by any stretch of the imagination.

"It's hard not to eavesdrop, sitting next to you, Kit. The way you talk, you and your best buddy here..." he jerked his thumb to point at Meg, "seem to think you're sitting in a priest's confessional rather than in the middle of a Senate office."

Meg let out a tiny gasp. I thought of all the times Meg and I had sat at my desk, chatting indiscriminately about all kinds of issues and people, with that weasel Trevor listening in on our conversations.

"Okay, you've made your point. You like to listen in on other people's conversations. So what's the big deal about the Carter Power decision?"

He smoothed his tailored pants and forced a fake smile. "Just a reminder. Your office transactions have not been exactly secretive."

"Trevor, if you know something about Carter Power, tell me right now." I turned my chair to face him directly.

"I find it ironic that we have hardly spoken all this time, and now you expect me to divulge sensitive information." No doubt about it. Trevor was enjoying this. He had watched Meg and me chatter away for hours on end, day in and day out. Was he jealous? Maybe Trevor just wanted a friend.

I tried a gentler approach. "Trevor, I just want to make sure I can carry on the senator's legacy after his death. Don't you think that's what he would have wanted? I need to know who else in this office knew about Carter Power."

Trevor's face softened. "It's not a person inside the office."

Had Carter Power's lobbyist Jeff Prentice told someone about our confidential discussions? If Prentice had opened his mouth, it might have sabotaged Regan's chance of persuading Langsford to join him. Veteran politicians like Langsford didn't appreciate being bullied over a big decision. Lobbyists had considerable power in Washington, but limits existed. Elected officials reacted poorly if lobbyists painted them into a corner. Besides, Langsford had sworn everyone to secrecy during the discussions. All participants had agreed to his terms, even Jeff.

"Who could have found out about this outside the office? Trevor, you didn't say something to a friend, did you?" This was a long shot, since I doubted Trevor had many friends.

He shook his head. "You're missing the obvious, Kit."

He was enjoying this riddle repartee, and he was going to make me work for the answer.

I looked at him blankly. I could tell from the expression on Meg's face that she had lost patience. She despised Trevor, and she didn't want to waste more time talking with him.

Meg extended a manicured red nail toward him. "Now listen here. Stop playing these silly games and tell us. If it was so obvious, we'd already know who it was, wouldn't we?"

"That's a leap of logic I wouldn't make," said Trevor.

As Meg glowered, Trevor leaned back in his chair. "I can see you two need some help on this. Who else advised Langsford on the decisions he made as a senator? Wouldn't it make sense he would have talked to *her* about such an important choice?"

He was right. It was so obvious, I completely missed it. If I was going to figure out who had murdered Senator Langsford, I'd have to hone my sleuthing skills.

"Vivian, of course. Senator Langsford hardly made a decision without talking to his wife."

Trevor beamed—a rare sight for a guy who didn't make smiling a priority. "Well, it's good to know you're not completely clueless." He turned back toward his computer and started pounding away.

Of course we could not be absolutely sure Vivian knew about Senator Langsford's decision concerning Carter Power. He had been more adamant about keeping his position under wraps than the other times he had sworn staff to secrecy.

I toyed with the idea of Vivian as a prime suspect. She had wanted Senator Langsford to retire from the Senate at the end of his term and get a high-paying job as a defense lobbyist, even though Langsford was eager to run for another term. Voting against Carter Power wouldn't endear him to most of the power players on K Street. Both his desire to remain in the Senate and revoke his support of Carter Power had to rub Vivian the wrong way.

Furthermore, she would have had access to the senator's office and Kara's area. She could have easily swiped my memo and put it in the recycling bin. Did she want to keep her husband's intentions regarding Carter Power under wraps so she could broker a sweetheart deal down the road?

My theory didn't matter if I couldn't confirm Trevor's contention. "Wait a second, Trevor. Are you positive Vivian knew about Carter Power? Or are you just assuming?"

Trevor stopped banging the keyboard and peered at me. "Kit, of course I'm positive. Would I provide you with less than concrete information pertaining to a murder investigation?"

"*How* did you know? I need specifics, Trevor."

"Quite simple. One day last week I was waiting to meet with the senator, and I took a seat in his waiting area." Trevor's language was so formal, it bordered on amusing. Who talked like that?

I prodded him, "Go on. Spit it out." If all my inter-rogations took this long, I might as well wait for the police and forensics to solve the murder.

"It was late in the day. Mrs. Langsford was also wait-ing for the senator so they could go to their evening en-gagement. Her cellphone rang, and she took the call. She was obviously upset about what the caller was saying. From listening to her end of the conversation, I could tell it was about Carter Power. She insisted she had tried to persuade the senator to support Carter Power, and she wasn't having much luck. She was distressed by her failure." He paused and stared at me. "Does that information suffice?"

It did, and I thanked him. But a crucial piece of in-formation was missing. "Do you know who the caller was?"

"She never referred to the person by name, so it would be impossible to come to a conclusion." He re-turned to his computer.

Even though Trevor couldn't identify the caller, what he'd told me was valuable. Vivian had known that the senator intended to deep-six Carter Power. Someone had been keeping her informed. She was also quite upset about Langsford's position. Vivian didn't seem distraught over her husband's murder. Was that because it wasn't news to her? Had she done it herself or col-luded with someone to kill him before he voted against Carter Power later this week at the hearing?

I shuddered as I considered the possibility of Vivian's involvement in Senator Langsford's death. All the din-ners, receptions, and campaign events together flashed before me. Maybe Vivian had grown tired of her life as a senator's wife. Perhaps she wanted to leave Washington altogether and live somewhere else. The possibilities were endless. But if that were the case, why not just divorce him? After all, the money was hers. Being divorced was no disgrace these days.

All I knew was she had access to his office and the opportunity to put my memo in the garbage. Whoever had tossed the memo was trying to cover up something important—a motive for killing Senator Langsford.

SEVEN

ALL OF A SUDDEN, I was ravenous. I turned to Meg. "I haven't eaten anything all day, and I'm starving. What about you?"

She smiled. "You know me. I can always eat."

That was an understatement. Meg was one of those enviable creatures who could consume whatever she wanted without consequences, including several drinks of choice at happy hour. Despite her seemingly endless indulgences, she remained slender. She rarely exercised and complained bitterly about it when she did. I, on the other hand, faced a constant struggle with the battle of the bulge. One bad week of overindulging, and I found myself with no alternative than to wake up at 6 a.m. for spinning class so my tailored suits still fit.

"Why don't we go to Union Station and get some lunch?" A huge food court resided inside the train station a few blocks away. It was an inexpensive dining option for hungry Senate staffers. I glanced at my watch. Two o'clock meant the lunch crowd would be long gone.

With a pained look, Meg said, "Kit, do you remember what happened today? Not only was our boss murdered, but until the Capitol Police solve this case, you're the prime suspect—at least as far as the media is concerned."

The picture Matt showed me online flashed before my eyes. By now, every blogger and newspaper under the sun had surely obtained it. Despite the best efforts of the police, a good Internet rumor doesn't get quashed in a few hours.

I sighed. "You're right. A stroll down Second Street wouldn't make much sense right now." Was I trapped in this office? I imagined spending days upon days here and felt a newfound sympathy for Edward Snowden.

Meg said, "Don't worry. I think I can get away with venturing outside. I'll buy us lunch; then we can sit in a smaller conference room and eat. You just sit at your desk and relax, okay?" She gently pushed me into my seat. "Don't look at the Internet. Don't turn on the television. Take a few minutes to unwind."

Meg was right. The tension had been building up all day, and now I had an enormous headache. Instead of my usual three or four doses of coffee, I'd barely finished one cup. "Meg, bring me a Coke Zero, will you? I need the buzz."

She whipped her head around. She was wearing large Jackie Onassis sunglasses and had pulled her blond bob into a ponytail. I was impressed. "I like the disguise. You look like Gwyneth Paltrow before her conscious uncoupling." An avid consumer of Hollywood news, she smiled and sped out of the office.

I should have listened to Meg's advice and relaxed for a few moments. I did avoid the Internet and television, but my email inbox was a different story. Many of the messages were from people who lived in Massachusetts and wanted to know what would happen to the legislation or projects we'd been working on. Lucinda would give us instructions soon about how to reply, so I ignored them. Other emails were from numerous Senate friends and contacts. It was comforting to know that a cadre of colleagues didn't believe I had killed Senator Langsford.

I opened an email from my mother. My parents were retired and spent half the year traveling the world. It was impossible to keep track of them. They were currently on a wine-tasting trip in California. That was perfect. Computer-savvy, they used an iPhone to maintain contact when they hit the road, but wine tasting was a favorite activity. Shocking news would at least be received in a muted fashion, particularly if they had started touring the vineyards early in the day. The email confirmed my suspicions. They had heard about Langsford's death, yet details about my status as a suspect had escaped them. There were more wineries to be visited, and the news hadn't upset them too much.

The train of thought involving my wine-mellowed parents led to another, less reassuring one. Doug's parents would respond differently to today's events. No one would describe their temperaments as mellow. With considerable resources at their disposal, Doug's family surely knew the stories posted online fingered me as a suspect. They were undoubtedly mortified. Doug probably had spent the better part of the day on the phone with them in an attempt to control the damage.

Meg reappeared at my desk, and we adjourned to an unoccupied conference room to eat our lunch. Usually, all three conference rooms in our Senate office were booked from 10 a.m. until 5 p.m. by lobbyists, constituents, and other policy advocates who wanted precious minutes of Senator Langsford's time. Today, the small conference room sat eerily vacant.

Nibbling on low-fat chicken tacos, my lunchtime staple, I watched with envy as Meg unwrapped her chorizo and cheese monstrosity, accompanied by a large side order of chips with guacamole. Some people had all the luck.

Meg took a big bite. After swallowing, she asked, "What are you doing tomorrow night after work?"

"Nothing much, except trying to avoid a murder charge."

"So clever! Well, I ran into Jeff Prentice on the way to Union Station. He wants to meet us for drinks tomorrow night at Lounge 201. I told him we'd be there."

Lounge 201 was a trendy bar near the Senate office buildings. Various happy hour specials made it a convenient watering hole for staff. Darkly lit with tiny tables, it was a good place to socialize and enjoy a cocktail, or two...or three. Since Lounge 201 boasted a wide selection of martinis, I didn't refuse invites often. Yet an evening with Prentice wasn't high on my "to do" list.

"After the conversation I had with Senator Regan today, I'm not sure I'm up for a night on the town with Jeff Prentice." After all, Jeff was Carter Power's chief lobbyist. I wasn't his favorite person these days.

"Kit, do you want to find out who killed Senator Langsford?"

"Of course I do. Then I can return to my life of anonymity."

She nodded. "That's right. We can leave this up to the police, who will take a week to figure out who the likely suspects are, then God knows how long to solve the case." She paused. "*If* they ever solve it. In the meantime, you're the one person ever mentioned as a suspect. It's Gary Condit all over again."

"Did they ever figure out who killed Chandra Levy?"

"Yes, seven years later, and it wasn't the good congressman. Doesn't mean his reputation ever recovered."

"But if the police can't solve the murder of the senator," I said, "how are we going to do it? Last time I checked, your college major was English, not criminology."

"Kit, think about what we do for a living. We make observations and reach conclusions. Sure, it's about political issues, but it's basically the same thing. We just have to use our smarts." She tapped her head. "And if we do that, we'll figure this out. Besides, don't you read a mystery novel a week? You should be an expert."

I winced at her mention of my favorite pastime. My Kindle bill rivaled Meg's monthly makeup expenditure. We both had our vices. Of course I had already decided to try my hand at sleuthing with regard to this case. However, reading about murder was one thing; solving a real crime didn't necessarily follow. I was also somewhat sensitive about my love of popular murder mysteries. While the rest of the Washington elite attended the opera, the symphony, and independent documentary films I had never heard of, I preferred the company of Carl Hiaasen, Janet Evanovich, and Dame Agatha.

"I'm glad you have such confidence in my sleuthing abilities. What's with this 'we,' anyway? You hate mysteries." Meg didn't share my love of crime novels. Her major pastimes were dating cute guys who worked on Capitol Hill and reading trendy fashion magazines.

Meg's expression turned serious. "I'm surprised at you, Kit. Did you think I could just stand by and watch your career go down the toilet because you were in the wrong place at the wrong time? Of course I'm going to help clear your name."

I had to fight back a tear. It had been a stressful day, and Meg's words tugged at my heart. Knowing Meg had my back made me feel a hundred percent better.

I gave Meg a quick hug. She grinned at me. "Should I text Jeff and let him know we're on for tomorrow night?"

"You bet. I have a hunch Senator Langsford's death is somehow related to Carter Power, and Jeff Prentice is ground zero."

We finished our lunch quickly and returned to our desks. After the morning's drama, the afternoon's deluge of calls and messages filled our time with a comforting bustle. Lucinda assigned all staff to answer the phones, since the office switchboard was lit up with calls offering condolences and inquiring about the senator's murder. We took message after message and dutifully provided the office mailing address for those who wanted to send sympathy cards to Mrs. Langsford.

At quitting time, I worried about the press corps, still holding vigil outside the office. But Matt came up with a brilliant idea. Instead of leaving our office through the regular entrance, I exited through the upstairs door of our two-floor suite, the one Senator Langsford had called his "secret exit." He used it when he wanted to avoid reporters, who usually camped outside our main office doors after a controversial vote. The exit was a few steps from a bank of elevators, which whisked him down to the parking garage. My departure was more complicated because I needed to leave Hart through the lobby. Much to my surprise, I left without fanfare. Keeping my head down, I walked through the building's lobby then jetted behind the long shadows of the Calder statue. I was outside in fewer than ten seconds.

Riding home on the Metro was no problem. D.C. social mores forbid eye contact on the subway. No one so much as glanced in my direction. Before I knew it, I was headed toward our condo building. At 7 p.m., it was still light out, yet the heat of the day had dissipated. Normally, I loved this time of year. If I arrived home at a decent hour, I liked to sit on the balcony, pour myself a glass of wine, and read a mystery novel. After dealing with constituents and other Capitol Hill staffers all day, I relished a few quiet minutes by myself. Usually Doug was buried in a book or his research and didn't mind my brief seclusion. There wasn't going to be much "quiet time" tonight.

As soon as I opened the door, Clarence greeted me with several "woofs," punctuated with sloppy doggie kisses. Clarence was a needy dog, although perhaps that's redundant. Doug worked at home part of the time, so Clarence was spoiled. He craved constant petting, admiration, rubbing, and feeding. Unless he was asleep, Clarence wanted attention, thanks to his origins as an adopted beagle rescue pup. We didn't mind. Clarence called the shots in our household.

I bent down to massage Clarence's floppy ears. His sparkling brown eyes glistened appreciatively, and he nuzzled my neck briefly with his wet nose. Clarence had a healthy appetite. Like most dogs, he was "food motivated." In short, he was obsessed with dog treats. Clarence must not have figured out that Doug and I discussed his food consumption, because Clarence always pounced on me when I came home, thinking I could be duped into serving him more treats or even a second dinner.

Tonight wasn't the time to argue with Clarence about

his obsession. I walked over to the drawer where we kept his treats—complete with a child safety lock so Clarence couldn't help himself. After giving him a biscuit, I leaned down to rub his neck and he snuck in a quick lick. That was the best part about having a dog. Even if the entire country thought I was a murderer, Clarence would remain devoted, especially if the treats kept flowing.

Doug came down the hallway with a book in his hand. Apparently, the fact that his live-in girlfriend was a murder suspect hadn't stopped him from continuing his research. He adjusted his horn-rimmed glasses and ran his fingers through his wavy brown hair. Doug should wear a t-shirt with the tagline "I'm a Professor" on it. He looked and acted the part perfectly.

"Tough day, huh?" He smiled and gave me a half hug.

I shrugged. "I've definitely had better. Where do you want me to begin?"

"Before you start, I think you need a drink," Doug proposed.

"That's the best suggestion anyone has made all day."

He uncorked a bottle of Virginia Riesling and grabbed two glasses from our vast collection. Like my parents, I enjoyed wine tasting, particularly in the surrounding countryside only a few hours from Washington, D.C.

I briefly sniffed my wine before settling into an overstuffed armchair, detecting a nose of aromatic peaches with hints of floral. I took a long drink.

Doug settled next to me on the sofa and stretched out, bringing the bottle of wine with him. "Now that you have the proper liquid refreshment, why don't you tell me how you ended up as the prime murder suspect of a prominent United States Senator?"

I recounted the day's events to Doug, with more details than during our frantic conversation earlier on the phone. He silently sipped his wine and poured me another glass. Like Meg, Doug was a good listener. He had calmed down considerably since our chat this morning. He didn't interrupt me as I told my story and avoided peppering me with questions.

I sat back on the sofa and rubbed my temples. Massaging my shoulders and neck, Doug said, "Kit, it's terrible what happened, but I think you're in the clear. You don't have a motive, and who would kill someone and stagger out of his office with the murder weapon? The police know that, and I'm sure they'll find the killer soon."

I shook my head. "I don't have much faith that the police will solve the murder easily. The killer is someone who knew Senator Langsford and had a personal motive for wanting him dead. It's going to take the police several days to develop a list of suspects. He had a lot of friends, enemies, and acquaintances. It's almost impossible for outsiders to understand the inner workings of a political circle. By the time they agree on a pool of suspects, the killer might already have covered his tracks."

"You might be right, but there's nothing you can do about it, is there? You're going to have to sit tight and provide the police with as much information as possible. Maybe that will help them solve the crime."

I poured myself a little more of the wine, which was making me bolder. "I'll help the police as much as I'm asked, but I don't think I should rely on them to solve this case."

Doug stared at me, bewildered. As much as Meg was adventurous, Doug was cautious. It must be the New England blue blood that ran through his veins. I liked to push the envelope; Doug played it safe. It was classic yin and yang. Doug's restraint was also one of the reasons why I sought out Meg. My best friend brought out the crazy side of me Doug tried to suppress.

"I'm not sure what you mean. Do you want my parents to hire a private detective to clear your name? I can call Father and see what he thinks, although I'm certain he's going to want us to steer clear of drawing more attention to your involvement in the murder."

I chuckled. "No, I definitely don't want your parents to hire a detective." I hesitated for a second, searching for the right words to make our plan sound less foolish than it was. "Meg and I think we might be able to put our heads together and follow up on some leads."

Now it was Doug's turn to laugh. "'Follow up on some leads'? Do I need to remind you that you're a Senate staffer, not Lord Peter Wimsey...or maybe Harriet Vane? Should I also remind you that you're soon to be unemployed, once Senator Langsford's replacement is named? How are you going to solve a crime...perhaps between interviews for a new job?"

Now it was my turn to ratchet up the emotions. "Doug, there isn't going to be another job for me on Capitol Hill unless I clear my name, and do it quickly. So I think it might be a good investment of my time to solve this murder." Hearing the last sentence come out of my mouth shocked me. Was I really serious about investigating Senator Langsford's death?

Doug's expression grew solemn. "You've already made up your mind. All I can say is you'd better be careful. If someone was angry enough to murder a sitting United States Senator as he sat in his office, that person won't be intimidated by a young Miss Marple and her trusted sidekick. If you poke around, you're going to bring attention to yourself, especially if the murderer is part of the 'inner circle,' or whatever you call it."

While I was sure Doug had heard from his father today about "damage control" and his family's need for me to distance myself from the murder investigation, that wasn't the main reason he wanted me to mind my own business. There was a murderer on the loose, and if my hunch was correct, the perpetrator was someone familiar. He or she would be watching my behavior and actions closely. As much as I wanted to find the person who killed Senator Langsford, I didn't want to become the next victim.

I smiled tightly. "Point taken. I'll be careful. Besides, Meg and I are just going to do some surface stuff. We won't dig deep enough to alert the killer. So I wouldn't worry about us risking our lives."

Doug put his arm around me. "I'm sure you're correct. Besides, it will give you something to do at work for the next couple of days before the office closes. You might as well make it interesting."

If only we had known how wrong our predictions would turn out to be...

EIGHT

THAT NIGHT I fell into an unsettled sleep. In my dreams, I was clutching the model helicopter that killed Langsford and running toward the exit of the Senate office building. People noticed I had the weapon and a crowd surrounded me. When I broke free and tried to escape, I couldn't open the heavy door. The mob grew bigger and louder behind me. I finally woke up, perspiring and wondering what had happened. The realization that it was just a nightmare ignited pangs of both relief and sadness.

Morning arrived too early. My less than stellar night's sleep provided a legitimate excuse to skip my usual morning jog. A nice relaxing breakfast at home was the better option. No reason to beat my colleagues to the office today. First, my boss was dead. Second, I had arrived to work early yesterday, and look what had happened?

Doug's soft, rhythmic snores indicated he was none the worse for wear. His relatively blasé attitude yesterday evening hadn't shocked me. Doug had a knack for blocking out the rest of the world when he was working on a project, and he'd started his latest research masterpiece a few weeks ago when the semester ended. Since he was a professor, he devised his own schedule in the summertime. That didn't mean he frolicked at the condominium's pool. Quite the opposite. Doug was the quintessential academic, with his absentminded approach to life, but he was also a hard charger who didn't blow off the time between classes. Furthermore, he didn't write about American history for financial security or the accolades. He had plenty of money that came to him annually as part of his trust fund. Doug was an intellectual purist, motivated by an infatuation with knowledge. He published his dissertation on the great Virginia dynasty of presidents soon after leaving graduate school. Immediately following that ground-breaking work came a book on the first Supreme Court. I envied Doug and the ease with which he forged a successful career path. Only since I started working for Congress in the policy world had I felt fulfilled.

Stifling a yawn, I ambled down the hallway of our spacious condo. My career plan was in jeopardy, given I might not have a job in the near future. Even if another position miraculously presented itself, I would miss working for Senator Langsford. Constant headaches came with the job, but they were eventually resolved, leaving Meg and me to share a good laugh.

I hustled Clarence outside for a brief morning walk. Upon our return, he raced into the kitchen, sat obediently at my feet, and licked my legs. Then he emitted a muted growl. Clarence typically started his shenanigans with a low decibel rumble. Ignoring him resulted in a gradual increase of volume. Scratching his ears would placate him momentarily while I made coffee.

Doug's parents had bought us a top-of-the-line espresso machine. We were lucky to live in a condo with enough counter space; the machine consumed an entire corner of our open kitchen. Normally I would have chafed at such an extravagant gift, but I craved coffee in the morning, and nothing beat a large dose of top-quality espresso. As I ground the coffee, Clarence gave me a reminder growl. He was still trying to be polite, but he was losing patience. I didn't have much time.

I wanted to toast my bagel, yet if I delayed much longer, Clarence would wake Doug with a full beagle howl. I left the espresso to brew and undid the lock on Clarence's food cabinet. He wiggled his butt in excitement as I poured the kibble into his bowl.

With Clarence momentarily satisfied, I popped my bagel into the toaster and steamed my milk for a monster triple-shot latte. Glancing toward our condo's mammoth ceiling-to-floor window, I saw more clouds than sun. It might be safe to enjoy breakfast on the balcony without suffering unbearable heat. Just as I was about to head outside, I heard Doug enter the kitchen.

"I'm surprised you're up this early," I said. "Aren't you on your summer schedule?"

He gave me a half smile. "Actually, I had a horrible night's sleep. I kept dreaming you were running away with a bloody helicopter in your hand."

I almost dropped my latte. They said people who lived together too long started to look like each other. I wondered if cohabitants also started to have the same dreams.

"Funny you should say that. I dreamt the same thing."

"Wow. Wonder why?" His voice dripped with sarcasm. I looked at my watch. The prospect of a serene balcony breakfast had gone by the wayside. It was time to gulp my bagel, shower and dress, and depart for work.

As I moved toward the bathroom, Doug asked, "Hey, where are you going in such a rush? Don't you want to make me a latte?" He grinned.

"No time for love, Dr. Jones. Got to get to it." Doug appreciated my movie quotes. They were appropriately placed and usually downright funny.

"What are you going to do at work today, anyway?"

Doug must have either conveniently forgotten our conversation from the night before or concluded I'd been tipsy, deranged, or both. I could remind him my main goal was to figure out who killed Lyndon Langsford, or I could let him think I'd given up on that adventure. Honesty is not always the best policy.

I chose my words carefully. "There will be a lot of loose ends to tie up in the office today. I want to make sure I'm as useful as possible."

He must not have noticed the vagueness of my words, because his only response was an uninterested nod. He already had his iPad fired up and was scanning the morning edition of the *Washington Post*. I used his distraction to my advantage, and in an effort to avoid further questioning, I made a dash for the shower. A few minutes later, I headed out the door for the day. I waved him a breezy air kiss and locked the door behind me.

It was time to get to work. That is, it was time to figure out who had killed Senator Langsford.

NINE

THE TRIP INTO work was uneventful, although I worried every Metro rider was staring at me. I fought back a wave of paranoia. According to Doug's iPad email debrief, the morning newspapers had reported that Senator Langsford's body had been "discovered by a longtime staffer." Reports also stated, "Police questioned the aide, who has been released at this time." It was far from a complete exoneration, but it might be enough to keep the press hounds at bay. No thanks to press secretary extraordinaire, Mandy Lippman. Without Matt's intervention, she wouldn't have lifted a finger to help.

I stopped by the downstairs café in the adjacent Dirksen Senate office building before heading upstairs to work. I was about to put my usual allotment of skim milk and sugar substitute into my second morning coffee when I almost collided with a familiar rival. Jerking my head to look up from my drink, I found myself face to face with Representative Jordan Jessop.

Jessop didn't look like a member of Congress. He was vertically challenged, although he probably had a few inches on James Madison, our nation's shortest U.S. president at 5'4." Some factoids were assimilated by osmosis while one dated a historian. Unlike most politicians, who plastered permanent smiles on their faces, Jessop usually wore a scowl. He wasn't a slight man. Today he was dressed in a summer suit that failed to flatter his chubby build. It was only 8:30 in the morning, and he looked as though he'd already run the Boston Marathon. Instead, he'd walked over to the Senate from the House office buildings, about fifteen minutes away.

Jessop's appearance didn't give me pause. After all, Washington was known as "Hollywood for ugly people," so physically unattractive people were par for the course. This was supposed to be a town that ran on smarts and savvy. Jessop had been Langsford's rival in his most recent Senate election. Working for Senator Langford's campaign, my sole focus for six months had been to defeat him and the values he espoused.

There was no escaping this encounter; I had almost doused Jessop with my coffee. I immediately put a smile on my face. "Hello, Congressman Jessop. I'm Kit Marshall from Senator Langsford's office." I extended my hand for a polite shake.

His stare identified me as a bug ripe for extermination. No doubt Jessop remembered I had worked for Langsford during the Senate campaign and held it against me. At the congressional delegation meetings Langsford hosted, he'd always looked at me with extra distaste. Meg insisted I had imagined this hostility, but his present reaction to me confirmed his revulsion was authentic.

He ignored my hand. "Yes, I certainly remember you. I flew in last night, and I'm heading over to your office in a minute to pay my condolences to Vivian and the others. It's a tragedy, yet the work for our state must continue." Jessop gave me a knowing glance.

I tensed at Jessop's obvious delight over having my boss out of the way. "Of course, of course. I'm headed to the office now. Do you need any assistance in finding your way around the Senate complex, *Representative* Jessop?" I put a slight emphasis on the "Representative" to remind him he was a House member and not a senator.

"No, no. I certainly know my way around the Senate, for all the years I've been on the Hill. I imagine I'll become much more familiar with your office in coming days."

I looked at him curiously. Jessop was tossing something back at me, and I was slow on the uptake.

He didn't wait for my response. "As you know, our great state has recently elected a governor of my political party. Therefore, it's altogether likely," he paused for dramatic effect as he drew in his large belly and puffed out his squat chest, "that I will be named as Senator Langsford's successor. I'll return home tonight to await the announcement."

I couldn't conceal my audible gasp. I had been so overwhelmed with the murder of Senator Langsford and the investigation swirling around me, it had slipped my mind that Jessop might be Langsford's successor. Jessop was certainly correct. He would be the leading candidate to serve the remainder of Senator Langsford's term.

I smiled meekly at Jessop, wishing I had shown more humility in our earlier exchange. Still, he wouldn't be hiring me, so I couldn't resist a small dig. "I wish you the best of luck, Congressman. Of course, right now, I'm only focused on grieving for Senator Langsford and hoping his killer is brought to justice."

Jessop's face immediately turned bright red. "Yes, of course. We must focus on finding out who committed this horrible crime. That's what I've been saying to every reporter who asked me for a comment."

I nodded curtly and returned to fixing my coffee. Stirring my drink, I realized I had just spoken with a prime suspect. What better motive for murder than a United States Senate seat? Jessop had almost made the big leap from the House to the Senate, yet Langsford was more congenial and friendly. An all-around better politician. There was no way Jessop would have beaten Langsford in a head-to-head rematch. Challengers typically got one shot for a Senate seat. After a candidate lost to a sitting senator, the state political party usually nominated someone else the next time around. The only way Jessop could move to the Senate would be if Langsford were removed. He would have to die, resign, or decide not to run for another term. Langsford was ethically pure, so it was unlikely he would ever resign due to a scandal. He'd recently come into his own with his "independent" streak and had gained substantial support across parties in the state for his unconventional policy positions. His reelection wasn't guaranteed, but the outlook was positive for another term. The only way Jessop could make his way to the Senate would be if Lyndon Langsford died. His wish had been granted, but by whom?

After putting my purse away at my desk and signing onto my computer, I made a beeline to Meg. I wanted to ask her opinion about my encounter with Jessop. To my disappointment, her cubicle sat empty. A half-eaten ham and cheese breakfast burrito rested next to her workstation. She couldn't be too far away. Once again, how did she remain so skinny? I returned to my cubicle and responded to emails until she showed up as "present" on our Instant Message system.

Next-door neighbor Trevor was sitting at his computer, pounding on his keyboard as usual. He had provided valuable information yesterday. It was time to lift the silent treatment.

Small talk wasn't going to work with Trevor. If I tried to engage him in normal conversation, he'd clam up. As awkward as it might be, the direct approach seemed best.

Without a "hello" or "good morning," I tilted my chair back, slid next to Trevor, and asked him point blank, "Who do you think is going to be appointed to Senator Langsford's seat?"

Trevor didn't miss a beat. Without a pause in his typing, he answered, "Jordan Jessop."

Bingo! A direct question resulted in an honest answer. Why had I allowed Meg's opinion to deter me from befriending Trevor? He was intelligent, and his bluntness was refreshing.

Pushing my luck, I asked another question. "Is there anyone else who might be considered besides Jessop?"

This inquiry required a more elaborate response and perhaps analytical thought. He stopped typing and turned his chair toward me.

"That question involves a good deal of speculation. Certainly, there are others who will be considered for the appointment. The governor may want to appoint someone who might do nothing more than hold the seat for two years until another election can be held. Or perhaps the governor will want to take the seat himself. You also can't forget Mrs. Langsford."

I almost spit out the coffee I had just sipped. The thought of Vivian Langsford as a United States Senator didn't fit. It was almost like picturing a leather-clad grandma on a Harley or a dog drinking a martini. Vivian had enjoyed the benefits of being a senator's wife, but she'd never seemed interested in the policy decisions and political horse-trading that transpired daily on Capitol Hill.

Trevor raised his eyebrows at my reaction. "You don't agree with my observations?"

I chuckled. "No, I appreciate your honesty, Trevor. But let's face it. I don't think Vivian Langsford is U.S. Senate material."

Trevor peered at me through the glasses that sat on the edge of his nose. "I would have to disagree with your assessment, Kit."

Of course, Trevor didn't offer anything else. It was just like him to leave me hanging. "You've got me interested. Why do you think Vivian Langsford would want to be a senator, when she's never shown concern with the daily operations of this office?"

Trevor shook his head. "I thought perhaps you possessed astute observational skills, Ms. Marshall. I've watched you for several years now, and I concluded you had a leg up on most of the people employed here. I admit, all the time you spent with your best pal Meg made me doubt your competency. Yet, I concluded you were one of the more valuable members of the senator's staff." He paused briefly to sip a bottle of Perrier water, placed directly to the right of his keyboard on his immaculate desk. "However, you're disappointing me lately with your apparent inability to connect the dots. Only yesterday, we spoke of Vivian Langsford's knowledge about the Carter Power decision. Do you remember this conversation?"

"Yes."

"We talked about this incident less than twenty-four

hours ago, yet you just stated Vivian Langsford hasn't shown any discernible interest in the everyday operations of this establishment. Do you see the contradiction in your conclusions?"

Trevor had a valid point. For some reason, Vivian had become involved in the decision concerning Carter Power. Perhaps Senator Langsford routinely discussed major decisions with her, if only in passing, or maybe Vivian had other reasons to sway her husband's decision.

There was another problem with Trevor's supposition. The governor was a Republican, and Senator Langsford had been a Democrat. Why would the governor consider appointing Vivian, the widow of a Democrat, to a seat that now belonged to the Grand Old Party? I asked Trevor this question.

"You're right on the politics. It's a long shot, but the governor could gain popularity points for appointing Vivian as a goodwill gesture. The addition of one more Republican won't tip the balance in the Senate. Who knows? Vivian could even make a deal to caucus with the other party in exchange for the appointment."

I shook my head. "No way. You're wrong on that account. Senator Langsford would never have joined the other party. He might have played fast and loose lately with his votes, but he was no turncoat."

"Kit, we're talking about Vivian now, not Senator Langsford, remember?"

I crossed my arms. Trevor's observations were helpful, but I still didn't know why Vivian was fascinated with Carter Power. It was worth another stab...no pun intended. "Trevor, do you know why Vivian intervened on the Carter Power decision?"

Trevor narrowed his eyes and leaned forward. "I have no idea, and I don't wish to speculate. I would think someone investigating the murder of Senator Langsford," he paused to look at me pointedly, "might want to find out the answer to that question."

Trevor returned to his computer and started typing furiously. My audience with the king had ended. The Wizard of Oz had spoken and disappeared behind the curtain.

I logged back into my computer and returned to answering email. Most were condolences from other staffers on the Hill. No one even hinted at the possibility of another job. Being a "person of interest" in the murder of Lyndon Langsford had decreased my stock considerably.

Mandy's smiling face suddenly appeared on my screen, accompanied by her whiny voice. Why on earth had she issued a daily video update about the senator's schedule? Sure enough, Mandy recapitulated the talking points she would provide today about the senator's death. She recited a paltry line, which Matt surely forced her to include, about "supporting all staff employed in the office at this difficult time." Her talking points were followed by instructions about handling inquiries concerning the wake, which apparently hadn't been scheduled yet. Nonetheless, staffers from Senator Langsford's office "were expected to attend" while "wearing proper attire." Mandy was a real piece of work. A prominent U.S. Senator was dead, and she was focused on fashion etiquette.

I hit the "close" box on the video window, and she vanished immediately. What if closing a computer window immediately shut people up in real life? When I wanted to silence someone, I imagined clicking a virtual "close" box, situated to the right of a person's head. I was daydreaming what it would be like to click "close" on my sadistic aerobics instructor when a familiar voice snapped me out of my reverie.

"Well, someone decided to take advantage of the situation and zone out." Meg towered over me.

"Oh, sorry. I must have been preoccupied for a moment." I didn't want to try to explain my fascination with clicking people shut to Meg. She had a literal mind and wouldn't appreciate my musings.

"Well, wake up, Kit! I need to tell you about my date last night."

She looked amazing today. Her highlighted blond bob was smooth and lustrous, and she was attired in a stylish black pantsuit with a white-buttoned collared shirt, and professional, yet sexy, three-inch heels. Her makeup was flawless. She was one of those women who knew how to apply eyeliner. Mine always had a messy outline to it, like I'd put it on while riding the Metro. Okay, more often than not, I did apply my makeup on the subway. Duplicating her slick presentation was beyond my realm of the possible.

Meg couldn't have had much sleep, but she still looked great. I was amazed she had ventured out on the town, given the murder and the fact we wouldn't have jobs in a week.

"You went on a date last night?" I tried to hide my incredulity. After all, who was I to judge? I lived with a Georgetown professor and an overweight beagle in a semi-luxury inner-urbs high-rise condo. Most of my Capitol Hill friends were unattached, and I liked to live vicariously through them. Still, the fact that Meg was partying less than twelve hours after our boss had been murdered seemed over the top.

"Don't give me that look, Kit," she said, and as if reading my mind, added, "Not all of us have a Prince Charming, remember?" Meg's taunt was justified. Doug was close to a saint, and I took him for granted occasionally. When this whole mess was over, I'd make an extra effort to let him know how much I appreciated him. He always wanted to attend evening cultural events at the Smithsonian. Rather than ignoring his forwarded emails about the next lecture series, I'd surprise him with tickets.

The relationship between Meg and Doug was occasionally rocky. Both competed for my time outside the office, and since they were polar opposites, activities as a threesome were out of the question. It was best not to press the matter.

"I didn't say a word. So tell me about your date."

"Well, if you must know, I did consider canceling, given the circumstances." She lowered her eyes and fiddled with her BlackBerry. "Really, I'm not heartless. I'm taking Senator Langsford's death as hard as anyone here."

I wasn't convinced that was an accurate statement, but people did express grief in different ways. I nodded, so Meg kept talking.

"Since I knew we couldn't start investigating until today, I figured I might as well keep my date. It was with Jerry, that guy who works on the third floor for Senator Martin. He covers banking and insurance for her. Do you know who he is?"

I shook my head. I knew a lot of people on the Hill, but mostly staffers in my issue area who worked for senators on the Appropriations Committee. I attended my share of happy hours and receptions because networking was an important part of the job. If I didn't meet the people who worked on the same stuff I did, it would be impossible to know whom to call when my boss needed something. Nonetheless, I didn't consider myself a D.C. socialite. Meg, however, was part of the Hill scene and consequently, her network was vast. Her electronic Rolodex extended well beyond her fellow compatriots who specialized in health care policy. Jerry was her latest victim.

Before I could ask how she had met him, Meg said, "You have to meet Jerry. He's a mover on Capitol Hill."

For Meg, any guy who was remotely cute was a "mover" on the Hill, giving her a professional reason to date every hot guy she could find in Congress.

She continued, "I met him in the cafeteria one day. We were both waiting for them to put out more sausage and pepperoni pizza. Isn't that amazing?"

What was amazing was that Meg could eat sausage and pepperoni pizza for lunch and still wear a size four. Apparently Jerry shared her passion for food, which was important in a relationship.

"What a coincidence. So what's so special about this Jerry?"

"First, he's extremely good looking."

This was no surprise. Meg wasn't completely superficial; she would never date someone who was attractive if he was also a jerk. That said, she favored guys who were close to her equal in physical appearance. That was a high bar. Without being an egomaniac, Meg never sold herself short. Her healthy self-confidence rarely wavered.

"He's tall, and he works out all the time, so he's in great shape. I wish I had a picture of him on my phone, but it's impossible to browse the web on this stupid BlackBerry. Oh, he's on Facebook, though. I'll show you his profile at my computer."

Prodding her, I tried to move this conversation along. "Great, I'll take a look sometime soon. Anything else notable?"

Her face became animated. "Wait, don't rush me. I'm getting to it. We went out for drinks, and he agreed to split a bottle of Prosecco with me."

This was pay dirt for Meg. She loved the Italian bubbly, which most guys considered a "girly" drink. Either Jerry shared her love for it, didn't care, or he wanted to see how far he could get by treating her to a few glasses.

"This certainly sounds like true love." I didn't bother to hide my sarcasm. Meg didn't pick up on it, or if she did, she ignored it.

"Well, he had a few drinks, which will help you understand what I'm going to tell you next."

Meg paused for effect. She had told me once that she'd acted in high school plays, and I believed it. She had a flair for drama. Although it could be annoying, it served her well in Congress. Constituents, in particular, liked the enthusiasm she displayed, and she often explained the lawmaking process with embellishment and intrigue to make it sound more exciting than it really was.

"Jerry shared an interesting piece of information. Once you hear this, you won't question my decision to keep my date with him." Meg's logic was a bit skewed, since I doubted she knew Jerry had any valuable information when she decided to keep their date, but I let it pass.

"Naturally, we talked about Senator Langsford's death. He had heard you were a suspect, and he thought you'd been taken into custody, but I set the record straight on that. Don't worry, Kit. I've been telling everyone I know you didn't do it." The strength of Meg's social network on Capitol Hill was formidable. Since she knew so many people, she qualified as a rumor mill in her own right. However, it did worry me that Joe Average Staffer thought I had been arrested for the murder.

"I appreciate your help, Meg. What did Jerry say that was so compelling?" At this point, I just wanted Meg to finish the story.

"You're going to love this. His brother works for an insurance company in the D.C. area. They sell policies to the elite Beltway crowd."

Maybe this was worth waiting for. "Go on."

Meg was practically bursting at the seams now. "Well, let's put it this way. Jerry wasn't surprised to find out you weren't the murderer."

"Okay, you got me. Why did Jerry assume I'm innocent?"

"I was just getting to that. Langsford's death was the biggest story yesterday on the news. Jerry talks to his brother all the time on live chat. Once his brother saw that Langsford had been killed, he messaged Jerry and told him the senator had recently taken out a big life insurance policy!"

Meg beamed at me. There was one piece of information missing. "Meg, do you know who was the beneficiary to that insurance policy?"

She smiled slowly. "Of course I do. It wouldn't be

that helpful if I didn't, right? Vivian Langsford is the sole beneficiary."

That sounded plausible, yet it was also a little too obvious. The motive was as mundane as it comes: the husband takes out a new insurance policy that increases the payout and the wife stands to benefit. If the husband suddenly ends up dead, the wife would be scrutinized for the murder, right? Regardless, it was a great lead, and given my latest conversation with Trevor, Vivian Langsford was a prime suspect.

I congratulated Meg on her impressive sleuthing and listened to a few more juicy tidbits about her night on the town with Jerry, which didn't end after his great revelation about Vivian's inheritance.

I spent the next several hours hunched over my computer, answering emails from staffers on the Hill, lobbyists, other contacts, and constituents. All the correspondence expressed deep sympathy and disbelief concerning Senator Langsford's death. He might have made enemies here or there, but he had earned the respect of many.

I got up to stretch my legs and take a walk around the office. Usually, a hefty number of meetings kept me moving throughout the day. I rarely sat at my desk for more than a twenty-minute stretch, but today I hadn't taken a break in hours.

As I turned the corner, I almost ran into Detective O'Halloran. The beefy cop looked like he'd seen better days. His eyes were droopy, and his clothes and hair were disheveled. He wasn't going to get a decent night's sleep until this case was solved. Besides a terrorist attack, the murder of a senator was the most serious crime for a Capitol Hill police officer. He would be burning the midnight oil until this got wrapped up.

"Ms. Marshall, just the person I wanted to see."

I gave a nervous laugh. "Detective, how is the investigation going?"

His tired face answered my question. He hadn't progressed very far. He stared at me for a second and then said, "We're narrowing down the people of interest."

I decided to fight fire with fire. "Very good. Can you tell me who is on that list?" As my conversation with Trevor had shown, the direct approach was often best.

Detective O'Halloran was taken aback. He crossed his arms in front of his chest. "And why would you want to know who's on that list?" He looked at me pointedly.

I had a good answer to his question. "Since I was your lead suspect yesterday and subjected to a high degree of media scrutiny, I deserve to know." I folded my arms across my chest. Two could play at this game, for sure.

O'Halloran met my gaze. "Our suspect list is police information, and I have nothing to do with the press." I wondered if the police actually had any suspects other than me.

Managing a smile, I decided to try another approach. "I'm sure it's difficult to wade through Senator Langsford's contacts. If you need any help with specific people, I'd be happy to assist."

He spoke in a clipped manner. "Thanks. If we come across anyone you might be able to tell us about, we'll ask you. Right now, we're just trying to get a handle on the big picture."

That was a euphemism if I had ever heard one. A "handle on the big picture"? My instincts were correct.

It was going to be extremely difficult for an outsider to develop a list of concrete suspects who had a reason to kill Lyndon Langsford.

"Does your big picture include Vivian Langsford?" I looked slyly at the Detective. I didn't want to divulge all my information, but I wanted him to recognize my familiarity with the cast of characters in Langsford's world.

O'Halloran gave me a hard stare. "And why would you ask that question about Senator Langsford's wife?"

If he wanted to be obtuse, that was fine with me. "Oh, no reason, really. I just heard she might have a motive for killing her husband." I tried to act nonchalant, as blasé as humanly possible while accusing my former boss's wife of murder.

O'Halloran shook his head. "I don't know what you've heard, but you shouldn't be poking around in police business. This is a job for the professionals. If you didn't murder Langsford, as you contend," he raised an eyebrow at me, "you should feel lucky to be alive. The autopsy concurred with the medical examiner's initial findings. Senator Langsford had been dead only a short while before you found him. Besides, we've already checked out his wife, and she's got an alibi for yesterday morning."

"Where was Vivian? She wasn't at home? I didn't know she was particularly active in the morning hours." I tried not to sound overly cynical. In the Senate office, Vivian wasn't known as an early riser. Our scheduler Kara had told me Vivian couldn't be booked for any appearances before ten in the morning. She simply wasn't willing to get up earlier for events with the senator.

"If you must know, and I'm not sure why I'm telling you this, she was working out with her personal trainer during the time period in which we think Senator Langsford was stabbed."

Vivian had several motives for killing her husband. First, she didn't like the decision he'd made concerning Carter Power. Second, Langsford had recently increased his life insurance policy. Neither motive put me any closer to solving the murder if she had an airtight alibi, although the personal trainer excuse seemed a little shaky. Like I said, Vivian wasn't known as someone who woke at the crack of dawn. I couldn't imagine her working out that early in the morning, yet Detective O'Halloran seemed convinced the alibi was legit.

I nodded vaguely. I didn't want O'Halloran to know quite yet that Meg and I were informally investigating Senator Langsford's death. The police never appreciated the help of amateurs. However, after talking to O'Halloran, I was more convinced than ever that we needed to keep snooping around for clues. O'Halloran had certainly figured out by now that Senator Langsford's network was vast and complex. An outsider might take days to figure out the most important people, then even more time to winnow that group down to suspects who had motive or opportunity. I could eliminate the entire first part of the process, given that I knew everyone of consequence in Senator Langsford's professional life.

Before I had a chance to get away, O'Halloran stopped me. "Wait a second. I almost forgot why I wanted to talk to you in the first place. We've been able to determine that Senator Langsford was probably killed less than an hour before you discovered his body. Possibly as short a time as half an hour."

I shuddered. I hadn't realized that Senator Langsford was so recently dead when I saw him.

"If you didn't kill Langsford, that means there's a slight chance the killer was still in the building when you entered to come to work." Another macabre thought, for sure.

"What I'm trying to say, Ms. Marshall, is I need you to think carefully about what you saw yesterday morning, especially while it's fresh in your mind. Do you remember seeing anyone suspicious or out of place in the Hart Building when you arrived? Anyone at all? Perhaps even someone leaving the elevator or headed into a restroom?"

O'Halloran looked at me with pleading eyes. I was starting to feel sorry for the man. He didn't have many leads, and pressure from his boss to solve the case as soon as possible was likely increasing. Right now, I was his only potential eyewitness.

I chose my words cautiously. "I wish I could help you, Detective O'Halloran. I just don't remember seeing anyone I knew that morning. If something comes to mind, I'll be sure to let you know." I reached out to shake his hand, and he politely took it.

I thought about our office's secret exit on the upper floor of the suite. If that was how the killer had escaped detection after committing the crime, it definitely had to be an insider or someone the senator knew very well indeed.

"Thank you, Ms. Marshall." He turned to walk away, then spun around abruptly. "Something else. Please be careful. You may not remember seeing anyone who left the building yesterday, but that doesn't mean you didn't see someone, or you don't remember you saw someone. In that case, the murderer might have seen you."

Nodding in acknowledgement, I felt the sting of the detective's words. Perhaps my sleuthing had taken on a new purpose. It wasn't only about clearing my name. It was about catching the killer before I became the next victim.

TEN

I HEADED TOWARD Matt's office. He had made himself scarce this morning, and I wanted to make sure I was attending to my duties. Given that we didn't really work for a living United States Senator anymore, I assumed our responsibilities were limited. But assumptions had a way of getting me in trouble.

Like Detective O'Halloran, Matt looked like he hadn't slept much last night. His tie was crooked, and his demeanor, usually vibrant and good-natured, seemed strained. Matt had known Senator Langsford for almost a decade. He had to be hurting both professionally and personally.

He smiled wryly when he saw me, though. "Kit, have a seat. I hope you're not still the prime suspect in our boss's murder?"

"Well, sir, it looks as though they're trying to identify other suspects, but I don't think Detective O'Halloran has cleared me yet."

"I just had a long interview with the police, and I must admit, I don't think they have any idea who killed the senator," Matt offered.

"I know what you mean. I just talked to Detective O'Halloran and I didn't get the impression they have a suspect in mind."

Matt winced. "I was afraid my suspicions were correct. I hoped the police would have several solid leads by now." He sighed. "I guess this case is a hard nut to crack. Who would want to kill Lyndon Langsford?"

Now it was my turn to smile wryly. Matt was the best boss I could ask for, but he had a blind spot when it came to Senator Langsford. Without fail, he cast Langsford's maverick positions in the best possible light, justifying them by saying a particular stance was "for the people" or "the right thing to do." Most of the time, Matt was right. He refused to believe that even Langsford occasionally made choices on the basis of pure politics. Matt chose to view Senator Langsford through rose-colored glasses. No wonder he had no concrete ideas as to who might have killed him. To Matt, Senator Langsford was the model public servant.

"Honestly, sir, I don't know who would want to kill Senator Langsford, either. But I hope, for everyone's sake, that the police figure it out soon."

Matt nodded. "Especially for Vivian's benefit. I don't know how she's coping with all this."

Matt's mention of Vivian gave me an opening. "Yes, and his death must be quite messy, given the recent increase in Senator Langsford's insurance policy." My words hung in silence for several moments.

Matt raised his eyebrows. "How do you know about an increase in his insurance policy?"

I hadn't been a detective for long, but something told me part of the gig was protecting my sources, much like a journalist. I didn't want to name Meg or her friend Jerry, even though I trusted Matt would never use that information inappropriately. Still, some things were better left unsaid. My instincts told me this was one of them.

I gave Matt my most innocent look. "Oh, you know,

COLLEEN J. SHOGAN 97

people talk. I heard someone mention it casually in conversation." At least that wasn't a lie.

With a stern voice, Matt said, "Kit, it sounds like gossip to me. I have no idea whether it's actually true. But you need to be careful dropping pieces of information like that. Someone might take it the wrong way."

He had a point. It didn't make sense to fuel any rumors. I only needed to share what I knew with those people who could help me discover more leads. Showboating wouldn't get me anywhere, except in a heap of trouble.

I saw an opportunity to change the conversation's direction. "Since we're talking about Vivian, do you know about the plans for a memorial service for Senator Langsford? Mandy didn't give us details this morning."

"Lucinda was going to announce the plans later today to staff. There will be a memorial service the day after tomorrow at the Langsfords' home in McLean."

The senator and Vivian lived in a distinguished home in the affluent Virginia suburb a few miles from where I lived. I had visited their house several times to drop off an urgent document or to attend the Langsfords' annual summer barbecue for staff. The house was beautiful. I always got nervous when visiting because if I broke anything, it would cost me an entire year's salary to replace it. Vivian brought considerable wealth to their marriage, and by the looks of their house, she never lost her taste for the finer things in life.

"Can I ask Mandy any specific questions about the wake? I'm getting a lot of inquiries from my contacts who had professional dealings with Senator Langsford."

Matt shook his head. "I would ask Lucinda. I'm not

sure Mandy is going to remain on staff for the duration of the transition."

That was news. "Did she find another job already?"

Matt averted his eyes. "As a matter of fact, she did. Mandy will be moving to Senator Regan's office, effective next week."

Mandy didn't waste any time. That conversation I had interrupted yesterday was her overture, which meant she had sealed the deal with Senator Regan in less than twenty-four hours.

"I guess that means one of us has found employment. At least she has somewhere to report next week. Who knows if we will?"

Matt rubbed his hands together nervously. "I hate to admit it, but you're right. The governor will probably wait an appropriate amount of time—maybe a week after the wake—then he'll appoint a successor. That person won't be from our political party."

I remembered this morning's conversation with Trevor. "There's no chance Mrs. Langsford will be appointed as a caretaker for the remainder of the term?"

"We thought initially that Vivian might be in the running. That would have given us a soft place to land until staff secured permanent offers from other offices. But we heard this morning from the governor's representative in Washington that he's headed in another direction. There's a lot of pressure on him to appoint someone who will be useful to the Republicans."

"Matt, who do you think will get the appointment?" He knew the state and its politics better than anyone in the office, so his opinion counted.

"The odds-on favorite is certainly Jessop. He ran for the seat and put up a decent fight. The governor knows

Jessop's House seat is a safe one, so it's likely to stay within his party if he leaves it and becomes a senator. There are other possibilities, of course, but most people expect Jessop will be occupying this office." He sighed and put his face in his hands.

I understood Matt's frustration, especially since Senator Langsford had defeated Jessop in the last election, and his victory had required the all-out efforts of many of the staffers currently employed in our office. It seemed like a moral defeat after such a hard-won race. Langsford had pulled ahead only a few days before the election. Jessop was close to becoming a United States Senator, perhaps the dream of every member of the House of Representatives. He'd had a glimpse of the brass ring, yet it had ended up out of reach. That glimpse made Jessop a bitter man. The relationship between the two politicians had not improved after the campaign, despite several attempts by Langsford to mend fences.

Matt needed an emotional boost. "Don't worry. It's only for a couple of years. Even if Jessop gets the appointment, he's going to have to run again to keep it, and we all know he wasn't successful the last time he tried to do that."

Matt gave me a small smile. "Thanks for putting a positive spin on an absolutely bleak situation." He paused for a second. "Let me know if you find out any more colorful gossip." He winked at me, and I grinned back at him. Matt had to give me a lecture about why gossiping was poor form, but when push came to shove, he wanted to know details about the murder investigation, too.

I left Matt's office and had only taken a few steps

outside when I nearly collided with Mandy. She appeared to have recovered from yesterday's maelstrom. She looked fantastic in high heels, a slim skirt, a freshly pressed white blouse, and a delicate pearl necklace with matching earrings.

"Mandy, I hear congratulations are in order." I gave her the biggest smile I could muster.

Instead of returning the pleasantry, she scowled. "What do you mean?"

She was going to make this difficult. I suppressed a groan. "I heard you got a new job with Senator Regan and you start next week."

Her eyes narrowed as she glowered at me. "How did you hear about that?"

There was no point in lying, and Mandy had officially annoyed me. "I just came out of Matt's office, and he told me. Is it a secret?"

She shook her head. "No, Miss Busybody, it's not a secret. I was going to announce it tomorrow on my morning video update, but there's no point. Now that you found out, everyone in the office will know soon." She tossed her hair over her shoulder and flounced down the hallway. She had only gone a few steps before she turned around and added, "If you haven't already noticed, this is a sinking ship, Kit. I wouldn't stay onboard too much longer."

What a drama queen! Goodbye and good riddance, Mandy Lippman. The less said, the better. Though I hadn't adhered to that mantra very well so far, I vowed to follow it in the future.

ELEVEN

THE REST OF the day passed uneventfully. I disciplined myself to finish up several administrative tasks and dutifully answered emails and phone calls as they came in. Finally I took a few minutes to call Doug and let him know I had scheduled drinks after work with Meg and Jeff Prentice, the lobbyist from Carter Power.

Doug sounded suspicious when I told him I wouldn't be home for dinner tonight due to happy hour plans. He knew I never jumped at the chance to spend time with Jeff Prentice. He also knew my involvement with Carter Power had died with Senator Langsford.

"That's curious. Why did you make plans with Prentice? As I recall, he was never your favorite lobbyist."

I gritted my teeth. One of the downsides of being involved with a professor was the impossibility of getting anything past him. He had an exceptional memory, and beyond his early morning fog, he rarely forgot a comment or detail. Some old-fashioned spin was in order so he wouldn't worry too much about my machinations. When in doubt, just blame it on your best friend.

"Well, it was Meg's idea." That wasn't a complete fabrication. Meg had suggested we have drinks with Jeff Prentice tonight.

Doug wasn't buying it. "Well, why are you tagging along? You're no longer involved with the Carter Power deal, are you?"

This was unusual behavior for Doug. He never cared about my happy hour exploits, and he understood that part of working on Capitol Hill meant I attended social events after work. He was being nosy because he suspected ulterior motives, which included snooping around for clues.

"You're right. I'm not directly involved with the Carter Power business anymore. However, I should be on the lookout for a new job, and I want to concentrate my search on senators who focus on issues similar to those that interested Langsford. I'd better keep all my relationships intact, right?"

Whether or not Doug still doubted my reasons for meeting with Jeff, he gave up. The argument about finding another job resonated with him. "I guess that makes sense. You'd better not burn any bridges."

"Exactly. I'm so happy you understand. I'll see you later tonight." I hung up quickly before he could ask more questions.

Glancing at the clock on my desktop, I realized it was almost 6 p.m. Normally this would have been the end of the official workday in the Senate, although staff often stayed later to write memos or other documents they couldn't finish earlier because they were busy with meetings or hearings. Without an elected boss, burning the midnight oil seemed irrational. I sent Meg an Instant Message: "Are you ready to go?"

"I can hear a Cosmo calling my name," she typed back.

My reflexive chuckle was followed by a wave of sadness. There wouldn't be many more evenings like this. It would be next to impossible to find jobs in the same Capitol Hill office, and one of us—me, most likely—

would have to look for employment somewhere other than Congress. We would both land on our feet, but those feet wouldn't be planted in the same place.

I gathered my purse and headed over to Meg's desk. She had apparently embraced the notion that our jobs weren't all that serious at this point; she was listening to her iPod full blast while playing Solitaire on her computer. I stood by her desk, and she paid me no attention. I poked her on the shoulder to announce my presence.

She said loudly to me, "Want to head out now?"

I nodded. Was I standing at her desk for the heck of it? Meg definitely marched to the beat of her own drummer.

As we walked out, we peeked into Lucinda's office. She looked even worse off than Matt. She was completely bent over, her upper body resting on the desk. Her telephone headset was dangling, like an askew tiara on a beauty queen. She'd been on the phone all day, and the weary drudgery of reciting the plans for the wake and telling well-wishers to donate to Senator Langsford's favorite charity had taken its toll. We both gave her a wave as we headed for the exit.

I daydreamed about becoming a chief of staff in the Senate one day in the future. Lucinda always had the senator's ear and the enviable capacity to catapult an issue or concern to the top of his agenda. Observing Lucinda that evening, however, I realized that a great deal of responsibility came along with a job as important as hers. I needed a few more years under my belt before assuming that type of position.

We walked into the evening air, which was still a balmy 85 degrees. Thankfully, Lounge 201 was only a short block away. Any longer of a walk and we'd have to take off our suit jackets to withstand the oppressive humidity. I spent all year waiting for the summer, yet when it arrived in D.C., I joined in with the familiar cacophony of discord and complained incessantly about the horrible heat.

I took advantage of the short jaunt to query Meg about meeting Jeff Prentice tonight. "Can you tell me again why we agreed to join my least favorite lobbyist for drinks? It's not like he can pay for us anymore, you know."

Ethics laws had changed drastically in recent years. Lobbyists used to wine and dine congressional staff on a routine basis, often resulting in so-called "working" lunches, dinners, and happy hours. That fun had come to a halt, and now lobbyists could only host staff and members of Congress at "widely attended events" that involved no chairs or forks. It made little sense to most staff on Capitol Hill. As long as the meat was on a stick and no one could sit down, lobbyists could still buy us a drink. The moment our bottoms hit the seat and we picked up a utensil, the lobbyists put their credit cards away.

"Kit, even you admitted yesterday that if Senator Langsford's death had something to do with Carter Power, Jeff Prentice was the best place to start digging."

"Wait." I thrust my arm out to make Meg stop in her tracks. "Let's take a moment to come up with a game plan."

She almost tripped when her body collided with my arm. Giggling, she said, "You sound like a high school basketball coach or something."

Laughing with her, I realized it was the first time

since Senator Langsford died that I had cracked a genuine smile. It felt good to relax for a moment.

"Let's get serious. What do we need to get out of this conversation?"

Meg thought for a few seconds. "First, we should figure out who had a motive to kill Senator Langsford."

"Good idea. Let's go through the list."

"There's Vivian Langsford. We know she stood to inherit a lot of money from the senator's life insurance."

"That's true. But I did learn this morning that she has an alibi. So we need to check that out."

"Besides Vivian, there's also Representative Jessop."

"Definitely. He wants to become a United States Senator more than anything else, and the only way he could have a shot would be if Senator Langsford resigned or died."

Who else was on the suspect list? "Consider Carter Power. The two people who might have wanted Senator Langsford out of the way are Senator Regan and Jeff Prentice. If Senator Langsford had voted the way he intended, Carter Power's longstanding contract with the Pentagon would be history. That would mean hundreds of lost jobs in California, and doomsday for Senator Regan's reelection campaign. It might also have cost Jeff Prentice his job, since he's Carter Power's main lobbyist in Washington."

Meg agreed. "Carter Power could be the main motive for killing Senator Langsford. Don't forget Trevor told us Vivian might also have been mixed up in Langsford's position on Carter Power."

I snapped my fingers. "I almost forgot about that. It gives her an additional motive besides the life insurance policy."

"Is there anyone we're missing?"

"I don't want to rule anyone out—and I mean *any-one*—at this point. Let's try to think creatively. Who else might have a motive to kill Senator Langsford?"

Meg said slowly, "I suppose any employee in our office. But I don't like saying that out loud, do you? That would mean we've been working alongside a murderer." Meg lowered her voice when she said the word "murderer," as if it was a dirty word.

I cupped my chin in a deliberate pause, waiting for two staffers to pass us by on the sidewalk. Meddlesome eavesdroppers were ubiquitous in Washington. Saying something juicy too loudly at the wrong time meant casual comments could end up in a *Washington Post* article the next morning.

"I see your point. But we don't have the luxury of eliminating anyone now. There may be more motives out there we need to uncover. I read in one of my mysteries that motive is the key to solving a crime. Motive will give us our possible suspects; then we'll take it from there."

"Can you tell me with a straight face we should consider Matt a suspect?" Meg put her hand on her hip and tilted her head at me.

"That's a tough one. It's unlikely he's on our short list. But let's not exclude anyone right now. For example, think about Lucinda. You and I don't know if she's got some crazy hidden motive to get Senator Langsford out of the way. Or even Kara! Maybe Mandy? Or could it be Trevor?" My voice was getting louder, as it usually did when I got excited. I thrust my finger into the air to emphasize my point. "We can leave no stone unturned!"

It was Meg's turn to laugh. "You've made your point.

We won't discount anyone right now, but let's focus on Jeff tonight. With any luck, he's already had one martini and is ordering his second as we speak. Remember how drunk he got at the Carter Power holiday party?"

I had a flashback of Jeff Prentice swilling down alcoholic drinks and stumbling past me at the annual event. "I remember, although I wish I didn't. This is a good environment to pump him for information. I have to admit, Meg, I didn't know how you'd adapt to this gumshoe role, but you've been resourceful."

My best friend blushed. "We've always made a great team, haven't we?"

Now it was my turn to blush. I reached out and gave her a quick hug. "Yes, we have. And I'm sure we have a lot of adventures still in store. Aren't you?"

"Definitely. Now let's go inside, have a drink, and figure out if Jeff Prentice murdered our boss."

TWELVE

WE WALKED DOWN the short staircase to Lounge 201, which was the quintessential Capitol Hill basement bar. A below street level bar was appropriate for bottom-feeders. Although there were more sharks at this bar than the Great Barrier reef, I still liked the place. The décor was garishly seedy, complete with leopard print high-back chairs and dim lighting, but it wasn't a bad place to hang out after a stressful workday. It was a Wednesday evening, meaning half-price martinis. That was always a popular night, which could make it difficult to find a seat. We arrived earlier than usual since we'd left the office right at six. Hopefully we wouldn't be standing by the bar, straining to hear every other word from Jeff.

I let my eyes adjust to the dark. We were in luck. The full onslaught of Senate staff thirsting for cheap libations wouldn't descend for another forty-five minutes. We had our pick of tables. I motioned for Meg to head to the corner of the lounge so we could maximize privacy with Jeff when he arrived.

We sat at the circular corner table and picked up the drink-special menu. I was ready to order, and I was sure Meg's mind was made up as well. Regular customers knew the best deals each day of the week. With a mission to accomplish, tonight wasn't the time to try out new drinks.

Our waitress came over to the table and asked us in a bored monotone if we had decided. I asked for the White Cosmopolitan, which was a deliciously crisp and refreshing substitute for the traditional. Meg ordered a Jamaicatini, reminiscent of her recent Caribbean vacation with its rum and mango blend.

As we waited for our beverages and Jeff's arrival, I reminded Meg we needed to extract as much information as possible from our guest. "I know it's hard to pry you away on discounted martini night, but we should sip one drink only and try to get him to 'fess up."

Meg strained to appear innocent as our cocktails arrived. "You don't have to remind me why we're here. I set this up, remember? I know we need to keep it under control tonight. But don't we also need to loosen up and act like we're having fun with Jeff? Otherwise, he's never going to tell us anything." Meg gave me a pouty look that made me think I was spoiling her evening.

I was about to tell Meg we could act like we were having fun without drinking Jeff under the table when I caught a glimpse of him entering the bar. Jeff certainly looked like a stereotypical defense lobbyist. He had short dark hair cut close—similar to a military-style trim, but suitable for a young professional. He was in his late thirties, I guessed. As he walked across the room, he took off his aviator style sunglasses and tucked them inside his suit pocket. He was certainly in shape, probably continuing the regimen he'd followed in the Army.

Like many in the defense world, Jeff was a veteran. Those who served in the military could speak the language of endless acronyms that permeated defense policymaking circles in Washington. DARPA, ICAF,

SAC-D, RTP, MLA, SOCOM. The abbreviations constituted a private language only a select few spoke fluently. Furthermore, veterans carried with them an air of unassailable legitimacy that helped them gain instant credibility with congressional offices of both parties.

Jeff had these advantages working in his favor, yet I still didn't trust him. Since I worked on all issues before the Appropriations Committee for Senator Langsford, I had solid relationships with lobbyists all over town. A day never went by that I didn't meet with or talk to a registered lobbyist. After four years of happy hours, meet-and-greets, and calorie-laden receptions, I could size up a lobbyist quickly and determine whether I trusted him or her. I had spent a considerable number of hours in the past six months with Jeff when Senator Langsford had begun to waver on the Carter Power contract. The whole time, my faith in him never grew stronger. If anything, I questioned his motives more. That was why I'd cringed when Meg suggested we meet him for drinks. He wasn't my favorite lobbyist, and I doubted I was his favorite congressional staffer.

Jeff finally spotted us in the corner and made a beeline to the table. He smiled widely as he approached, almost like he'd just won reelection in a landslide. "How are two of my favorite ladies of Capitol Hill today?"

His affable demeanor threw me off. For months I had become accustomed to Jeff's morose attitude as we negotiated regarding Carter Power. Langsford's death might explain the change in his outlook. He'd been down in the dumps when he thought Carter Power might lose its contract and preferred standing. Now that Langsford was dead, there was a good chance Carter

Power would be offered another lucrative contract, and that meant Jeff stood to collect a big bonus.

Jeff must have realized his super-friendly greeting was inappropriate for the occasion. He took one look at our blank faces before backpedaling. "Hey, I'm sorry about what happened to Langsford. You know I loved the guy. It's such a shame to see a talented senator die in a horrible way."

He paused, and when we didn't respond, kept talking. "I guess the police don't have many leads, or if they do, they're not being made public." He looked at both of us. Jeff wanted information from this meeting, perhaps to find out how much we knew about the murder. Our objective was to give him little, while trying to get him to give us as many details as possible.

Before Meg could respond, I said, "We understand the police are chasing down several leads and may be close to an arrest." Meg gave me a questioning look, but I kicked her under the table so she would stay quiet. Baiting Jeff to see if he'd squirm at the prospect that the police were zeroing in on a suspect seemed like a smart way to start the interrogation.

He seemed alarmed at my white lie, but it was hard to tell if he was confused or simply surprised. "That's news to me. I stopped by your office a few minutes ago to chat with Lucinda, and she didn't think the police were far along at all."

He shrugged and motioned for our waitress to take his order. Jeff gave her a thousand watt smile, his eyes wavering between her face and fitted blouse. "I know it's half-price martini night, but I'm in the mood for a nice red wine. Do you have any Pinot Noir from Oregon?"

The cocktail waitress made a funny face. This wasn't a place for a wine connoisseur. "We have six red wines on our menu, and we do have a Pinot Noir, but I think it's from California."

Jeff sighed. "That will have to do. I'll take a glass."

I raised my eyebrows. As long as I knew him, Jeff drank whatever was on special, usually not drifting too far from the Budweiser or Coors category. I glanced at the menu and confirmed, as I suspected, that the Pinot Noir was the most expensive wine on the menu.

I couldn't resist asking about his selection. "So Jeff, have you been watching *Sideways* lately on cable, or what? I've never seen you order wine before, especially a nice wine."

Jeff's face clouded over, almost as though he'd been caught doing something naughty. I was willing to bet he had seen *Sideways* lately and had picked up the Pinot Noir reference, but I wasn't going to push it. It was more intriguing that this former cheapskate's palate had drifted from domestic tap beer to a $14 per glass wine.

He grimaced. "I've spent time in California recently with Senator Regan, and we toured some vineyards. I guess you could say I've been bitten by the wine bug."

The waitress approached with his glass of wine, which Jeff carefully swirled, then sniffed deeply. That exchange led me to two conclusions. First, Jeff had either come into money recently or thought he was going to see an increase in salary soon, thereby explaining the expensive change in taste. Second, he had spent a considerable amount of time with Regan in California. Senator Regan didn't seem the type of politician who would just invite a lobbyist to tour the local vineyards.

There had to be another reason why Regan had gotten so chummy with Jeff Prentice lately.

With the waitress lingering at our table, Meg ordered us another round of drinks. She was getting antsy. I'd have to incorporate her into the conversation soon or she'd end up finishing her second drink way too quickly. Two martinis in rapid succession had the potential to send the evening into an intoxicated tailspin.

Jeff carefully studied his Pinot, raising the glass into the air and scrutinizing it from different angles. I took the opportunity to text Meg, using my BlackBerry underneath the table. Only the Senate maintained a contract with BlackBerry; the rest of Washington, D.C., and the world used more sophisticated smartphones. The sole advantage of the antiquated BlackBerry was the built-in keyboard, which made it easy to type messages without mistakes.

I typed, "Ask him Y he spent time w/ RGN in CA." I hoped she understood my shorthand. She was usually adept in deciphering my shortcuts in texts. Her Black-Berry buzzed a second later, and she discreetly glanced at it underneath the table. I'd let Meg take the lead on the next round of questioning.

Meg took a big sip of her second martini and batted her eyelashes at Jeff. Oh boy. I had requested the full treatment when I gave Meg the green light to take the reins.

She smiled at Jeff and subtly licked her upper lip. "I like your new interest in wines. Tell me more about what you've seen in California." She patted his hand with her carefully manicured nails. He edged slightly closer to her.

Meg let Jeff prattle on about several wineries he'd

toured in California. Affirming my *Sideways* hypothesis, he explained he'd started liking Merlot but had moved on to Pinot Noir once he had "refined his palate" and "trained his nose" to appreciate the "full arsenal of scents" from various grapes. Jeff had clearly picked up the appropriate vocabulary during his winery tour with Senator Regan.

Once she had lured him in, Meg asked, "So tell me again why you were visiting Senator Regan in California? Was it business? Or *pleasure*?" She emphasized the word "pleasure," which sent a variety of subliminal messages to Jeff.

Her flirting must have achieved the desired effect, because Jeff didn't hesitate in answering. "Oh, it was business, although I certainly had a lot of fun."

Meg smiled again at him and took a seductive sip of her martini. "I see. Were you on business from Carter Power, then?"

Jeff paused for a second, presumably realizing the conversation was veering in directions he hadn't anticipated. With a smirk, he leaned back and put his hands behind his head. "I suppose it can't hurt to let the cat out of the bag now."

Meg giggled, which I could tell was fake, but I bet Jeff couldn't. "Please, let the cat out of the bag. After all, you're among friends and we're all sharing secrets, right?"

He nodded. "Sure. I mean, it can't hurt, and you guys don't even work for Senator Langsford anymore, do you?" He gave a short laugh.

We both responded with tight, forced smiles. He didn't seem to notice our tense reactions. Meg chimed in, "Right, we're barely even Hill staff anymore. Right, Kit?"

"Yep. I imagine we'll have to turn in our Senate identification badges any day now."

Jeff leaned forward again. "Well, I went to California to visit Senator Regan because we were discussing Carter Power business officially. We did talk about the contract renewal when I was out there. But just between us, Senator Regan wanted to talk with me about coming on board to work on his legislative staff when he's reelected. He wants to shake things up and bring in some people with real world experience, if you know what I mean. So we used the visits to get to know each other better and talk about my job prospects in his office after the election in November."

The pending offer of employment gave Jeff a substantial incentive to ensure Senator Regan's reelection. And Regan's reelection was directly tied to the renewal of Carter Power's contract. No contract, no reelection, no job for Jeff. I also noticed that Jeff said "when" Senator Regan was reelected, not "if." Was that confidence warranted, or had Jeff acted to guarantee his prospective boss's victory?

Of course, that motive was only credible if Jeff knew Senator Langsford planned to vote against Carter Power in the upcoming committee vote. That decision had been heavily guarded. Jeff hadn't attended every meeting with Senator Langsford and Senator Regan when crucial discussions took place. Despite Senator Regan's contention that Langsford was going to vote to support Carter Power, all the meetings had showed my boss was skeptical at best. Had Regan told Jeff that Langsford was going to sabotage the vote? If so, did Jeff want to work in the Senate so badly that he killed Langsford to ensure Regan's reelection and the continued prosperity of Carter Power? My next line of questioning for Jeff would aim to determine if he knew about Senator Langsford's intentions.

"Are you going to be working on defense issues for Senator Regan?" I tried to smile sweetly at Jeff, but it was a pathetic effort. On my best day, I couldn't hold a candle to Meg. Added to that, even when I was single, I was terrible at flirting. It was a miracle I had found Doug, except that he was as nerdy as I was clumsy. In that sense, we were a perfect match.

It must have been my lucky day, or Jeff was simply feeling good after his glass of wine. "That's what it looks like. I'll be staffing him on defense appropriations. You know—all the good stuff."

I decided to try to keep the conversation rolling. "The first big issue will be the contract with Carter Power, right?"

Jeff agreed. "That's part of the reason Senator Regan wants to hire me. He knows I understand that issue inside and out, and he needs to get a win on it."

I kept pushing. "I'm curious. What was your plan of action with my former boss?" I winced slightly at the term "former boss," but I needed to get over it and keep grilling Jeff about what he knew. "If he'd voted against Carter Power, that provision wouldn't have made it out of committee."

Jeff didn't miss a beat. "It's a moot point now, so there's no reason why we can't talk about this. We knew Langsford might not vote for Carter Power."

"If that was the case, then how did you think you were going to win the committee vote?"

"We may not have had the votes there, but Senator Regan was confident that if the issue went to the Senate floor, we'd be able to get enough senators to amend the bill and put Carter Power's funding back in. That's where I was going to work my magic. I have contacts with almost all the Senate offices, and it was going to be my job to secure the necessary votes later on if Langsford screwed us over."

It was a plausible explanation, but something bothered me about it. Losing in committee was never a desirable outcome. Putting it to a floor vote was risky because the outcome was unpredictable, especially in times of budgetary hardship. Senators from both parties ran away from votes that added more dollars to the ballooning federal deficit.

"Weren't you concerned your strategy might fail? It seems like a high stakes game to play."

"You're right, but we don't have to worry about that, since your boss isn't going to have the chance to vote in committee now. I don't mean to be insensitive, but whoever murdered Lyndon Langsford made my life a lot easier."

Now it was Meg's turn. "That's a nasty thing to say, Jeff. Senator Langsford might have just been a vote on a committee to you, but we liked our boss, and we're sad he's dead. Just because he wanted to save the taxpayers some money didn't mean he deserved to die." She stared pointedly at Jeff.

"Ah, jeez. I didn't mean for it to sound that way. You know I didn't want Senator Langsford to get killed. But the fact that he was giving us so much trouble on this vote…" his voice trailed off, then he finished his thought, "Let's just say Langsford was going to make

Regan's reelection unnecessarily complicated. You can understand that, right?"

Meg didn't give Jeff the courtesy of an audible reply. I had to step in and salvage the rest of this conversation if we were going to learn anything else from Jeff. Meg was charming, but she had a short fuse. Jeff had pushed her buttons.

Acting as if nothing had happened, I asked Jeff, "Was Regan positive that Langsford was going to vote against Carter Power?"

Jeff seemed happy to avoid the awkwardness brewing with Meg. He turned back to me. "He had a pretty good sense from those meetings, although he would never admit it. But I had my own sources."

Fortunately for us, Jeff seemed unable to keep his big mouth shut. Who had told him Langsford had settled on a final position? It hadn't been me. "I don't recall that we ever discussed Senator Langsford's decision on the Carter Power issue."

Jeff smirked. "Sorry to disappoint you, Kit. You played that card close to the vest. I knew I wasn't going to get any information out of you. But you weren't the only person in the office who knew about Langsford's plans."

I thought quickly. The only other people in the office who knew were Matt and Lucinda. I mentally crossed Matt off the list. He had sworn me to secrecy and counseled me about keeping Senator Langsford's intentions unknown until the last possible moment. That left Lucinda.

I wanted to confirm that Lucinda was the leak in the office. If Senator Langsford had been killed because of his upcoming vote on Carter Power, it was critical to have an accurate list of everyone who knew that Langsford planned to throw Senator Regan under the bus.

Before I had a chance to ask him about it, Meg took the reins again. She turned the charm back on and smiled at Jeff. She knew the leak had to be Lucinda. First, she patted Jeff's hand and grabbed his wine glass, which was empty. Then she motioned for our server to come over and promptly ordered Jeff another glass of wine. Jeff seemed to like the fact that Meg had taken charge and returned the favor by ordering her another drink. If this had been purely a social outing with no murder investigation in mind, I would have been steamed at Jeff's willingness to ignore me when it was convenient. Since we needed information from him and Meg seemed to have a talent for extracting it, I was perfectly satisfied to let her take another swipe at him.

The drinks arrived quickly, and they both took a sip. Meg inched closer to Jeff in the booth and said, with a slight purr in her voice, "Now, what were we talking about again?" She paused for a second and then kept going before he could get a word in edgewise. "I know. You were saying Lucinda told you about Senator Langsford's Carter Power decision." Meg looked at Jeff innocently.

She had caught him off guard, but he didn't slip up. He laughed nervously. "I don't remember saying it was Lucinda."

Meg twirled a lock of her short hair around her finger. Did guys really go for this stuff? It seemed so obvious.

"Of course, silly. I know you didn't mention Lucinda specifically, but we both know it was her, right? She was the only person who knew about Senator Langsford's intentions besides Kit. Isn't that right, Kit?" Meg was bluffing. Matt also knew. This wasn't the time for the unvarnished truth, though.

"You're absolutely right, Meg," I said. "Only Lucinda had that information."

Meg turned back toward Jeff. "It had to be Lucinda. Don't worry. We won't tell anyone, and it doesn't matter anymore, does it?" For good measure, she batted her fake eyelashes at Jeff.

Jeff's wine was almost gone. He had to be feeling rather loose by now. "Yeah, what the heck. You guys guessed it. You're pretty good at this stuff, you know? It was Lucinda who told me which way Langsford was leaning. It confirmed what Senator Regan suspected all along. His good buddy Lyndon Langsford was going to sell Carter Power and his reelection prospects down the river."

I could tell by Jeff's cutting remark he was losing patience with this conversation. I still needed to get a crucial piece of information out of him before calling it a night. I glanced at my watch. Almost an hour had gone by, and Lounge 201 was filling up. Soon, the place would be replete with Senate staff, and Jeff would recognize acquaintances. Even Meg's alluring presence wouldn't keep his attention when key contacts arrived for happy hour. I decided to plunge forward and go for broke.

"Jeff, where were you yesterday morning, between seven and eight o'clock?" I shot my question at him, hoping to catch him off balance.

He stared at me for several seconds, then burst out laughing. "Do you think I killed Senator Langsford? Is that what this interrogation is all about?" He shook his head in apparent disbelief. "I guess the Capitol Police are desperate to solve this case. Have you decided to join their ranks now that you might be out of a job in a few days? Or are you afraid the police might not find another suspect and will decide to pin the murder on you?" He belted down the rest of his wine and signaled the waitress to bring him another drink.

I didn't let Jeff rattle me. "Don't be ridiculous. I'm confident the police will find out who did this." I straightened in my seat and looked him squarely in the eye, hoping he didn't call my bluff.

Meg interrupted, "If you have an alibi for the murder, Jeff, then why not tell us? There's no harm in sharing that information, is there?" She sat back in her seat and crossed her arms.

The server came with his refill, and he took a sip. "Since none of this matters one bit, I don't mind telling you I have an ironclad alibi for yesterday morning."

I asked, "Which is?"

"I was sharing the company of a woman, if you must know. In fact, I believe the police have already verified my whereabouts."

This piqued Meg's interest. She couldn't resist a follow-up. "Who were you with, Jeff? I didn't know you had a girlfriend."

He sighed. "I don't have a girlfriend, Meg. Don't be naïve. But believe me, my alibi is rock solid, and my acquaintance has already attested to that." He smirked at his attempt at a dirty double entendre.

As far as I was concerned, that was too much information, and it signaled an end to happy hour. We had discovered several pieces of valuable intelligence, and I wanted to head home and process what we had learned.

I seized on the lull in conversation and said, "On that note, I think it's time for Meg and me to take off. It was nice seeing you again." I cringed at the word "nice," but I made myself say it. Jeff's penchant for divulging information could come in handy in the near future. Meg and I each threw down a twenty for our drinks and gathered our purses to leave the booth.

Jeff grabbed Meg's arm as she was trying to leave. "One more thing, ladies. I suppose neither of you is thinking about staying on board when Senator Langsford's replacement is named, right?"

I replied, "I seriously doubt it, Jeff. You know the governor will pick someone who shares his beliefs, and I doubt our services are going to be required when a senator from the other party is appointed."

"I thought I would offer my recommendation if either of you decided you wanted to stay on board as a Senate staffer and not hit the unemployment line."

I stopped dead in my tracks. "And just who would you be giving this recommendation to, exactly?"

Jeff put his hands behind his head and leaned back. "I believe the next senator from the great state of Massachusetts is going to be none other than Jordan Jessop."

Meg and I both bristled at Jeff's brazen announcement, even though it was no surprise. Having been on the campaign to reelect Senator Langsford and keep Jessop out of the Senate, it was a bad political nightmare to see our boss's former adversary rise to that office.

I stated emphatically, "No, Jeff. I don't think Meg or I will seek employment from Jordan Jessop. How do you know for sure he's going to be selected by the governor for the appointment?"

Jeff shrugged. "It's not official, but let's just say that

in certain circles, we know Jessop is on the short list, and the governor's only considering one candidate."

I didn't want to continue this conversation any longer. "Well, good luck with Senator Jessop, I guess. You'll need it."

"Oh, I look forward to a beneficial partnership with Jessop. He's sympathetic to Carter Power, and I'm sure his vote in committee will be much appreciated by Senator Regan."

Ugh. I could hardly stand it. Our boss was dead, Meg and I were losing our jobs, and we were going to be replaced by a repugnant politician we had worked hard a few years earlier to defeat. Politics could be a killer—no pun intended.

We needed to leave now. Meg and I fled Lounge 201 without speaking to anyone else, although we knew half of the staffers who now filled the bar. We hurried up the stairs and huddled outside.

"Well, that's ninety minutes of my life I'll never get back."

She smiled. "I know you don't like Jeff, but you have to admit we learned some valuable stuff from him, right?"

I gave her a quick hug. "You were great, by the way. I loved how you reeled him in by batting your eyelashes."

Meg beamed. "He was an easy mark. He hardly put up a fight."

I giggled. "I've got to run. Doug will wonder what happened to me, and Clarence is probably yowling for dinner. We're an impressive team, aren't we?"

Meg's eyes glistened with moisture. "We are. I'm sad this might be the end of our time working together. What's going to happen to us?"

"I don't know what's going to happen to us, but let's try to see if we can't tackle this one last challenge together and find out who killed Senator Langsford. Wouldn't that be the best way to leave the Senate?"

We gave each other a quick fist bump to seal the deal.

THIRTEEN

I WALKED SEVERAL blocks to Union Station to take the Metro home. The rush hour traffic had subsided, and I pulled out my iPhone and listened to upbeat pop songs during the ride. After a few minutes, I could feel the tension leave my body as I let myself get lost in the music. My mind drifted back to the conversation with Jeff Prentice. What had we learned? Was this whole idea of solving our boss's murder a pipe dream? Maybe we should leave the sleuthing to the professionals.

Visions of prison jumpsuits flashed before me. Although those women on the Netflix series didn't look bad, orange wasn't my new black. Rationally I knew I wasn't a credible suspect, but until the murderer was found, the fear remained. With a renewed focus, I pulled an old-fashioned paper notebook from my purse and created a written inventory of what we knew about the case.

First, who were our suspects? Certainly, Senator Regan and Jeff Prentice had motives to kill Senator Langsford. Jeff claimed he had an alibi; I wasn't sure about Regan.

Who else? Senator Langsford's wife, Vivian, earned a spot on the list. She didn't want Senator Langsford to run for another term, she disagreed with his position on Carter Power, and she had recently increased the insurance policy on her husband. However, Vivian also had an alibi. Perhaps she hired someone to kill her husband. That possibility preserved her status as a suspect.

Could I add anyone else to the list? I couldn't rule out Lucinda. After all, it was curious she had told Jeff Prentice about Senator Langsford's position on Carter Power, when Matt had made it crystal clear the decision was extremely hush-hush. Was that a motive for murder? Perhaps it was, particularly if Lucinda had wanted to leave her job in the Senate and secure a lucrative job as a lobbyist, maybe in the defense industry. Lucinda remained on the list, at least for now. She'd been clearly upset yesterday when she'd learned of Senator Langsford's death—or had that been clever acting on her part?

Matt didn't have a discernible motive, and neither did Trevor or Kara.

Mandy was a downright nasty individual, yet a plausible motive for why she would want Langsford dead escaped me. She had secured a job with Senator Regan already, but she could easily have quit her job and gone to work for Senator Regan without resorting to murder. Hill staff bounced from office to office as opportunities arose, and her departure would have been nothing but a momentary blip in the long string of Senate staffers employed by Lyndon Langsford over the years.

That left Representative Jordan Jessop. He certainly had the motive to kill Langsford. After getting his ox gored by Langsford in the last election, he knew beating him in a one-on-one rematch was unlikely. If Langsford had decided to retire, Jessop would have been free and clear to run for the Senate seat, but word on the street was Langsford was gearing up to run for another six-year term. That would have ruined Jessop's chances of ever becoming a United States Senator, since he wasn't getting any younger. Did Jessop take matters into his own hands and kill Langsford so he could receive an appointment to the Senate? It wasn't far-fetched. The campaign four years earlier between Jessop and Langsford had been acrimonious. Perhaps Jessop had gone over the edge and murdered Langsford so he could move from the House to the Senate.

As the subway arrived at my home station, I tucked away my notebook and boarded the long escalator to the street. I definitely knew more about the murder now than when I woke up this morning, but was I any closer to figuring out who had killed Senator Langsford? What was my next move?

These questions weighed heavily on my mind as I strolled toward our condo building. Even though it was past eight, the oppressive heat of the summer persisted. The nice part about this time of year was the plentiful daylight, even when I got home later than expected from work. For the remainder of the walk home, I pondered whether the sticky weather was a fair trade for the longer days.

In the lobby, I greeted my doorman and pressed the elevator button for the fourth floor. We lived in a twenty-five-story "high rise" in the heart of trendy Arlington. We would have preferred a condo closer to the top, since the view of the Washington Monument was outstanding from those units. Nothing else had been available when we moved to D.C., so we'd had to settle for the fourth floor. With the ongoing housing recession and mortgage crisis, we could now afford two condos next to each other on the 25th floor, but Clarence the beagle wouldn't have appreciated living so high up.

Lofty living meant a longer ride on the elevator, which already made him nervous.

We adopted Clarence from a shelter, and his lineage wasn't known to us. When in doubt, rescue organizations usually labeled dogs of an unknown origin as "beagle mixes." He exhibited several excitable, puppy-like behaviors he hadn't shed in adult doghood, such as jumping up on our guests. Great care had to be exercised when opening the door, because Clarence was usually on the other side, having sprinted the length of the living room when he heard my key in the lock. Clarence seemed to know the hallway was off limits, since he consistently tried to escape. He wouldn't get far down the long, carpeted corridor, so there was no danger in losing him. However, our next-door neighbor wasn't a fan of Clarence or any pet, as far as I could tell, and she had publicly threatened at a condo board meeting to report any sightings of unleashed dogs to our "condo sanctions" committee, which would undoubtedly levy an absurd fine on our account. I imagined Mrs. Beauregard poised at the peephole every time I came home from work, ready to document the exact time and date of Clarence's latest escape.

Just as I expected, Clarence was underfoot as soon as I entered the condo. I hastily closed the door so he had no time to dash into the hallway. He barked twice to say hello, then jumped up and down next to me as I fell heavily onto our plush sofa in the living room.

Doug emerged from the hallway. By the looks of his disheveled hair and rumpled clothes, it might well be his first venture outside his home office in hours. He usually divided his time equally between Georgetown and our condo. Although an increasing number of historical documents, books, and academic journals were now available online, Doug believed in a traditional approach to research. Colleagues who were jealous of his success referred to his methods as "antiquated" or "old-fashioned." He preferred journeying to the library to collect what he needed for the day; then, after teaching his classes or meeting with students, he'd return to our condo in the afternoon and write as much as he could.

This regimen satisfied him deeply, both professionally and intellectually. For me, the predictability and repetitiveness of the routine would be too mundane. His obsession with sticking to a schedule had its benefits. He was terribly productive and churned out a new book every other year, making him the crown jewel of the history department.

Doug removed his glasses, which he had recently come to rely upon for reading and using the computer. Noticing it was dusk, he asked blankly, "What time is it?"

I chuckled, since he'd been staring at a computer screen for the past several hours, which clearly displayed the time. When Doug became immersed in work, almost nothing could distract him.

"I think it's time you took a break and had a drink."

He smiled wryly. "Not a bad idea." He popped over to our wine refrigerator, conveniently located next to our monster espresso machine, and removed the bottle of Riesling we had sampled yesterday.

"Shall we finish this bottle?" He pulled the wine stopper.

"I'll have just a small pour. I already went to a happy hour." I lightly touched my belly. Alcoholic beverages accounted for the extra pounds I perpetually tried to shed. It was a losing battle. Every time a few inches came off, another round of obligatory evening events would present themselves, and the cycle repeated itself.

"Did you go out with Meg?" Doug poured me a half glass and emptied the remainder of the bottle into his own.

I reminded him, "Yes, and Jeff Prentice, as well."

Doug raised his eyebrows. "I thought you couldn't stand that guy."

I might have escaped Doug's scrutiny this morning and later on the phone, but now that I was face to face with him, honesty was the best policy. I couldn't lie to Doug about my sleuthing. Besides, his super brain could be useful. I recounted my day to Doug in as much detail as possible, starting with my morning Jessop encounter and ending with the revelations at happy hour. He listened attentively as he sipped his wine.

After thinking for a moment, Doug leaned back and set his wine glass down. "From what you've told me, you have three possible motives for the murder of Senator Langsford." He ticked them off with his fingers with a slight pause between each point. "First, you have a power motive. Carter Power, to be exact. If Langsford backed the company, several people would stand to benefit, not just financially but by proving their influence and their ability to get things done. Second, there's the political motive. Several people would move up in the world, one to the Senate. Third, you have a personal or financial motive, such as the insurance money."

"That's what I've been able to uncover so far. Don't forget that a few suspects had multiple motives. Vivian might have had all three. She didn't want her husband to abandon Carter Power, she wanted him to retire from the Senate and get a more lucrative job, and she benefits from the increased insurance policy."

Doug nodded. "That could be important. Jessop might have more than one motive, too. Given what Jeff said at your happy hour, he might have been in cahoots with Carter Power, and he certainly wanted to be a senator."

Doug had a knack for making a complicated situation sound simple. That's why he was such an accomplished history author. He eliminated the unnecessary information and told the story as crisply as possible.

"If I understand what you're saying, then do you think we need to focus on Vivian and Congressman Jessop?"

He shrugged. "It couldn't hurt. Right now, they're the suspects who have the most to gain from your boss's death. Even if neither of them did it, investigating those motives should get you closer to figuring out who did."

I pondered Doug's suggestion. "I don't have regular access to Vivian, at least until the day after tomorrow when I go to the wake. So I guess we need to turn up the heat on Jessop in the meantime."

Doug put his arm around me. "Just how do you think you're going to make that happen? As I recall, you worked on the Senate campaign that defeated Jordan Jessop. I can't imagine you have too many friends in common with him."

"Then I guess I'll just have to get creative, won't I?" I smiled mischievously at Doug, who clearly wished he'd kept his mouth shut.

FOURTEEN

THERE WAS NO morning delight I cherished more than a real breakfast in the Senate cafeteria before work. In an effort to avoid the necessity of buying a new set of business suits due to an expanding waistline, I ate a calorie-conscious breakfast most mornings. This Spartan repast consisted of nothing but a protein breakfast bar, which typically kept me coherent until lunch. For my lymphatic body type, which seemed to gain weight at the mere sight of food, a meager breakfast seemed to be the best option.

However, there are days in which the best-laid plans must be cast aside. This was one of those days. I was tired, stressed out, and ravenous. A treat of eggs, carbs, and bacon was well deserved. After all, I had jogged almost four and a half miles instead of my usual four. I would head directly to the Senate cafeteria as soon as I'd checked in at the office.

I signed on to my computer and immediately heard Mandy's whiny voice pop up as part of her insipid video blog. From what I could tell, there was actually important information in the video, because she was talking about Senator Langsford's memorial service tomorrow. Listening was mandatory, but it certainly wouldn't be the first thing I did this morning.

I minimized Mandy's face and instead opened an Instant Message window and asked Meg if she wanted to join me for breakfast. Always a fan of comfort food, Meg never turned down an invitation for a satisfying meal. Before I knew it, she was standing next to my cubicle with her designer wallet in hand.

We took the elevator to ground level of Hart and walked from there to Dirksen. A long, dreary hallway with worn carpeting connected the two Senate office buildings. Thousands of staffers had made this trek before us, eager to seal a deal over breakfast or fight off a hangover lingering from the previous evening. We descended one more level to enter the bowels of the Dirksen cafeteria.

My plebian roots were reflected in my general appreciation for cafeteria food. Sure, it wasn't the best cuisine, but I loved picking and choosing my favorite victuals with reasonable predictability. It also reminded me of college and the fun times I had with my roommates in the cafeteria. Our craziest exploits, ranging from hilarious prank phone calls to complex plots exposing cheating boyfriends, had been hatched over Sunday brunch in the cafeteria. The Senate cafeteria was not much different. Countless political strategies and landmark pieces of legislation had been devised and negotiated at the tables in Dirksen. Lunchtime was best for witnessing these deals. It was also the busiest time and next to impossible to find a table. Therefore, I had come to appreciate Dirksen at a quieter time of the day, namely breakfast.

For less than five dollars, a hungry Senate staffer could get a great meal, which included scrambled eggs, bacon, hash browns, rye toast, a cup of coffee, and a small orange juice. For someone who normally ate a power bar the texture and taste of firm sawdust for breakfast, it was heaven. I rarely finished my whole plate, yet I always felt incredibly fortified for the rest of the day.

I went through the line and got my usual plate of assortments. Meg opted for a cheese omelet, wheat toast, and grits. What can I say? Some of us have all the luck. I noted for the record that Meg's outfit consisted of a form-fitting linen sheath, a beautifully styled short, yellow blazer, and a pair of second-hand Jimmy Choo espadrilles. Linen was not a forgiving fabric for most, yet on her, it fit in all the right places.

Once we were settled in at an empty table, I told Meg about my conversation with Doug and the latest game plan. We needed to focus on Vivian and Jessop. Both had unquestionable motives to kill Senator Langsford.

Between bites, Meg listened intently. She finally stopped chomping and said, "We need a strategy, and we need to put it into action now if we want to figure out who killed the senator. We don't have much time to spare. I heard the governor might announce Senator Langsford's replacement next week. Once that happens, we'll be out of a job, and without United States Senate ID badges, it's going to be hard to poke around."

She sighed before continuing, "Besides, I need to start looking for my next job. Once I'm unemployed, I won't have much time for solving Langsford's murder."

The loss of our jobs put Meg in desperate financial straits. Doug's generous trust fund supplemented both his and my incomes, so I could afford to take more time to find a new position. I had already decided to start a full-scale search once my job in Senator Langsford's office ended. While my immediate situation wasn't dire, if I didn't clear my name as a suspect, no Hill office would hire me. The lingering effects of an unsolved murder and the persistent D.C. rumor mill could ruin my career.

"We can work on Vivian when we go to Senator Langsford's memorial service tomorrow. I'd like to hear more about this appointment with a personal trainer she claimed as an alibi. As far as I know, Vivian isn't an early riser. I find it hard to believe she was doing sit-ups at eight in the morning."

Meg nodded. "Access to Vivian and the people she knows shouldn't be too difficult tomorrow. The harder nut to crack is Representative Jessop, right?"

Meg had hit the nail on the head. I'd considered how to investigate Jessop earlier during the morning commute, and I didn't have any great ideas. We weren't exactly popular in that office.

Meg asked, "Is the House of Representatives in session this week?" Usually, the House and Senate stayed in session, when members of Congress debated and voted on legislation, during the same weeks of the year. But the schedule had been screwed up lately, with the House and Senate meeting during different weeks of the year.

I checked my BlackBerry and told her the House wasn't in session.

She smiled and said slowly, "I might have an idea."

"Tell me about it. It's got to be better than anything I've come up with, which is nothing."

"It's risky, and I'm not even sure it'll work. When we're out of session and the boss isn't around, the office is much more relaxed and not as crazy, right?"

"Of course. I think it's like that in both the House and Senate. When the Senate's not in session, I feel like it's a completely different job."

"Since the House isn't in session, there might be a chance I could distract Jessop's chief of staff so you could sneak into the congressman's office and look around."

Meg wasn't exaggerating when she said it would be risky. Even though I had been accused of killing Senator Langsford, I hadn't committed a crime. Rifling through a member of Congress's personal papers had to be a felony of some sort. Orange jumpsuits flashed before my eyes again.

I narrowed my eyes. "How do you plan on keeping Jessop's chief of staff busy while I'm in the office?"

"It shouldn't be too hard to do. He's always eager to buy me a drink when I see him at the Capitol Lounge." The Capitol Lounge was a bar on Pennsylvania Avenue, close to the House office buildings. It was on the other side of the congressional complex, which wasn't far away, but a place that Senate staffers rarely patronized.

"Do you go to the Capitol Lounge often?"

"Only when I get tired of the same old happy hours and events on the Senate side. You know, sometimes I like to see how the other half lives." Meg cracked me up. If she had been in Marie Antoinette's shoes, she wouldn't have seen anything wrong with the "let them eat cake" line.

"When you decide to slum it and head over to the House side, you see Jessop's chief of staff and convince him to buy you drinks? That's your plan?"

Meg shrugged. "His name is Kyle. He always says we need to let bygones be bygones, and we should work together for the good of the state. He feeds me those kinds of lines. Since he wasn't involved with the Jessop campaign for Senate, I don't think he holds a grudge against me." She paused to take a big bite of omelet and grits.

Her plan was so far-fetched, it might work. When I talked to Jessop yesterday morning, he said he was leaving town. That meant he would be out of the office. Also, it was critical that Kyle hadn't worked for the Jessop for Senate campaign. All those people knew us and would bristle at our presence.

I thought for a second. "Maybe we can use the senator's death as an excuse for making the trip to the office. We have a lot of constituents we are trying to assist, and since we aren't going to work in Congress much longer, we want to let Representative Jessop know about those people in his congressional district."

Meg snapped her fingers. "That's a fantastic idea! I don't even have to lie about it. I know exactly the constituent case I can pass off to them. I can say it's too complicated to explain on the phone, so I'd like to walk over to Jessop's office and meet with Kyle about it."

Meg beamed at me. She had been more than a mere confidante when it came to figuring out who murdered Senator Langsford. So far, she'd been downright indispensable. She'd obtained valuable information and come up with several creative ideas about how we could pick up more clues along the way.

More importantly, her enthusiasm was infectious. I grinned widely, despite the fact we were strategizing to break into the office of a member of Congress. If I stopped too long to think about how ridiculous it sounded, I was afraid I'd lose my nerve.

I paused to sample my eggs and a piece of toast. "Okay, so that's our plan for this afternoon. Do you think you'll be able to keep Kyle occupied so I'll have enough time to sneak into Jessop's office?"

"It's hard to say until I start talking to him. I know his shared office is next to the congressman's. If I can catch his attention, you could slip away and investigate. I could get you maybe ten minutes in which Kyle wouldn't realize you'd gone missing. Do you think that's enough time?"

"Given the fact I have no idea what I'm looking for, it's an eternity. Don't get me wrong. I wouldn't be surprised to learn Jessop had a hand in Langsford's murder. But it's not like I'm going to find a note on his desk that says, 'I'm the murderer,' right?"

"No, but you can snoop around for any incriminating evidence. Maybe a note or a business card will provide a link to Langsford. Who knows? You might see something that will point us in the right direction."

"I guess you're right. I won't know what I'm looking for, but hopefully I'll know when I see it."

Meg took the last bite of her omelet. "That's the spirit! Let's face it. It's not like anyone else is making significant progress on this case."

Just as Meg finished her last sentence, Detective O'Halloran stood behind our table, materializing out of nowhere. "Well, if it isn't my two favorite Langsford staffers." He had just bought a doughnut at the cafeteria, and powdered sugar was speckled on his tie and dress shirt. So much for moving beyond stereotypes.

I could tell Meg was worried about what he might have overheard. She hurriedly said, "Hello, Detective. How's the investigation going?"

O'Halloran smirked, as if he knew she would ask this question. He pulled up his pants with his belt while chomping on his pastry. "I can report we're getting closer. People need to have a little faith in their public servants."

Meg took a big gulp and gushed, "Absolutely, Detective. I couldn't agree with you more."

O'Halloran gave her a knowing glance. "I'm glad I ran into both of you. Forensics took another look at the senator's office, and we found a possible piece of evidence. I'm asking all the people who knew Senator Langsford about it, so I can figure out if what we found counts as a credible lead."

This was welcome news. If the police were on the right track and could find Senator Langsford's killer, my name could get removed from the suspect list and we could all move forward with the next chapter in our lives, whatever that might be.

O'Halloran continued, "We found a blond hair in Senator Langsford's office. At first, I thought that made blondie here," he pointed at Meg, "the prime suspect. It made sense, since you," he pointed at me, "found the body. I figured you two were in cahoots for an unknown reason and had devised a way to cover for each other." He stuffed the rest of his doughnut into his mouth and ran his stubby fingers through his hair. Now there was a streak of powder in his hair that made him look almost distinguished.

I didn't like the direction this was going. While he was swallowing, I interrupted. "I thought the timing cast doubt on that, since Senator Langsford was killed before I entered the building."

He took a big gulp. "That's right...when we thought you were the murderer. But with the blond hair, we naturally assumed that she," he motioned toward Meg, "was the actual killer. Maybe you were just an accomplice to throw us off the trail."

Now it was Meg's turn to interrupt. "That doesn't make any sense." She got up from her seat at the table and put her hands on her hips. "Why would Kit and I want to kill our boss? We loved Senator Langsford. You can ask anyone!"

"Yeah, yeah, I know. I've heard it all before. It was a regular love fest in Senator Langsford's office, apparently. Your boss Matt told me all about how you saved Langsford's hide four years ago when he was running for reelection. My answer to that is that four years is a long time ago. Maybe you two weren't real happy with the direction the office was taking. Lyndon wasn't quite as liberal as he used to be when you pounded the pavement for him, right? So your reputations as Capitol Hill staffers were taking a nosedive. Quitting might be messy, but if Langsford suddenly died, you both got a chance to start over. Sounds plausible to me. Nothing shocks me when politicos are involved in this city. You're all out for numero uno."

"How would I have gotten in?" said Meg. "You certainly won't find me on the video surveillance entering the building before the murder."

"How did the killer get in?" he replied. "He or she wasn't on video surveillance either. We've examined the footage from earlier that morning, and it hasn't yielded any plausible suspects."

O'Halloran's attention shifted. He eyed the vestiges of my breakfast, which included a piece of rye toast and half a strip of bacon. Clearly, the doughnut hadn't been enough to satisfy him. I ignored his hard stare at my plate. "Did you track us down so you could get a

DNA sample from Meg to match her hair to what you found on the scene? Even if it was a match, Meg has been in that office at least ten times in the past month. She could have easily shed a hair or two during a meeting with Senator Langsford."

O'Halloran put a hand up to silence me. "That won't be necessary. Like I said before, you both got carried away. I'm asking everyone in Langsford's office about it. At first, I did think it might have been a case of the dynamic duo," he gestured toward us, "killing their dear boss. But then we had some preliminary tests done on the hair, and it's synthetic."

Meg had a confused look on her face. "So it was from a wig. Is that what you're saying?"

"Good job, junior detective. The hair is from a wig. So unless Blondie here is faking it, I think she's in the clear."

Meg reached up and gave her bob a quick tug. "Nope, I'm afraid this is all natural. No hairpieces for me."

O'Halloran sighed. "I didn't think so. It's a good clue, but I'm back to square one. We're combing through Senator Langsford's appointments in the last seventy-two hours of his life, and no one who was in that office wore a wig. The cleaning staff vacuumed in there every other day, so going back three days is generous. I don't get it. There just isn't anyone who met with Senator Langsford who could have shed that hair." He paused, perhaps for effect. "That leads me to believe the artificial blond hair might have come from the last person to see him alive, which would have been his killer."

O'Halloran's reasoning sounded on the mark to me. Kara kept tight control on access to Senator Langsford's office. She sat immediately outside, and no one got inside who didn't have a legitimate appointment with the senator. I asked, "I assume you talked to Kara about this. She knew the senator's schedule backward and forward."

"I might not be a fancy Capitol Hill staffer like yourself, but I've worked here for years, and I know how a congressional office works. Of course I talked to the scheduler. She pulled all the records for me, and we went over them together. There was no one on his appointment schedule who could have been wearing a blond wig. Since Kara leaves with the senator each evening, there's no chance a late night visitor might have made an appearance without her knowledge."

I stood alongside Meg. "Thanks for the information, Detective O'Halloran. We'll let you know if we come across a blond wig."

He shrugged. "I can use all the help I can get. It's the best lead we've got. So far, it hasn't led me anywhere concrete, though." He gave us a mini salute and headed out of the cafeteria.

Meg and I looked at each other. "It's a valuable piece of information. I don't know how it fits into our theories about who might have killed Senator Langsford, but we need to keep it in mind as we gather more clues."

Meg sniggered. "Well, I guess we know what you're looking for in Jessop's office. Keep your eye out for a blond wig!"

FIFTEEN

WASHINGTON, D.C., A CITY with approximately five million people residing in its metropolitan area, was no Mayberry. But despite its considerable size, Washington boasted several attributes consistent with a small town. The most significant was the swiftness with which gossip spread. When I started working on Capitol Hill, I had no conception of this phenomenon. Innocently enough, I'd have a conversation one evening at a happy hour, assuming naïvely that what was discussed would be held in confidence. By lunch the next day, I would hear remnants of that conversation quoted back to me, sometimes with new information sprinkled in to increase the juiciness of the story. After this happened a few times, I realized D.C. was no place to share secrets. Sooner or later, people divulged information they possessed in exchange for other information that would further their own causes. It was a dog-eat-dog world inside the Beltway, and getting mauled once or twice was par for the course. Luck of the draw determined whether those rookie mistakes were fatal. Capitol Hill was riddled with stories of staffers who had shown great promise but made a dumb error early in their careers and ended up blacklisted or fired.

Given my rough and tumble political education, I shouldn't have been concerned when Mandy gleefully recounted my conversation with Jeff Prentice from last night. After all, she was the communications director, and the press folks had the worst reputation for gossiping and sharing prized intelligence. In fact, their jobs routinely depended on their ability to push valuable tidbits out and gain insight into the plans of politicians. Press was a competitive game, and idle chitchat turned into valuable currency.

Mandy waited until I had settled into my cubicle before sauntering over. She had a self-satisfied smirk on her face, and if I had been more astute, I would have guessed she was on the hunt. Mandy rarely sought me out for conversation, unless it was to deliver a "gotcha" moment like this.

"I heard you had a great time at happy hour last night," she drawled. In spite of myself, I admired her black pinstripe suit, complemented by a white fitted blouse adorned with an elaborate frilled collar. Even though it was incredibly stylish, if I had tried to pull it off, I would have looked like Elizabeth the Virgin Queen. Mandy was a Barney's mannequin come to life.

"I had a few drinks with Meg." *Play it cool and don't take the bait.* I returned to my computer screen.

She stared at me with her steely dark eyes. "And with Jeff Prentice."

I turned back toward Mandy. "Yes, Jeff was there, too." Sometimes feigned boredom would discourage an annoying interrogator. Mandy was more persistent than our most skilled CIA operatives at Guantanamo Bay, so I should have known I wasn't going to be let off easy.

"I heard from a source that you pumped Jeff for information about Senator Langsford's murder."

I sighed loudly. This was headed in a bad direction.

"Actually, I wanted to have a drink with Jeff before we lost touch."

Suddenly I realized I could turn the tables on Mandy and see what she knew. "I found out he's going to be your coworker in Senator Regan's office. I suppose you already knew that, though."

Mandy made a face. "Of course I knew that. Jeff and I are hardly strangers." Mandy was the kind of woman who liked to kiss and tell.

I leaned toward her and put on my friendliest smile. "No, I didn't know you and Jeff were acquainted. Just how close are you two these days?"

Mandy seemed torn between wanting to divulge the intimacy of her relationship with a hottie and telling me to mind my own damn business. She opted for a combination of both.

"Not that it concerns you," she snapped, "but Jeff and I are in an exclusive relationship. So you'd better tell your best friend to keep her wandering hands off him."

Mandy must have good sources. Jeff wouldn't have told her Meg had put the moves on him. As a press secretary, Mandy had informants everywhere. Someone at Lounge 201 must have seen Meg's aggressive flirtation with Jeff.

In a breezy voice, I said, "I wouldn't worry about Meg. She's not interested in Jeff."

I returned to staring at my computer, satisfied I had extracted enough information from Mandy for the time being. I decided not to tell her that Jeff had denied having a girlfriend. He must have omitted that part of the conversation when he recounted last night's conversation to Mandy. Her conception of an "exclusive relationship" was obviously much different than his, but she'd have to figure that out on her own.

Mandy huffed. My comment could be construed as a dig directed at her pedestrian taste in men. I hadn't meant it that way, although now I realized that's how it sounded. I wasn't going to lose sleep over it.

Apparently, Mandy wasn't finished with our conversation. "I also heard you were fishing for information about Senator Regan."

"Not really. Jeff told us about his new position with Senator Regan, and we talked a bit about Carter Power and his work with Senator Langsford."

Mandy eyed me suspiciously. "That's not the story I heard. Were you trying to point the finger at Senator Regan for Langsford's murder?"

She had my full attention. "Mandy, I never came close to accusing Senator Regan or anyone else." That much was true. There had been no blatant indictments on my part.

Mandy glared. "You'd better be careful poking around. Some people might take it the wrong way. It's not my problem the police haven't cleared you as a suspect. I start my new job as Senator Regan's press secretary next week, and if you're trying to cast guilt on him, it'll be my business to put an end to it." She thumped her chest for emphasis.

Her last comment struck me as hilarious. The idea of skinny Mandy defending Senator Regan, who was probably twice her size, seemed utterly ridiculous, and I stifled a laugh. Mandy could tell I wasn't taking her seriously.

Since she was clearly annoyed with me, maybe I could catch her off guard. "If that's the case, then you won't mind telling me if Senator Regan has an alibi for Tuesday morning, say between the hours of six and eight in the morning?" I looked innocently at Mandy.

Her face contorted in anger. "You certainly have a lot of guts accusing a sitting United States Senator of murder." She put her hands on her hips. "Senator Langsford always sang your praises, and I could never figure out what he saw in you. I guess it was the fact you worked for him during the reelection campaign. He must have felt some sort of puppy-dog loyalty to you. I never thought you had the discretion to succeed in politics. Now I know I'm right. I'm betting that after your recent media blitz, you'll never work in the Senate again."

I decided to press on. People made a lot of mistakes when they were furious and unable to control their emotions. "That might be true, Mandy. But you still haven't told me if Senator Regan had an alibi for the murder. Are you trying to avoid my question? I would think Senator Regan's future press secretary would be able to answer it."

Her skin had an unhealthy flush that told me I had pushed her last nerve. Calling into doubt her insider knowledge about Regan had done it. "Of course I can answer that question. He told the police the truth. He was with his wife on Tuesday morning. Will that shut you up?"

It was painful, but at least now I knew the identity of Regan's alibi. In mystery novels a spouse was never considered a reliable alibi. I would deal with his flimsy defense if we found other clues that led us to believe Regan was our killer.

Satisfied I had gotten what I needed from Mandy and

even more than I'd bargained for, I said, "Yes, that'll shut me up. I'm more than happy to return to my work now. Thanks, Mandy." I gave her my sweetest, most angelic smile.

As she walked away, she called out, "Don't be late tomorrow for the memorial service. It's all hands on deck to make sure the VIPs are treated well and everything goes smoothly."

I hadn't paid attention to the details for tomorrow's event. "Wait, Mandy. How am I supposed to know where to show up and when?"

Mandy didn't even turn around to answer me. She kept walking and yelled over her shoulder, "If you watched my video blog, you'd know what was going on, Kit. I shouldn't have to tell everyone twice. I'm looking forward to working in an office where people actually listen to what I have to say!"

I muttered, "Goodbye and good riddance."

As soon as the words left my mouth, I heard someone say, "Now, now. Play nice in the sandbox."

I looked up to confirm the identity of the speaker. "Hello, Trevor. I almost forgot you were there."

"Yes, I know. It's been that way for the past four years."

I leaned back in my chair. "It's too bad we're only getting chummy now, when it looks as though we're out of jobs."

"My dear Kit, the only reason we've become friendly is because we're no longer going to be working with each other."

Trevor was right. I hadn't paid much attention to him in four years. If our boss hadn't been murdered, that détente would never have happened. Trevor and I had come together in the face of tragedy. Nothing more, nothing less.

"Well, better late than never, I guess." What else was I supposed to say?

Trevor wasn't one for small talk. "Have you made any progress in your discreet inquiries?" He peered over his glasses. Though twenty years younger, he gave me a look that reminded me of my college philosophy professor when I confessed I didn't have the faintest understanding of Heidegger or any other dead, famous white guy we'd read during the semester.

"Yes and no. There's no shortage of suspects, but I'm not close to figuring out who killed Senator Langsford."

"Sometimes it's darkest before the dawn."

"You're right. My boyfriend always says that when he's completely frustrated with whatever history book he's currently writing, he's close to finishing it."

"Charming. What's your next plan of action?"

I hesitated. Perhaps I shouldn't tell Trevor too much? I didn't think he was a credible suspect, since he had no obvious motive, but my intuition told me that being a blabbermouth might not be the best idea, either. On the other hand, Trevor was smart, and I could benefit from talking to a colleague who had something on the ball. I loved Meg, and she'd been invaluable in securing information from Jeff Prentice and other relevant male interlocutors. That said, I wasn't sure she qualified as the next Dr. Watson, or even Trixie Belden.

I took a deep breath and decided to tell Trevor about our plans to infiltrate Representative Jessop's office. I had to face facts. If I wanted to figure out who killed Senator Langsford, I needed to work with the cards dealt me. Trevor had many obnoxious faults. He possessed the social graces of Attila the Hun, but every conversation we'd had since Langsford's murder had proven informative. Also, I privately wondered if Meg's extreme dislike of Trevor had biased me. Maybe he wasn't such a bad guy, just socially awkward in an annoying way, like Anthony Michael Hall in a John Hughes movie.

I recounted to Trevor our plot to gain access to Jessop's office by using Meg's "close friendship" with Kyle to divert attention. If Trevor thought this was a crazy plan, he didn't let on. His demeanor was impenetrable. That's why he had the reputation of being such a valuable Capitol Hill staffer. He never let anyone see his cards.

I started to wrap up. "Even if this works, I'm not exactly sure what I'm looking for in Jessop's office. It's kind of a wild goose chase." I laughed nervously, then fell silent, signaling to Trevor that I was finished talking.

He fixed an unyielding stare on me again, and I shifted nervously in my seat. A normal person understood that a pause in conversation meant I was finished speaking, and would respond. Instead, he let me sit there uncomfortably for several seconds. Finally he said, "Are you finished?"

I nodded. How did Trevor have the ability to make me feel like such a dope? His superiority complex knocked me off my game.

He leaned back in his chair before he started to speak. Although Trevor wasn't a hunk in the classic sense, he might have an appeal for a refined segment of Washington women. He'd be a catch among those who liked power-hungry, self-confident, upwardly mobile policy wonks. I wasn't sure if that was a category a single woman could check off at eHarmony or Match. As I took another look at him, I concluded that he would be a desirable commodity in the Beltway dating market.

Trevor's reply shocked me back to the present. "This might be the craziest harebrained scheme that's ever graced my ears," he said. He picked up his pencil and started to fiddle with it. I'd seen him do that when he was working on something that puzzled him. "But I have to say, if you can pull it off, you should go for it."

Trevor's support shocked me. I was certain he would try to convince me that Meg and I were playing with fire and we should mind our own business. "I'm surprised at your reaction, Trevor."

"Believe me, I don't often endorse breaking the law, especially given our position as employees of the United States Senate." Leave it to Trevor to lay a guilt trip on me. "Nonetheless, sources tell me the police are making little progress solving this case. I agree that Representative Jessop has a clear motive for wanting to see our boss dead, and the connections you've uncovered may tie him to Carter Power. To search a member of Congress's office would require a serious challenge to the speech or debate clause of the Constitution. However, you are not the FBI or the police."

Trevor was referring to a little known provision in the Constitution that shields legislative branch work from executive interference. Members of Congress had successfully invoked criminal immunity before, although the alleged charges in those cases were corruption or bribery, not murder. Law enforcement's ability to search congressional offices was severely limited.

"You're saying Meg and I need to illegally do what federal investigators can't accomplish legally?"

His eyes narrowed. "Yes, in a sense. As I said before, this gives me great pause." He stopped for a second, as if to enhance the dramatic effect of his constitutional concern with the situation.

Perhaps I had underestimated Trevor's capacity to push the envelope. "Even if our plan works perfectly, I'm not sure what I should be looking for in Jessop's office."

Trevor nodded. "I think you need to look for an item that appears suspicious. Focus on calendars, date books, or anything else that might connect Jessop to a suspect who might have been involved."

"That's a wide range of suspects. After all, Jessop and Langsford did represent the same constituents. They have a lot of common ties, simply by virtue of that fact."

"You are right, of course," answered Trevor. "However, use your analytical skills. What else has been a common theme since you've started your inquiry?"

I thought for a few seconds. Then I snapped my fingers. "Of course, it's Carter Power. Even Mrs. Langsford may have some ties, if what you overheard is true."

Trevor actually smiled. I was starting to think he liked playing a muted "behind the scenes" role in this ragtag investigation I was conducting. "Everything you've uncovered thus far points in the direction of Carter Power. However, you may be completely wrong." Leave it to Trevor to bring me down to earth, just when I thought he was starting to enjoy being a team player. He went on, "But Carter Power is a better motive than anything else I've heard so far." Then he added, "By the way, don't forget your memo."

I looked at him quizzically. "My memo?"

He heaved an exasperated sigh. "I hope this hasn't

gotten too complex for you, Kit. Obviously I have some degree of confidence in you and your sidekick, or I wouldn't invest time and energy trying to determine your next move."

I couldn't count on Trevor to indulge me forever. He had his limits.

His eyes widened. "The memo that disappeared on the day of Senator Langsford's murder?"

I hit my forehead with my hand. "Oh, that memo!"

"Does any other memo actually matter these days?"

"You're right. I'd forgotten about that memo. It could have ended up in the recycling bin by accident, but that's too much of a coincidence. Someone was deliberately trying to get rid of it."

"Correct. Which gives credence to your theory that Carter Power is at the center of this conundrum." He raised his eyebrows at me.

Trevor's formal style of speaking, in which he frequently avoided contractions and used the most arcane, stilted language possible, gave him a certain cachet with the intellectual Cosmos Club crowd in Washington, D.C. In New York terms, he hearkened back to the Dorothy Parker gang who met at the Algonquin during the hotel's heyday. I appreciated it, and I admit to sipping a martini or two in hope of channeling the Round Table and all the great wit of the era, but the Algonquin wasn't my scene and never would be.

I tilted my chair back and looked at Trevor. This had been a profitable conversation. "Thanks, Trevor. I think you've helped focus my efforts."

Trevor rubbed his chin thoughtfully. "Yes, the memo could be quite significant." He pushed his chair away from his desk and leaned back to put his hands behind his head. "As you said before, it might be nothing more than a coincidence. Yet somehow I doubt it. Too much else points to Carter Power, which as we've already discussed, is the tie that binds, I'm afraid."

If Trevor was right and Carter Power was the linch-pin, then there was no better suspect than Jeff Prentice, their chief lobbyist, or Senator Regan, their chief political benefactor. A sinking feeling came over me. Had Meg and I had the murderer in our crosshairs last night?

If that was the case, there wasn't much we could do about it now. "So my goal should be to find anything that connects Jessop to Carter Power or proves any knowledge of the decision that was coming before Senator Langsford's committee."

Trevor gave a small smile. "Something about Carter Power is the most obvious clue. I would stay on the alert for anything that seems out of place or corroborates a motive for Jessop."

"Thanks, Trevor. I'll keep you in the loop." I stood and pushed in my chair.

He shook his head. "No need to do that. The less I know, the better."

Yet another lesson from Washington, D.C., that Trevor had mastered. Being in a position to deny everything was the key to survival.

SIXTEEN

THE REST OF the morning passed quietly. Lucinda and Matt were in a closed-door meeting for several hours. I confirmed with Matt when I saw him emerge that our days as Senate employees were indeed numbered. After Senator Langsford's memorial service tomorrow and his subsequent internment, the governor would appoint a successor to the office. Since the governor hailed from the other political party, he was under pressure to waste no time filling the vacant Senate seat.

Matt corroborated what everyone had been whispering: Representative Jessop was the hands-on favorite to get the nod. This news gave my quest with Meg this afternoon added urgency. Besides Senator Regan and Jeff Prentice, Representative Jessop had the strongest motive for wanting Senator Langsford dead. With Langsford out of the way, his path to becoming a senator was clear. If not for Langsford's untimely death, Jessop would have been relegated to the House of Representatives for the foreseeable future.

I ate a quick lunch at my desk while sifting through more emails and returning phone calls. Unfortunately, I didn't have good answers for the eager constituents who were awaiting funding decisions by the Appropriations Committee. Senator Langsford's successor would likely get a seat on Appropriations, but since I wouldn't be working for the new senator, I was in no position to make promises. Several worthy projects for towns and cities in the state hung in the balance, and I felt bad about letting down the many hardworking people I had shepherded through the convoluted federal funding process.

My phone rang, and I glanced at the number that popped up on my caller ID. Doug's cellphone. Should I screen him or not? I felt instant guilt for even thinking about ignoring his call. We had left things ambiguous this morning, and he probably wanted to make sure I hadn't gotten myself arrested.

With a sigh, I picked up the phone. I might as well face the music. I wouldn't be able to keep Doug in the dark for long about our planned escapade later today.

After saying our hellos, Doug immediately asked, "How is the investigation going?" I knew him pretty darn well.

I tried to play nonchalant. "Oh, we haven't made too much progress today. We did run into Detective O'Halloran, and he told us the police found a hair from a blond wig at the scene of the murder. It might be an important clue."

Doug let out a low whistle. "That's big news. It should give the *police* a lot to go on, right?" I noticed his distinct emphasis on the word "police."

"I suppose so, although Detective O'Halloran didn't seem too optimistic. They haven't located the wig itself yet."

"At least it's a break in the case. Does this mean you and Meg are going to suspend your efforts to solve the murder? It sounds as if the official investigators are making progress."

Doug definitely wanted me to back off. Even though

he'd shown genuine interest in the clues we'd uncovered, he thought we were both out of our league, and I was pretty sure he'd fielded a phone call from his father earlier this morning, who undoubtedly wanted an update that confirmed I was in the process of separating myself from the whole messy business. Senator Langsford's murder had continued to be front-page news and the lead story on every cable news network. Without another hot prospect, I was still the only person named publicly as a suspect. I imagined Doug's father, dressed in his velvet smoking jacket with a crystal glass of vintage port in his one hand and his pipe in the other, clicking through various channels and praying not to stumble across my cheerful face in a televised news story about Langsford's death. Doug's father had good intentions. He wanted the best for me, but the fact I was attached to his son, and consequently, the sacred family name, was the real reason for his concern.

Fiddling with the phone cord, I wondered if I should tell Doug what he wanted to hear. Namely, that Meg and I had decided to end our informal investigation and chalk up the whole murder of Senator Langsford to bad luck. That would make Doug happy in the short term, and it would get his father off his back, for sure. Somehow, it didn't seem the right choice.

I took a deep breath. "Actually, we may have figured out a way to obtain some inside information in Jessop's office, and we're headed over there later today," I hesitated as I searched for the right words, "to poke around."

"Poke around? How are you going to do that in a congressional office?" Doug sounded noticeably alarmed.

"Well, Meg has a friend over there, and she may be able to keep him occupied while I take a..." I hesitated again as I racked my brain, then blurted out, "quick peek."

" 'Quick peek'? Kit, I never tell you what to do, but you'd better be careful." Now I'd done it. He was exasperated.

"I know, I know. Don't worry about us. I doubt this plan will even work. We'll probably walk over to Jessop's office, Meg will flirt with the guy she knows, and that'll be it. We owe it to Langsford to at least try, right?"

Doug reluctantly agreed, and I got off the phone after promising to give him a blow-by-blow account later this evening when I returned home.

I spent several hours on the phone catching up with Senate colleagues while casually mentioning I would have to find a new job soon. Once my current position ended, it would become more difficult to find another Hill job. I had to alert contacts now about my plight and would have to keep reminding them in the upcoming weeks. D.C. had a stunted memory. I hoped other Senate offices or committees might take pity upon Langsford staffers and find good jobs for us when his successor was appointed. Of course, if the murder wasn't solved, it would be next to impossible for me to find a new job, given the suspicion that hung over me like a cloud. I detected hesitancy in the voices of the people I spoke with on the phone, compounding my worries about my employment prospects.

I was about to Instant Message Meg to find out if she'd made contact with Kyle about paying him a visit later this afternoon when I thought of Senator Langsford's memorial service at his house. All staffers were expected to attend, and I wanted to pay my respects. It might also be my only opportunity to speak with Mrs. Langsford to determine if her alibi was legit.

As Mandy had so rudely reminded me, I needed to watch her video blog about the memorial service. I reluctantly found the link to her daily diatribe. At least I wouldn't have to suffer through these missives much longer. I clicked on the link, and Mandy's face appeared on my screen. I put on the headphones I kept attached to my computer. Just because I had to listen to Mandy's shrill voice didn't mean I had to subject the rest of the office to it. Any other press secretary would be satisfied with sending out an email about the senator's daily activities, but not Mandy. She had convinced Lucinda and Matt a video blog was more "responsive to the digital age." I doubted that was true. Mandy simply wanted to appear on everyone's computer on a regular basis so we could all be reminded of how beautiful and important she was.

Only Mandy could appear perky when talking about a memorial service. No, we didn't have to wear black, but dress was "professional attire." Screw Mandy and her contemporary fashion advice. I was going to a memorial service, my boss was dead, and I was sad about it. Black seemed altogether appropriate. We had to be there at ten sharp tomorrow morning.

Senator Langsford had lived with his wife Vivian in a sprawling house in McLean, which wasn't easily accessible by Metro. I'd have to make sure my car had gas in it. I almost never drove it during the week, and frequently when the weekends came, I discovered it was nearly on "empty." Thankfully, environmentally concerned citizen that I was, I owned a hybrid vehicle.

This meant I could usually drive at least thirty miles on fumes with no problem.

Something seemed vaguely out of place, but I couldn't put a finger on it. The fuzzy remnants of a thought was batting around in my brain. I couldn't grasp what bugged me, so I shrugged it off and sent Meg an Instant Message, "Are we set for this afternoon?"

She wrote back immediately, "Let's leave in 15 minutes."

I responded: "Are u going to mem service?"

She answered, "Y. Need ride." I smiled. Meg took the "environmentally responsible" citizen label even more seriously than I. She didn't own a car.

I typed, "OK. Metro out to me and we'll leave at 930. C U in 15."

I busied myself with tidying up my workspace for the remaining few minutes before our departure for the House of Representatives. I had accumulated a lot of crap in the past several years working for Senator Langsford. A good deal of the paperwork would need to be boxed up for his archives. The personal stuff would get thrown out or come home with me. I fingered several photographs from our staff costume Halloween party last year, a couple key chains that constituents had given me to remind me of their causes, and my souvenir coffee mug from the downstairs gift shop that displayed all the names of the senators. I vowed to restrict myself to one box to take home, hopefully by the end of the week.

I had been daydreaming about my time in the office when Meg woke me out of my reverie. "Ready to go?" she asked cheerfully.

I quickly bounced out of my stupor. "Oh! Sure. Let's go."

She laughed at me. "Were you taking a nap?"

"No, but I was daydreaming. I was thinking about the past four years working in the office. Meg, I can't believe it's over." I put my BlackBerry into my purse and smoothed my hair.

Meg put her arm around me. "I know. It's surreal. I always knew we wouldn't get to work together forever. I guess I just wasn't ready for the end to come so soon."

"Well, I'm sure Senator Langsford would agree, especially since I'm positive he wasn't ready to die. Let's get going and see if we can figure out who did this to him."

Meg grinned. "I couldn't have said it better myself."

SEVENTEEN

SENATE STAFFERS RARELY visit the House of Representatives. The same is true of our brethren on the other side of the Capitol. For most staff, having an appointment or meeting in the other house of Congress is like going on a field trip. In reality, the walk through the basement tunnels over to the House takes only fifteen minutes. Walking outside makes the trip even shorter.

Since today was another scorcher, Meg and I agreed that if we wanted to arrive without sweat dripping off our faces and drenching our clothing, we should stay indoors. After taking the Senate subway to the Capitol, we weaved our way through the sea of humanity at the newly built Capitol Visitor Center, known as the CVC. We found the passageway leading to the Cannon House Office Building tunnel and reached Representative Jessop's office none the worse for wear.

As we walked into his office, I was reminded how small House offices are compared to Senate offices. It makes sense, since House members only represent one congressional district, and senators represent entire states. Three Senate office buildings accommodate the staff for one hundred senators and committees. Three House office buildings provide office space for 441 members and delegates, plus committees. House offices are considerably smaller in size and appear quite crammed, beyond the front desk area welcoming visitors.

I let Meg take the lead since she was the one who had set up our meeting today. Meg cleared her throat and approached the young woman manning the receptionist's desk, who stood as Meg approached. She was barely twenty years old—likely an intern and not a full-time House employee. Nevertheless, she had perfectly styled blond hair and an expensive-looking string of pearls around her neck. She wore a slightly tight sweater and a business-like, yet suggestive, straight skirt that barely reached the top of her knees. Three-inch designer heels polished off the look. Leave it to Jessop to put his best eye candy on the front desk. Blondie would probably replace our staff assistant as the front desk person when the governor appointed Jessop to the Langsford's Senate seat.

Meg announced, "Hello, we're here to see Kyle Tarnoff."

Blondie assessed Meg, her expression slightly annoyed. I gathered she knew we weren't constituents and so automatically judged us to be second tier visitors.

She responded, "And you are…?"

I remembered the *Saturday Night Live* skit with David Spade in which a bitchy gatekeeper assistant asked famous people the exact same thing. I suppressed a snicker. If I acted snotty, we might get shown the door, given we were Langsford staffers and not the most popular people from Jessop's perspective. Furthermore, even if I could explain to Blondie why I was laughing, she wouldn't understand the reference. She wasn't old enough.

Meg cleared her throat in annoyance. Motioning toward each of us, respectively, she said, "My name is

Meg Peters and this is my associate, Kit Marshall. We work for Senator Langsford."

For a second, Meg looked confused. She caught herself and shifted to the past tense. "Rather, we *worked* for Senator Lyndon Langsford. Kyle is expecting us." Meg dug into her purse and produced her business card, and I did the same. We gave them to Blondie, who seemed unfazed by the fact that our boss had just been murdered.

"I'll let Kyle know you're here." She went back to staring at her computer screen, likely checking the latest status updates on Twitter. A little empathy might have been in order, but we were in Jordan Jessop's office. These people wanted to take over my boss's job; condolences were out of the question.

We sat in the small waiting room, and I took note of the décor. Since working in Congress, I had made a point of scrutinizing every congressional office I visited. From a purely anecdotal, non-scientific perspective, the way a member of Congress chose to decorate his or her office revealed a great deal. Members who had big egos tried to hang impressive photos of themselves taken with as many important people as possible. Even if the president had a popularity rating lower than Herbert Hoover's, members of Congress with an inflated sense of self still proudly displayed a photograph with him in the Oval Office or at the White House holiday party. Members who wanted to portray themselves as down-to-earth "guy next door" types usually had photos with their families and frequently with their dog. Golden retrievers were especially popular.

Members who liked to emphasize the work they did for voters chose to decorate their waiting rooms with constituent artwork or with prints proudly displaying popular local attractions. Members who came from places without particularly scenic areas displayed local sports memorabilia or other collector's items.

I looked around Representative Jessop's office. As I could have predicted, pictures of Jessop were everywhere. In addition to his smiling visage, almost every photograph featured a famous person or a powerful politician: Jessop with former Presidents, Jessop with Cabinet secretaries, Jessop with the current and former Speakers of the House. There was even a picture of Jessop with Kermit the Frog. The message came through loud and clear: Jordan Jessop was an *important* person, and he spent time with *important* people—and occasionally Muppets. I groaned inwardly as I thought of Senator Langsford's office, adorned with beautiful landscapes of the Boston Harbor, Cape Cod, and the historic industrial factories of Lowell. Except for a few candid shots with Vivian, Senator Langsford had decorated the office to commemorate the people he represented and the landscape he treasured. He hadn't been egocentric—not for a politician—and his office décor testified to his lack of hubris. His likely successor, it appeared, didn't share his humility.

I was awoken from my musings by a sing-song voice announcing, "Hello, fellow Bay State brethren!" I willfully restrained myself from muttering WTF under my breath.

Standing before me was a smiling man dressed neatly in stylish black suit pants, a perfectly pressed white shirt, and an American flag tie. He was in his early thirties and had short blond hair. His wire-framed glasses screamed, "smart, not nerdy." Welcome to Mr. Joe U.S.A., the typical chief of staff in the U.S. House of Representatives. He looked as earnest and patriotic as could be. That wholesome look was rare in the Senate, where the senior staff was usually older and had grown chiseled and wizened, for better or for worse.

Much to her credit, Meg was ready to play her part. She jumped out of her seat and greeted Kyle with an enthusiastic hug. Now the obligatory expressions of sympathy would start. Kyle might be blond, but he had a greater sense of propriety than Blondie at the front desk.

Just as I predicted, Kyle gushed about how sorry he was about Senator Langsford. As he launched into his torrent of missives and testimonials about Langsford's greatness, he ushered us back to his small office, which I noticed was adjacent to Jessop's private suite. So far, so good.

As Kyle went on and on, describing Langsford as a "true American patriot" and a "great fan of the state," I contrived a plan of action. If Meg could get him to move out of his office and into the area where the rest of the staff worked, I could slip into Jessop's office undetected. Kyle was clearly the gatekeeper, and it would be Meg's job to keep the gatekeeper sufficiently occupied.

I started to pay attention to the conversation again. We had moved on from sympathetic pleasantries to a discussion about the constituent request Meg ostensibly wanted to pawn off. It was a good excuse. If Jessop thought he was headed over to the Senate, he would want to establish a statewide constituent casework operation swiftly.

I caught the end of Meg's remarks to Kyle. "We wouldn't want any interruption of service, so I'm eager to make sure this concern is passed along to another congressional member of the delegation."

He nodded his earnest agreement. "Exactly. We're here to serve the citizens of our great state, aren't we?" Kyle looked for affirmation from Meg and me. How many times would Kyle use some variation of the term "great state"?

We both hung on his every word, although it required serious acting on my part. Meg supervised constituent requests related to her issue areas, but we had casework staffers who took the lead on those matters. Members in the House, however, represented single congressional districts and not states. Every staffer who worked in the House had to develop a solid repertoire for handling constituent complaints, concerns, and requests. Their bosses were up for election every two years, as opposed to six for the Senate. That meant Election Day was at most one year and 364 days away. As the founding fathers had intended, the Senate had a greater degree of insulation from constant voter evaluation. Meg and I needed to play along to get Kyle away from Representative Jessop's office. I doubted that under any other circumstances Meg would have been so eager to collaborate on a constituent request, especially with a staffer from the other political party.

Meg took advantage of the window Kyle had opened with his last comment. "Did you want me to talk to a staffer in your office specifically about this request? You mentioned on the phone you had someone in mind who could take the initiative on the matter." She batted her eyelashes at Kyle; then, for good effect, she added, "And after we're done talking about constituents, I thought we could discuss your happy hour plans for tonight." She giggled and flipped her hair.

I'm sure Kyle was a conscientious chief of staff. He

dressed the part, and he certainly talked the right game. Regardless, he was putty in Meg's hands. His repeated past efforts to get Meg to have a drink with him had probably frustrated him immensely, and now Meg was offering a golden opportunity Kyle wasn't about to turn down. I could have announced green Martians had just landed on the Capitol lawn, and it would have made no difference. The man looked like he'd just won the lottery. Kyle had no idea I was still in the room.

He responded by stammering, "Sure, Meg. Let's go chat with the person who can serve as the new point of contact on this matter." He paused for a long moment. "And then," he touched Meg's arm lightly, "we can talk about tonight."

Meg beamed at him. "I thought you'd never ask, silly!" Even though her answer made no sense, Kyle ate it up and they left his office.

As predicted, Kyle paid me absolutely no mind. Even though he was aware on some conscious level I was present in the office, he had completely fixated on Meg and her charms. She had done her job and bought me the time I needed. I had at least ten minutes to sneak into Jessop's office and snoop around.

I peeked around the corner to make sure Meg had kept Kyle conveniently disposed. She was leaning against a desk, smiling at him and giggling at his jokes. The way Meg was piling it on, maybe I had more like twenty minutes to investigate.

I tiptoed into Representative Jessop's office. Congressional office suites were nothing to write home about. As much guff as the public sector took from taxpayers, those of us who worked for members of Congress didn't work in the lap of luxury. Congressional workstations were small, and only the head honchos had private offices. However, in both the House and the Senate, the one spot of regality was the member's office. Both representatives and senators claimed the crown jewel of the congressional office suite. Member offices were large, but necessarily so. Since many meetings took place there, they needed enough room to entertain visitors, conduct briefings, and host other politicians.

Just as the front waiting area of any congressional suite said a great deal about the elected representative, a member's personal office space provided a good read on the person who sat behind the desk. After all, this space wasn't really a private area, since members conducted a considerable amount of business inside their office sanctuary. I took a look around Jessop's inner sanctum. Even though he represented a district from the same state as my former boss, I had never set foot inside Jessop's private office before today. After the stinging campaign four years earlier, Jessop and my boss had only traded terse, yet moderately cordial, remarks. Many of those exchanges were made through competing press releases about parochial issues concerning the state.

Several sofas and chairs framed Jessop's dark wooden desk, with a coffee table in the middle. I looked to see what he'd chosen to place on the coffee table. It was a large book of famous presidential photographs. Was I surprised? Jessop might have his sights on the Senate for now, but he clearly aspired beyond the legislative branch of government.

I moved toward Jessop's desk. If I was going to find

anything linking Jessop to Senator Langsford's murder, it would likely reside in his personal workspace.

Jessop had the obligatory picture of his perfect family adorning his desk. His wife strongly resembled Blondie at the front desk, only age appropriate, which meant roughly twenty years her senior. Was it the ambition of the Blondies of the world to marry male members of Congress? It wouldn't be a bad gig if the opportunity presented itself. The spouses of members of Congress, whether male or female, had a certain cachet in Washington, D.C. If channeled properly, their influence could be considerable. For example, a non-profit or issue advocacy group would never allow a congressional spouse phone call to go unanswered. I had no idea what Mrs. Jessop's professional career entailed, but whatever it was, it couldn't hurt to be married to a powerful House member who was likely to become the next Senator of the United States.

I had no time for whimsical thoughts about the Jessop family unit. His darling photograph wasn't getting me any closer to solving the murder. In fact, his desktop was a bit messy. Papers were strewn everywhere. I would have to shuffle some things around if I wanted to thoroughly examine the scene.

I moved swiftly back to the entrance of his office, so I could peek around the corner to check on Meg's relentless charm offensive. Meg was engaged in an animated discussion with another staffer from Jessop's office. I took that to mean she was explaining her "complicated" casework situation. Kyle stood nearby, hanging on her every word. Kyle wouldn't leave Meg's side as long as she chose to keep his attention. Then I felt a sudden stroke of panic. What if Kyle's desk phone rang? He was only fifteen feet away! He would rush back into his office and realize I was no longer innocently waiting for my friend to finish her business. I couldn't let that happen.

I impulsively snagged his phone from its cradle and placed it on his desk. Kyle wasn't going to receive any phone calls at his extension for the next couple of minutes. I hoped the United States could survive Kyle's brief period of being incommunicado. After all, I was trying to figure out who murdered a senator. In this instance, didn't one tiny wrong make a right? Besides, his iPhone was permanently attached to his hip, so a truly important person would have no trouble reaching him.

I rushed back into Jessop's office. I couldn't just look at what lay atop the desk. Digging was in order. I took a deep breath and mustered all the courage I could before shuffling the papers around. Everything I had read about adrenaline was true. Fight or flight? Well, I was ready for a fight.

There would be no other opportunity to investigate Jessop. If someone had asked me a week ago what I'd be doing at this moment in time, I would never in a million years have guessed I'd be rifling through a member of Congress's desk while my best friend flirted with a high-ranking staffer from the opposing party.

I picked up a big stack of papers and looked underneath. Jackpot! A black leather appointment book. No big surprise. Jessop hadn't embraced the technology revolution yet. He still had his scheduler keep a written appointment book listing his meetings, hearings, and other obligations. Being old-fashioned had its disadvantages, like increased vulnerability to amateur sleuths who managed to infiltrate congressional offices.

I flipped through the pages to find today's date. When I got to the right page, I started reading and scanning backward. Jessop's movements during the time leading up to Senator Langsford's murder were critical pieces of information. If I had enough time, I wouldn't have minded reading the whole appointment book, but I had less than five minutes if I wanted to avoid further risk of detection. Meg had Kyle under control, but there were others who worked here, and who knows if Meg could keep them tied up as well. Meg's allure was formidable, but it wasn't miraculous.

I turned to Tuesday's page, the day Senator Langsford had been murdered. I looked at the entry for the early morning hours. Representative Jessop had visited a senior center in his home district for breakfast. I stifled a groan. This would be easy to confirm. If Jessop had been munching on bagels with the blue hairs, he couldn't have killed Senator Langsford. Even the great Jordan Jessop couldn't be in two places at once. I paused for a moment. Did I hear voices growing louder, coming closer to the entrance of the congressman's office? I thought about diving underneath the desk, although if I was caught in that position, my photo would certainly grace the front page of the Hill rags, and it wouldn't be a mistake this time. But the voices faded away, moving farther into the depths of the office suite. The message was clear. My time was almost out. I had only a few more minutes before releasing Meg from her rapturous conversation with Kyle.

Nothing else on Jessop's desk looked remotely interesting, so I kept paging through his appointment book. At the very least it would satisfy my curiosity about how my former boss's archenemy spent his time. I plowed through the days leading up to Senator Langsford's death. Nothing grabbed my attention. As one might expect, the pages were filled with typical constituent meetings in his office, fundraisers, and consultations with other members of Congress.

Jessop met frequently with a large number of campaign donors off-site. Sitting members of Congress couldn't raise reelection funds on the Capitol grounds, including inside office suites. This regulation pushed fundraising to locations off Capitol Hill, but not too far away. Members could attend a fundraiser or "dial for dollars" for their reelection effort, then jump into a taxi to whisk them back to the Capitol for a vote or important meeting. For a member of Congress who was almost guaranteed to win again in the House, Jessop had done a lot of fundraisers. He might have been raising money for other co-partisans seeking office, although I never thought of Jessop as a particularly generous man who wanted to give thousands of dollars to others who shared his ideological beliefs. In fact, Jessop had mounted a competitive campaign against Senator Langsford because Langsford hadn't been a minion who had subscribed to all the dictates prescribed by those who led his party. Politically speaking, Jessop was middle of the road, which made him appealing to many constituents in a statewide contest. That also meant he wasn't likely to get tapped to raise a ton of campaign money for his political party.

These revelations were noteworthy, to say the least. If Jessop wasn't raising money for himself or his colleagues, why was he attending daily fundraisers? Did he know he would be mounting a statewide race for the Senate after being named as Langsford's successor? If that was the case, the circumstantial evidence against Jessop had grown.

After paging back two weeks, I unearthed a puzzling notation. His appointments were written out on his calendar in detail, for example: "Jane Smith from Boston police union on pay issue" or "Selectmen from Dedham on wastewater improvement grant."

One meeting stuck out: "JR—CP." It didn't take a rocket scientist to figure out the shorthand meant "Jonas Regan—Carter Power." If I was correct, this might indicate a connection linking Jessop to Carter Power. Could it possibly also link Jessop or Regan to the murder of Senator Langsford? Just as that thought registered, I heard voices coming my way. This time, they were getting louder, and they were accompanied by footsteps.

EIGHTEEN

WITH SECONDS TO SPARE, I ducked into the small bathroom in the corner of Representative Jessop's office. Making a snap decision, I flushed the toilet, then took a deep breath and opened the door slowly. Kyle was standing in front of me, with Meg behind him, along with another person I didn't know, presumably the other staffer Kyle had asked Meg to meet concerning the casework file she'd proposed to turn over. All three of them looked as if they had just seen the ghost of Speaker Joe Cannon. At least no one made a move to call the Capitol Police, although they were clearly waiting for me to explain why I had just used the private bathroom of a member of Congress.

I addressed Kyle, the presumed authority figure. "You and Meg were so involved in your conversation, I didn't want to bother you. I needed to use the restroom." I shrugged sheepishly.

The anonymous third staffer, a nondescript young man, replied, "That's Representative Jessop's bathroom. It's not a public restroom."

Duh. I wasn't born yesterday. So this guy was going to make it difficult. I'd have to fight fire with fire. "I know, but it was an emergency." I paused for a moment to increase the dramatic effect. "A *female* situation, if you know what I mean."

Instantly, Kyle and mystery man's faces turned a

dark red. That was the end of the conversation. Kyle could barely stammer a response. "Of course, if there was an emergency, it makes sense for you to find a bathroom. Don't worry about it."

He motioned for us to leave the office, and the three of us followed, Meg and me lagging behind. Jabbing me in the ribs, Meg whispered, "Female troubles? Was that really the best you could do?"

I muttered, "Shut up. It worked. Now let's get out of here."

Meg went into wrap-up mode and gushed at Kyle about how kind he was to welcome us into the office and how impressed she was with the quality of the staff, and so on. I willfully suppressed any appearance of incredulity because Kyle seemed to buy her line of bull.

As we were about to leave, Kyle glanced at his desk. Good gracious. Since I'd fled to the bathroom, I never had the opportunity to put his phone back on the receiver. Frowning, Kyle said, "Why is my phone off the hook? How could that have happened?" He looked over at us with what I hoped wasn't suspicion.

Maybe it was the pressure I had been under lately or the fact I felt like I'd been lying constantly during the past seventy-two hours. At any rate, I was speechless. I had run out of fibs, fabrications, or downright falsehoods. A little voice inside of me wanted to shout the truth. YES, I TOOK THE DAMN PHONE OFF THE HOOK. I WAS SNOOPING IN YOUR BOSS'S OFFICE BECAUSE HE MIGHT HAVE KILLED MY BOSS.

Fortunately Meg's real voice drowned out my little one. She must have taken one look at me and figured out I had been the one to put Kyle's phone out of commission. Without losing a beat, she piped up, "Oh, I knock my phone off its cradle on a daily basis. If I'm not careful, it happens a couple times a day. These phones they give us in Congress are so flimsy." She giggled coquettishly.

I looked over at Kyle. Surely, he wouldn't buy this?

Remarkably, it seemed he had. His brow furrowed. "It never happens to me, but I guess you're right. If you're looking for papers on your desk and you happen to brush the receiver, there's not much to keep it in its place."

Meg breathed a sigh of relief. "Of course. And your voicemail isn't blinking, so you didn't even miss a call. No harm done!" She rewarded Kyle with her most radiant smile.

He returned her grin with one of his own. "Meg, I wish you belonged to my party. I'd hire you in a second! You always focus on the positive side of any situation. Your boss died unexpectedly, and yet you took valuable time to walk over here and talk to us about a constituent problem. You're truly a laudable public servant."

I turned away in case the grimace I felt coming on surfaced. This charade needed to end so I could get out of here with a straight face. We had come to investigate his boss for killing our boss, and now Meg was being nominated for Capitol Hill Staffer of the Year? It was time to get the heck out of Dodge. "Kyle, you're one hundred percent correct. Truly, there's no congressional staffer like Meg. Thanks for taking the time to meet with us today."

I turned toward Meg. "Shouldn't we return to our office? People might start to miss us, right?"

Meg got my drift. "Yes, absolutely. Kyle, it was great to see you!" She turned to leave.

Kyle wasn't going to let her off that easily. "Aren't you forgetting something, Meg?"

She looked at her purse and checked to make sure she had everything. "No, I don't think so. I have my BlackBerry, and I gave the casework file to you and your staff." She smiled sweetly at him.

He shook his head. "We were so busy talking business, you didn't tell me where we're going after work tonight." Kyle's hopeful gaze reminded me of Clarence when he begged for a doggie treat.

I prayed Meg wouldn't dump Kyle right at this moment. First, it would be incredibly uncomfortable to watch. Second, it might seem suspicious to Kyle that she'd had such an abrupt change of heart. Third, I wanted to get out of that office before someone figured out I'd been snooping around the Congressman's desk while Meg had been flirting with the chief of staff. I didn't need to feel the cold steel of handcuffs on my wrists twice in one week.

Meg must have decided to avoid a scene. She flashed her pearly whites and touched Kyle lightly on his arm. Drawling sweetly, she teased, "Of course. Don't you worry. I didn't forget about our plans. You're not getting off that easy."

Relief washed over Kyle's face.

She offered, "Why don't I text you closer to six so we can figure out what makes sense?"

Kyle looked skeptical. He clearly would have preferred a game plan before he let Meg out of his sight. He said, "I guess that makes sense. Do you have my number?"

Meg winked at him and tapped her BlackBerry. "All your info is right here."

He looked slightly relieved that Meg had his number already programmed into her mobile device. Kyle obviously had little experience with women such as Meg, however. I had witnessed her moves over the years, and this was a replay of her classic brush-off routine.

We bid our final farewells and cruised out of the office. Before debriefing, we waited until we had exited the elevator—a notorious Capitol Hill location for eavesdropping. When I told Meg what I had found in Jessop's appointment book, she was giddy with excitement. "Can you believe our plan worked perfectly?"

"I can't believe we didn't get caught. How did you manage to keep Kyle busy for all that time?"

"It was easy. I took a relatively simple constituent problem and turned it into something as complicated as the national debt. Every time he thought we had wrapped it up, I mentioned a new wrinkle. It will probably keep that poor guy who inherited it in Jessop's office busy for the next month!" She threw her head back and laughed.

I turned to face my friend, hands on my hips. "If I didn't know you better, Meg, I'd conclude you actually enjoyed breaking into a member of Congress's office."

Her face lit up. "You know, it's funny you should say that. Although I was nervous, especially when we found you in Jessop's bathroom, I did enjoy myself. This afternoon was the first time in months I actually felt alive!" The look on her face was as serious as I'd ever seen on Meg. "Have you ever thought Senator Langsford's death might give you a new career opportunity?"

Even though our conversation had been light in tone

until this point, Meg wasn't kidding. Though she was a notorious flirt who placed too much importance on her social life, she was no slouch. All joking aside, Kyle had been right. Meg was an impressive Capitol Hill staffer. Senator Langsford had always thought of her as a valuable policy advisor. Meg was no stereotypical Capitol Hill party girl. Sure, she liked her happy hours and moved from guy to guy like they were going out of style, but that in no way diminished the formidable depth of her abilities and intelligence. As she had demonstrated in the past several days, she could think quickly on her feet and had a sharp wit that would serve her well, no matter where she worked in Washington.

"I need to start thinking about a new job," Meg said, "but to tell you the truth, I haven't focused yet. It's pretty irresponsible. The truth is I haven't come to terms with the fact we're not going to be working for Senator Langsford anymore."

Meg and I were walking the block separating the House from the Senate. We had just passed the Library of Congress on our right and were almost directly across from the East Front of the Capitol. So far I had kept my emotions in check since the senator's death. I had been obsessed with clearing my name, then finding his real killer. The preoccupation with these two goals had driven all thoughts of sorrow out of my head. Suddenly I was overcome with sadness, and tears started streaming down my face. Slightly embarrassed, since there were gaggles of tourists surrounding the public entrance to the Capitol Visitor Center, I tried to wipe away the waterworks.

Meg stopped in her tracks. "Hey, Kit, I'm sorry I brought up our next jobs. I know you were attached to

Senator Langsford more than I was. I didn't mean to upset you."

I shook my head at Meg's apology. She had worked on the Hill for other senators before coming to Langsford's office, and she knew what it was like to leave one Capitol Hill office for another. This was new territory for me, but it wasn't her comments that had brought on my tears. My own suppression of the dark feelings I had about ending my tenure as a Langsford staffer had triggered the emotional outburst, along with my genuine grief over my boss's terrible fate and my unknown and possibly nonexistent future in Washington, D.C. Doug was settled in his job, and he would always have his colleagues at Georgetown. Now I would be forced to find a whole new professional home, and it wasn't a change I ever thought I'd have to consider.

Panic seized me. What if I couldn't find another job in Washington? I doubted Doug would leave his appointment at Georgetown to take a job at another university. We weren't married, and that was another source of worry. With no firm commitment from him, a long span of unemployment could doom our relationship.

I had to stop thinking this way. Negativity had the power to paralyze me, and I couldn't afford a mental breakdown right now.

"It's not your fault, Meg. I haven't made plans beyond working for Senator Langsford because on some level, I don't want to think beyond this job. If I leave this job..." I paused to correct myself. "*When* I leave this job, I'll need to start over. Most likely, that new job will mean moving onto an office without you. And to tell you the truth, the prospect of facing Capitol Hill without you scares me!"

It wasn't easy baring my soul, even to Meg. On one hand, I was grateful for the opportunity to tell her how I truly felt. On the other hand, it was tough for me to admit my deepest insecurities about my career and future.

Meg faced me directly and put her hands on my shoulders. I had gotten her attention, since this departure from my typical even-keel approach was unusual. "Kit, I should be the scared one. You've always been the voice of reason for me in Langsford's office. I worked in other places on Capitol Hill before Senator Langsford, but no office was as high profile. Anytime I came close to trouble, you had my back. We've had four years to work for one of the best senators in recent history. Don't you think we've learned something during that time? I didn't want Senator Langsford to die. We can't control the fact that his life was taken from him. Now we have to move on. As I look at it, we need to count our blessings for the time we had together and use that experience to figure out our next step."

My tears had dried, and I grasped Meg's hands in mine. "You're absolutely right. Instead of focusing on the fact that we no longer work for Senator Langsford, I should have been thinking about the good times we had together."

Meg put her arm around my waist, and we continued to walk toward our office. On our way back, we talked about the great moments we'd witnessed as staffers for Senator Langsford. He'd been a major player on several landmark pieces of legislation, and it had been extraordinary to share those victories as part of his team.

We also talked about the fun times we'd had together as a staff. Matt had been a constant source of inspiration as our legislative director and immediate boss. It would be hard to find another supervisor like him. Lucinda had her quirks, but demonstrated the value of loyalty in Washington, D.C. When I thought about her relationship to Carter Power and any possible connection to Langsford's death, I remembered the tears she shed on the morning of his death, when others who were close to him showed little or no grief. Despite Meg's opinion of him, I would even miss Trevor. I had gotten used to his wisecracks, and in the past few days his practical wisdom and sound advice had helped with the investigation.

As we neared the Hart Building, for the second time today I had a strange feeling I had missed something important. I couldn't put my finger on it. Nothing Meg and I had discussed during our stroll down memory lane had been particularly riveting. I pushed aside the nagging internal voice as we returned to our office suite. Emails and phone messages required my attention, but I made a mental note to revisit my odd premonition later when I could focus on it.

For the next several hours, I provided information about tomorrow's wake or an address for condolences. Several supplicants asked who my successor would be when Senator Langsford's replacement was named. I deleted those messages out of pure annoyance. There were only so many mental tribulations one person could endure in one day.

I glanced at the time on my computer and decided it was time to go home. I was gathering my possessions when the phone rang. I didn't recognize the number.

That wasn't surprising since I barely knew many of the people who had called today about the wake.

With my purse in tow, I picked up the phone with my left hand and balanced the receiver under my chin. Fiddling with my mouse to shut down the computer for the night, I answered, "Kit Marshall speaking."

There was a pause on the line. I could hear faint breathing. Then a robotic voice came on the line.

"QUIT SNOOPING AROUND OR YOU'LL BE NEXT."

NINETEEN

IT TOOK ME several seconds to realize the voice on the line had been digitally altered. I stammered, "What d-did you say?" The next sound was a dial tone.

I glanced at my desk phone. As I suspected, the call had already disconnected and no number was visible on the screen. I had no idea who had called me. It hadn't come from inside the Senate since no identifying name had popped up with the number. There was absolutely no way I could recall the row of digits that had flashed before my eyes.

Abject fear would have been a normal reaction, yet my response was quite the opposite. I slammed the phone down in its cradle. My side of the office suite was empty. I asked loudly, "Meg, are you there?"

Almost instantly, she was standing right next to me. "How did you get here so fast?"

"I was walking over to say goodnight. What's up?"

She listened intently, her eyes growing wider as I recounted the mysterious caller's ominous threat. "Kit, this is serious. You need to contact Detective O'Halloran right away. Your life could be in danger." She wavered a second. "I mean, *my* life could be in danger, too."

My angry defiance hadn't subsided. "Not so fast, Meg. Do you know what this phone call means?"

"That Langsford's killer wants to make us the next victims?" she asked.

Meg had conveniently interpreted a brazen threat on my life as synonymous to a threat on her own. There was no point in calling out her self-centered behavior at this point.

"No. It means more than that. It means we're on the right track, and the killer knows it."

Meg grabbed my shoulders and gave me a gentle shake. "Kit, when the killer isn't happy about something, do I need to remind you what happens? Someone dies."

"No one else is going to die, especially if we ask the right questions. We're going to figure this out before that can happen. If we tell O'Halloran about the phone call, he'll forbid us from any further investigating. If that happens, how long is it going to take for the police to catch the killer?"

"You're right. If we tell the police, we're off the case." She rubbed her chin, seemingly deep in contemplation of our options.

I interrupted the silence. "This phone call should be our little secret for now. Let's see what we can find out tomorrow at the wake."

"Aren't you going to tell Doug about it?"

"No way," I answered immediately. "He'd be worse than O'Halloran. He wouldn't let me out of the condo for a week if I told him. Like I said, I think we should keep this between us for now." I gave her arm a squeeze.

My reasoning appealed to several of Meg's personality foibles. She treasured secrets and the exclusivity that came with them. She also loved knowing something I wasn't going to share with my boyfriend. At times, Meg and Doug competed with each other for privileged status. Meg often lost to Doug, but sharing this secret with only me gave her a huge advantage.

A smile slowly spread across Meg's face. "I'll make a deal with you. I'll keep your secret, but if you get another threatening phone call, you have to promise to call Detective O'Halloran right away." She grabbed my hand in hers. "I mean it, Kit. No fooling around. Will you promise me?"

I clenched her hand in response. "I promise. It's not going to come to that, though. We're going to find out who did this to our boss. We're making the killer nervous, and that means we're closing in."

Meg's BlackBerry buzzed, and she glanced at it. "I should have known. Guess who?"

"I wouldn't even want to venture a guess, given your long list of suitors."

Meg grinned. "It's Kyle, of course."

"Are you going to try to come up with an inventive excuse to avoid meeting him tonight?"

Meg fiddled with her device, and I thought I saw her blush. "Actually, I might go out with him. He's not a terrible guy."

I raised my eyebrows, since Meg's taste in men usually ranged from burly Capitol Hill police officers to attractive and sophisticated lobbyists on K Street. From what I had seen, Kyle didn't fit within the realm of hunks Meg regularly entertained. Nonetheless, Kyle did seem like a nice guy. Maybe Meg was starting to cast her net a bit wider. If I pressed her, she might change her mind. The less said, the better. I exclaimed with as much enthusiasm as I could muster, "Why not? Have fun tonight!"

I reminded her that the pick-up time was early tomorrow morning at the Metro if she wanted a ride to the senator's wake. We finalized our plans, and I decided it was time to head home to Doug and Clarence, who were no doubt awaiting my arrival with bated breath. Before we parted, she reminded me once again to be careful. My three-fingered Girl Scout promise acknowledged her warning.

TWENTY

AFTER PROFILING EACH rider anywhere near me on the Metro, I convinced myself the killer hadn't decided to make good on the issued threat—at least not tonight. My mind meandered about the case. Thanks to the menacing phone call, I hadn't fully considered the relevance of finding the "JR—CP" entry in Jessop's appointment book. It was impossible to determine if the appointment had any connection to Senator Langsford's murder.

On the significant side, it was suspicious that Jessop had met with Regan on a monumental issue only a short time before the homicide. If Carter Power was the reason behind Langsford's demise, the timing of the meeting was another piece of circumstantial evidence implicating Jessop or indicating his involvement.

Had Regan told Jessop that Langsford was unwilling to "play ball" on Carter Power, thus leading Jessop to decide it was time to kill him before the critical committee vote? It was possible. Or maybe Jessop gave Regan the idea that Langsford should be eliminated. Even if Regan had an alibi, he might have enlisted Jeff Prentice to do his dirty work for him and Jessop.

On the other side of the coin, Carter Power was a huge defense contractor. Regan might have simply paid Jessop a courtesy visit about the status of the company. Jessop served on the Armed Services Committee in the House of Representatives, so he had a general interest in all large-scale defense contractors, including the biggest nationwide supplier of the military's batteries. For all I knew, Jessop might have requested the meeting, not Regan.

How did our already identified suspects jive with the threat I received earlier this evening? I had no recall of the phone number, so that was a dead end. The voice on the phone had been mechanically altered beyond recognition. Anyone might have placed the call, likely with a so-called disposable "burner" cellphone that could be purchased at any large retail store. Jeff Prentice and Senator Regan might have reason to threaten me if either, or both, was the guilty party.

My mind drifted back to earlier today in Jessop's office. Perhaps my clever excuse for snooping hadn't fooled Kyle. Had he shared my exploits with Jessop, who had placed the call to scare me? Even worse, had wholesome Kyle somehow been coerced by Jessop to do his dirty work for him? Meg was on a date with Kyle right now. As soon as I got off the subway, I needed to text her to make sure she was safe.

In the meantime, I pulled out my notebook to jot down a few notes. Matt had given me sound advice when I began working for Langsford. If a problem was perplexing and the details overwhelming, get out of the weeds and look at the situation as an outsider. Could I apply that approach to Langsford's murder?

The culprit knew Langsford would be in the office early that morning. It was a Tuesday, and he wasn't always present in the office at such an early hour. That meant the perp, or an accomplice, had access to accurate information about Langsford's schedule.

Another important clue was the murder weapon, the

stainless steel model military helicopter that had been on display inside his office for as long as I worked there. It had proven a lethal weapon, yet only someone familiar with the senator's inner sanctum would have known its location—tucked away in a corner alcove several feet away from his desk.

The more I thought about the crime, the more it seemed premeditated. The only fingerprints on the helicopter were mine, or the police would have followed that lead. The murderer had likely worn gloves to hide his or her fingerprints, which implied the person had come to the office that morning to commit the crime.

Furthermore, the killer didn't bring a weapon. It was an important detail, and no doubt a critical piece of the puzzle I hoped the police had fully analyzed. It was difficult to carry any "weapon" into a congressional office building these days. Security was tight, and every person entering Hart passed through a scanner. Bags, purses, and coats needed to be removed and placed on the conveyor for X-ray screening. Anything that could be used as a weapon wasn't allowed inside the building. Only someone who regularly visited or worked within the congressional complex would understand the extent of these restrictions. The would-be murderer would have to rely on obtaining the weapon inside the building. My intuition had told me all along this was an inside job. Someone close to Langsford had killed him, and likely for strong political or personal reasons.

Unfortunately, everyone who had a motive for killing Senator Langsford appeared to have an airtight alibi. I crossed Jessop off the list after confirming that he had, in fact, visited a senior citizens center the morning of the murder. There were photos and a press release on his official website to prove it. Several theories and motives were plausible, but few people had the opportunity to kill Langsford. Except me, of course, which made it even more imperative that the real killer was discovered. If the police were similarly stymied, how long would it take Detective O'Halloran to circle back to me as the prime suspect, despite my lack of motive and late arrival on the scene? He had already tried to connect the one piece of physical evidence, the blond synthetic hair, to Meg. That deduction made perfect sense to him because he could then link the murder to yours truly.

After texting Meg, who assured me she was perfectly safe with Kyle and a delicious glass of bubbly, I put my key into the lock for the door to the condo and braced myself. Sure enough, as soon as the door cracked open, Clarence appeared out of nowhere, poised to bolt down the hallway to freedom. After I blocked his escape route, he issued several loud protest barks and ran toward the kitchen. If he couldn't make a mad dash out the door, then Clarence was always amenable to the next best thing, namely doggie treats or more food in his dish. I called for Doug, but there was no response.

After placing my purse on our countertop, I scrutinized a hopeful Clarence, who was seated politely at my feet with his ears and tail at attention. Clarence firmly believed good manners would get him anything he wanted in this world. For him, good manners meant sitting on command and putting on the saddest face he could possibly muster up. Clarence's belief system wasn't flawed; he got exactly what he wanted ninety-nine percent of the time when he looked at me with his wide eyes and expectant gaze. In fact, Clarence's behavior might be the most predictable part of my day. If I woke up one morning and Clarence didn't try to use his wiles to cajole me, I would wonder if there was something drastically wrong with him or if I had woken up in someone else's apartment. His unsurprising behavior was endearing. Throughout the vast majority of my day, I interacted with unpredictable, fickle, and often untrustworthy people. Clarence's routine provided comfort in a world that was anything but.

After rewarding Clarence's patience with a biscuit, I wandered into the bedroom and office area and found Doug. With iPod earphones in place and books strewn all over the room, the mad professor at work was oblivious to my arrival. Since he clearly couldn't hear anything besides the music, he seemed startled when I walked in front of him. His face brightened, however, and he stood to give me a welcome home kiss. I returned the favor with even more enthusiasm. Shocked, he pulled his headphones off quickly.

I laughed at his eager reaction. "Don't get too excited. I'm famished and I need to eat."

He looked behind me. Clarence had ambled into the room, quietly sitting behind us. He looked at us optimistically. Clarence understood several English words, and his favorite was "eat."

"You're not the only one who's hungry. Let's get Clarence his dinner and you some wine."

I gave him my broadest smile and said, "That's the best offer I've gotten all day!"

TWENTY-ONE

NEITHER DOUG NOR I like to cook much. From time to time, we've invited friends to our condo for wine and cheese. Home cooked dinners typically involve the pizza stone, frozen dough, and toppings hastily found in the fridge's remote vestiges. For routine sustenance, we patronize the numerous restaurants that populate our suburban corridor. Many are within walking distance, and several deliver their full menus to nearby condo dwellers. A Thai place recently opened a block away, and it promised speedy delivery. Living in the Washington, D.C., region has a lot of positives, yet amazing cuisine isn't one of them. It's hit or miss, and restaurants have a short shelf life, mimicking the attenuated attention spans of the young urban professional clientele.

A few moments later, Clarence had been fed, at least his first course before the human food arrived. He hunched over his bowl, wolfing down doggie food as hurriedly as he could. I sat in our comfortable armchair sipping a local Chardonnay, taking a moment to savor the crisp tartness of the vintage. I had changed from my work clothes into a pair of shorts and an old t-shirt with the slogan "Don't Assume That I Cook" next to a picture of a pizza box. After locating my cellphone in my purse, I searched for the Thai place's delivery number. In sixty seconds, we had a delicious meal of sesame noodles, green curry, spring rolls, and mango sticky rice coming our way. With its light touch and slightly fruity taste, the wine would complement our dinner perfectly.

As we sipped our libations, I recounted the day's events to Doug, with a few select omissions. I conveniently left out the detail in which I was almost uncovered as a snoop and had to seek refuge in Representative Jessop's bathroom. I also "forgot" to mention the sinister phone call at the end of the day. Was withholding information the moral equivalent of lying? In this instance, the ends justified the means. We had to keep up the hunt for Langsford's killer, and if Doug knew about the threatening phone call, he would make sure my gumshoe days were history, no pun intended.

Doug agreed the evidence of Jessop's association with Carter Power was suspicious, while still falling short of the smoking gun needed to pin Langsford's murder on the guilty party. After our food arrived, we sat at our sleek black dining room table and discussed tomorrow's wake. To my surprise, Doug said he would accompany me.

Don't get me wrong. Doug was a supportive significant other. He enthusiastically endorsed my off-the-wall idea four years ago to join Senator Langsford's tough reelection campaign. At the time, he had recently accepted an appointment as an assistant professor at Georgetown and was completely absorbed in writing his first book. Because of his fixation on tenure, I didn't know if it even registered I was gone from Washington for six months straight during the campaign. He flew to Boston for a visit whenever he took a rare day off from working on his manuscript.

After Senator Langsford won the race, I lobbied the

senior campaign staff about a policy job in Washington, D.C. Langsford's reelection meant I would have a job and hopefully a career in the same city as Doug. It didn't take long for the pieces of the puzzle to fall into place. The same day Senator Langsford was sworn into office for another term as senator, I took the federal employee oath and joined his staff.

Academics have a love/hate relationship with politics. Some prominent professors apply their intellectual knowledge to public affairs, and the highest level of policymakers seek out their expertise. Most of these professors are economists, political scientists, or international affairs experts. It's the rare historian who deigns to derive scholarly relevance from current events.

Doug's research was steeped in academic debates concerning the historical periods, people, and institutions he studied. His primary audience was other academics. While his colleagues weren't oblivious about what transpired in the world around them, academic careers did not typically soar due to the latest buzz from Capitol Hill.

Given this divide, Doug supported my career as a Senate staffer simply because I needed a job in D.C. Besides, working for the Senate was a prestigious position that served routinely as adequate cocktail conversation fodder at the various events we attended around town. Those two reasons surely contributed to his approval, but Doug went beyond such perfunctory encouragement. He routinely asked about the trials and tribulations of my work and kept abreast of the various lively characters I encountered daily. All the while, he refrained from injecting himself into my Capitol Hill life, always one step comfortably removed.

The arrangement was almost perfect. There was one wrinkle, which I avoided discussing like the plague, even with Meg. All that was missing was an engagement ring on my finger. Good things come to those who wait, and I had waited patiently. Doug's reluctance to take the plunge was a sore point. Since he was otherwise devoted, I tolerated his commitment phobia...for now.

So naturally I was taken aback when Doug mentioned he would accompany me to Senator Langsford's wake. Doug usually came with me to "official" events, such as a holiday party or an office picnic. Somehow, Senator Langsford's funeral seemed more intimate than those other occasions, and I hadn't expected him to come. Nonetheless, he was intent on attending, which led me to wonder whether his father had urged him to go, perhaps to represent the family and keep an eye on me. My recent brush with the law still didn't sit well with the family. That couldn't bode well for future wedding bells, either.

We made our plans for tomorrow, which included picking up Meg before heading out to McLean for the wake. After confirming that the car did indeed have gas, we decided to watch a made-for-TV mystery movie. The rest of the night passed peacefully, with Clarence happily snoozing between us on the sofa, snoring softly as we gave him all the attention he felt he deserved. As I watched the movie, that nagging feeling colored my thoughts once again. The plots for these cable movies weren't terribly sophisticated. This particular mystery featured a sleuth who figured out whodunit after realizing one of the suspect's stories contained a key detail that was woefully out of place.

I, too, had an annoying and persistent feeling a key

piece of information resided in my brain, just beyond the grasp of consciousness. Maybe I should have ignored those thoughts, turned off the television, taken an Ambien, and gone to bed. Instead, I kept trying to unearth the fuzzy detail eluding me.

TWENTY-TWO

I SLEPT FITFULLY AGAIN. I had not yet solved Langsford's murder and my remaining time as a Senate employee was rapidly disappearing.

After chugging a big cup of coffee and feeding Clarence, I searched my closet for appropriate attire. I briefly considered wearing a black dress instead of a suit. It was the middle of summer, and at least part of the wake included a reception outdoors on the beautiful grounds of the Langsford estate. I decided to go with my instincts and wear my most stylish black suit. Since it was July, no pantyhose were required and my dressiest pair of silver and black sandals would work with the outfit. In case someone thought my bare legs pushed the envelope, I donned my pearl necklace and matching earrings. Nothing said "traditional Washington" more than cultured pearls. Doug had taken less than half the time to get ready and was waiting in the living room.

His face lit up when he saw me. "You look terrific. Good enough, in fact, to attend a senator's wake." Doug meant it as both a compliment and an attempt to bring levity to a sad event.

I smiled back. "Would you mind getting the car out of the garage and picking me up in front of the building? I'd like to minimize my walking in these sandals." I pointed down at my heels.

He agreed, and after saying goodbye to Clarence,

I headed downstairs to the drive-up carport at the entrance of our building. I texted Meg to let her know we'd pick her up shortly at the nearby subway station. Doug pulled up and we made our way through the busy streets of Arlington to arrive at the Metro. When I saw Meg emerge from the escalator, I got out of the car to wave. Otherwise she might not be able to spot us from among the many other hybrid vehicles in trendy Arlington.

I saw Meg's reaction when she realized Doug was driving and would be joining us. It wasn't full-scale disappointment, yet it was definitely gloomy. Depending on the situation, it could be exhausting to mediate between Meg and Doug when we spent time together. Today's event would be stressful enough. I said a prayer asking for a blessing of short-term serenity.

Meg got into the car and said to Doug, "Imagine my surprise seeing you. You decided to slum it with the political hacks for the day?"

I sighed. So much for peace among the troops.

Much to his credit, Doug didn't take the bait, as he often did. "I liked Senator Langsford, and so did my family. I thought it would be appropriate to pay my respects, and of course, support you and Kit as you mourn the loss of your boss."

Meg couldn't come up with a witty retort. "That's nice of you."

Time to intervene. I asked Meg about her "date" last night with Kyle. Once again I was surprised at her lack of a clever response. I expected her to blow it off or provide us with a long-winded story about why she found him supremely annoying. After all, she only went on the date because she couldn't figure a way out of it. Instead, she simply answered that she'd had "a good time" and Kyle was a "pleasant guy." This was an interesting development, since Meg rarely missed an opportunity to dish about her evening social outings.

Meg abruptly changed the topic. "Don't you think we need a plan for today?"

I turned around from the front seat to look at her. "A 'plan' for attending the wake?"

"Of course, Kit. All the suspects will be there. There's a chance that Senator Langsford's murderer will be one of the attendees."

If our working hypothesis was true and someone Senator Langsford had known well had killed him, it was altogether likely, or even certain, that his killer would attend the wake. Meg had snapped me back into "investigator" mode. I thought about what we needed to accomplish today.

"Meg, you're absolutely right. We need to chase down several leads at the wake. We'll never again have all our suspects in the same place at once."

Doug had been listening carefully as he drove. "What do we need to do?"

I turned away from Meg and faced him. "Are you sure you want to get involved in this? I thought you weren't exactly thrilled with our investigation. You've been telling me since the first day to leave it to the police."

He took his right hand off the wheel, placed it on my knee, and gave it a gentle squeeze. "I want to find Senator Langsford's killer for a number of reasons, but the top reason is making sure nothing happens to you. The sooner the murderer is caught, the better for everyone involved. Am I right?"

A wave of happiness enveloped me. Doug felt an ob-

ligation to attend the wake, and his father might have
encouraged it, but the real reason he'd decided to come
was to keep me safe. It was times like this I knew I
wouldn't trade Doug for anything in the world, engagement ring or not.

Grabbing his hand, I said softly, "Thank you, Doug."
I felt a little guilty about hiding the threatening phone
call from him, but I pushed those feelings away. This
wasn't the time or the place to tell him about it.

Meg watched all of this unfold without comment.
After a few minutes, she broke the silence. "Now we've
had a tender moment, can we get back to who we need
to speak with at the wake? We're getting close to Senator Langsford's house."

We had just turned into the posh housing plan where
the Langsfords lived in suburban McLean.

"Let's divide up the suspects, so no one draws attention by pumping too many people for information."

Meg and Doug agreed. I proceeded with my assignments. "Meg, I need you to talk to Jeff Prentice. You
have a better rapport with him than I do, and I think it's
more likely he'll divulge information to you. We need
to figure out how Carter Power is connected to Langsford, Regan, and Jessop. I still think we're missing an
important detail."

"You got it. Prentice won't be difficult to break!"

I grinned. "Remember, this isn't an interrogation.
We can't look too obvious, and above all, it's a wake.
We're supposed to be in mourning. Of course, we want
to honor Senator Langsford's memory, but we have an
ulterior mission."

I turned to Doug. "Can you track down Senator
Regan and try to find out if he has an alibi? Mandy

claims he was with his wife at the time of Senator Langsford's murder, but I don't think we should trust her. Regan had a prime motive for killing Langsford, and if his alibi is wishy-washy, we need to know about it."

Doug gave me a mock salute. "Aye, aye, Captain. I don't think that should be too hard."

Meg asked, "Who are you going to hunt down, Kit?"

"I need to see what the deal is with Vivian. We've forgotten her lately, but she stands to gain from that insurance policy, and according to Trevor, she's tied up in the Carter Power business as well."

Doug said, "Good idea. But she might be hard to track down. Remember, this is her husband's wake."

"I know. I'm going to have to keep careful tabs and find an opportunity to speak with her. If I can do that, my next target is Lucinda. Matt led me to believe Senator Langsford's position on Carter Power was a well-kept secret. But now I'm not so sure Matt's intentions were carried out. It seems like many people knew about Carter Power and which way Senator Langsford was leaning at the time of his death. Now that he's been gone a few days, Lucinda might be straight with me about who knew what."

Doug looked at me in wonderment. "You two certainly have a knack for this business. When you told me you wanted to investigate Langsford's murder, I figured it was the result of some form of post-traumatic stress. Especially since you, um…" he trailed off.

I finished the sentence for him. "You mean since I discovered the body."

He shrugged. "Right. Since you were the first person to come across the senator after the murder, I thought you might have a strong psychological need to solve the murder." He took his hand off the wheel to nervously straighten his glasses.

I narrowed my eyes. "I didn't know you also had a doctorate in psychology, in addition to your history degree. I must have missed those graduate years."

He sniffed. "I don't profess to have a degree in psychology. But believe me, there are some helpful and informative websites out there that um, eh…" he trailed off again.

I finished his sentence once again. "Some websites that gave you enough information to diagnose me with having a neurosis."

Doug bristled at my sarcasm. "Don't get defensive, Kit. I merely thought your need to solve Langsford's murder might have been driven by the unfortunate circumstances that started your week. Now I see that no matter what the motive, you and Meg have made real progress."

Doug knew flattery would get him a long way. I relaxed and gave him a small smile. "I'm not sure we've made any earth-shattering discoveries. To tell the truth, we're long on suspects and theories, and short on facts and substantiated alibis. Unless we can do better, we're not going to solve the crime. This might be the last time we have the murderer in our sights. Let's not waste the opportunity."

Meg interjected herself into the conversation. "And don't forget, we can't look too obvious. Let's remember first and foremost, we're here to mourn Senator Langsford."

Doug made the final turn onto Senator Langsford's street. Having been there a handful of times in the years

I had worked for him, I knew his house was only one short block away. As we approached, the valet motioned for us to stop. We exited the car, and Doug turned the key over to the valet, who gave him a claim ticket. He promptly handed the ticket over to me. Doug was good at many things, but holding onto important items such as valet tickets wasn't one of them.

As we made our way across the manicured lawn toward the Langsford home, I was struck again by the grandeur of the place. McLean was a wealthy Virginia suburb of Washington. Its close proximity to downtown, beautiful homes, upscale shopping, and a stellar school system made McLean a magnet for prominent residents. As I understood it, Mrs. Langsford selected their house and had insisted upon living in McLean when Langsford first won election to the Senate. That was no surprise; McLean had long been the most upscale and socially exclusive bedroom community for elected officials, high-ranking military officers, intelligence leaders, and wealthy corporate players. Mrs. Langsford was a woman who didn't necessarily want to be bothered with the boring details of government—at least in my experience—yet she liked living among those who occupied powerful positions and possessed the authority to make critical decisions facing our country. Vivian was still top on my list of suspects.

I gazed at the house, a striking three-story colonial. Most of it was white stone, but the right corner, which comprised an entirely different wing, was a natural beige stone. The two-toned approach to the exterior made the house look older than it really was. Achieving both the contemporary and antiquated effect wasn't easily accomplished, and it explained the high resale value of the house.

Leading to the entrance was a beautiful limestone walk, lined with perfectly trimmed small shrubs. There were flowers between the shrubs that supplied a perfectly accented dose of contrasting color to the deep green lawn. As we walked toward the front of the house, I felt another intense wave of grief. Senator Langsford hadn't grown up in a wealthy family. Much like myself, he'd been the product of a middle-class upbringing. Hard work and a bit of luck had led him to his position as a United States Senator, and his marriage to Vivian had provided him with considerable resources and money. He'd had it all.

The image of him sitting in his chair with that stupid model helicopter sticking out of his chest was forever seared in my memory. Langsford had gotten up Tuesday morning in his stunning house in McLean, driven himself to work, and been murdered a short time later. How did someone who lived a privileged and prestigious existence die such a violent death?

Doug must have noticed I was in a daze. He touched my arm. "Are you okay?" he asked delicately.

With newfound resolve, I said, "Yes, absolutely. Let's go inside."

The main door was open, and we walked into the large entrance foyer. I've always admired the welcoming openness of this room. Immediately opposite was the grand staircase, which led to the bedrooms and living quarters. According to Zillow, it was a five-bedroom, five-bathroom, two million dollar home, but I had never been upstairs. However, the grounds and first floor were more than enough to telegraph the extent of the Langsfords' wealth and advantaged station in life. To the left of the foyer was the spacious living room, which had several pristinely elegant sofas, picture windows that ran from ceiling to floor, and Oriental rugs. I had never seen anyone actually sit on the sofas. The room was used for entertaining, and whenever I had been here for formal events, I was too preoccupied with not spilling my drink on the rugs to appreciate the décor of the room.

To the right of the foyer was the dining room, which was accented by a fireplace and a round dining room table. Kara, the senator's executive assistant, had once told me the round table was the one piece of furniture Senator Langsford had insisted Vivian purchase for the house. Apparently, when they had dinner guests, the senator preferred sitting at a round table, facing his guests to facilitate a lively conversation. I smiled when I recalled how he'd loved robust, spirited policy debates. Over the past year, he had found himself embroiled in many contentious political ones. Staring at the round table, I wondered if his passion for asking the hard questions had ultimately led to his death.

Behind the foyer and to the right of the staircase was the senator's library and study. When Langsford had summoned me here for Senate business—usually because work needed to be done over the weekend in preparation for an imminent hearing or vote—I had met with him in the study. This was certainly "his" room in the house. He had decorated it with keepsakes gathered during his service as a senator. Photographs from trips he'd taken abroad and mementos of successful campaigns covered the walls. Since he had enjoyed reading, he also owned a large collection of books. The last time I had been in his study, the senator had taken a moment to show me he had recently purchased Doug's latest book and was excited to read it.

Next to the study was the "family room." The term could be applied loosely, since to me, a "family room" connotes relaxation and fun with a family. However, Vivian had decorated the room with white sofas and settees—not exactly the color I'd have picked for a functional "family room." A huge flat-screen television had been built into the far end of the wall. The TV was never actually turned on, although Vivian would have surely chosen top of the line. Had Senator Langsford ever felt comfortable watching football in the family room? I doubted it. Chuckling to myself, I imagined the challenges of hosting a Super Bowl party in a room full of white furniture. Only the foolhardy or unusually dexterous would ask, "Please pass the salsa."

An exquisite stone patio stood in back of the house. On the other side of patio, an in-ground pool was situated next to a small gazebo. The Langsfords had hosted an annual summer party for staff each August, and the pool was open for attendees who wanted to take a dip. Since I had a firm rule that no one I worked with should ever see me in a bathing suit, I never had the pleasure of swimming in the pool. Others, like Meg, didn't suffer from such hang-ups and had enjoyed the pool several times. I would miss those parties. To foster a collaborative workplace, Senator Langsford had always encouraged those in his employ to socialize and celebrate important occasions. It was tragic our last staff gathering was his wake.

Kara, likewise dressed in black, hurried over to us. I silently congratulated myself for staying with tradition and not taking Mandy's advice that colorful business attire was perfectly acceptable. Kara greeted us, and the strain on her face showed how stressful it must have been for her to help with the planning. As the executive assistant, she was also friends with Senator Langsford and Mrs. Langsford. Kara was always perfectly poised, so only someone who knew her well would see the extent to which the past several days had worn her down.

I asked how she was feeling, and she managed a small smile. "Thank you for asking. I can't wait for this day to be over. Between this event and the vigil this evening, I can hardly keep up."

I looked at Kara with a puzzled expression. "Am I missing something? I didn't know there was a vigil this evening."

Kara tapped her BlackBerry, which she held in her hand. "Did you check your email this morning?" In the course of getting ready for the wake, I had never looked at my device.

"I'm sorry, I didn't even glance at my messages this morning."

"Totally understandable, given the circumstances. There will be a vigil for Senator Langsford this evening, right off the Senate floor in the Capitol. All senators are expected to stay in town to attend, and of course, staffers in our office are encouraged to go, too. It should start at seven, since last votes will take place around six thirty today."

Meg and I told Kara we'd plan to attend. She motioned for us to move into the dining room, where a short service would begin in a few minutes. After the formal program, Mrs. Langsford would host a reception with refreshments, taking place both inside and outside on the patio.

We walked into the dining room, and I quickly surveyed the attendees. Just as I had surmised, the so-called "usual suspects" were present. In addition to speaking with Vivian, I needed to observe if anyone's demeanor implied he or she had threatened me last night. How might a person act if he had recently made a menacing phone call? I had no clue, but I'd look for out of the ordinary behavior.

Since a Senate vigil was scheduled for this evening, I worried briefly that Senator Regan might have chosen not to attend this event. Fortunately I had no problem spotting him, along with Jeff Prentice. Of course Mandy glued herself to both Prentice and Regan. She wanted to keep close tabs on both of them, although for different reasons. Detective O'Halloran was also in the crowd with a purpose similar to my own.

The Langsfords' minister called the service to order and said several kind words about the senator and his spiritual beliefs. I had never known Senator Langsford as a deeply religious man, yet the minister attested to his church participation and devoutness. After he was finished, he hugged Mrs. Langsford, whom I watched closely. She was a hard woman to read. Certainly, she displayed more sorrow than she had immediately after the senator's death. Dressed in a slim black dress, black designer sandals, and an immaculate string of pearls, she certainly looked the part of a grieving widow. She clasped a small white handkerchief and dabbed at her eyes every minute or so. I wasn't close enough to determine whether she was faking the tears, although her heavy eye makeup looked none the worse for wear.

After the minister's words, there was no formal eulogy. Instead, a steady stream of people close to the senator offered brief vignettes about his numerous contributions. I listened carefully to the comments, both to appreciate their meaning and analyze them for clues. If there was a veiled message about Langsford's killer hidden in one of the speeches, I couldn't detect it.

A handful of mourners wept during the service, including my bosses Matt and Lucinda, who together told a heartwarming story about Senator Langsford. There were several poignant moments during the service, and at its conclusion, I stole a glance around the room and noticed there was nary a dry eye. It had been a worthy tribute, leaving me wondering whether I had the emotional energy to endure another heart-wrenching set of speeches this evening from his Senate colleagues. Mrs. Langsford didn't say anything, except to thank everyone and urge all in attendance to stay for an early luncheon.

After the formal program ended, as if on cue, a small army of servers emerged from the rear of the dining room that led to the kitchen. They carefully balanced loaded trays of appetizers while others carried flutes of what looked like orange juice. I took one and was pleasantly surprised to discover it was a champagne mimosa. At least we wouldn't have to struggle through this difficult day without the appropriate liquid refreshments.

Apparently Meg agreed with me. She smacked her lips. "I think it's Dom Perignon!"

Doug looked at Meg with suspicion. "How could you possibly tell, since the taste of the champagne has been absolutely eviscerated by orange juice?"

Undeterred by Doug's quasi-snotty tone, Meg shrugged. "I have a discerning palate when it comes to champagne. Identifying the good stuff has always been a talent of mine."

Doug appeared unconvinced, but the lull in the conversation allowed me to say, "We should enjoy the champagne, no matter what it is. But more important, we need to split up and try to complete our assignments. Are we ready?" I gave Doug and Meg my biggest smile in an effort to motivate the troops.

Their eager expressions indicated no pep talk was necessary. Meg said quickly, "I've been tracking Jeff Prentice since the service ended. He already went outside, probably to get food."

"Was Senator Regan with him? He was standing with Jeff earlier."

Meg stared over my shoulder to report our suspects' whereabouts. "No, Regan was with him during the service, but now he's waiting to talk to Mrs. Langsford, probably to offer his condolences in person."

I turned around casually to confirm Meg's report. She was right. Talking to Mrs. Langsford might prove more challenging than I thought. An informal line had already twisted around her. I'd have to stay vigilant and wait for the right opportunity.

Doug said, "I'll keep an eye on Regan. He doesn't have anyone with him right now, so after he talks to Mrs. Langsford, it might be the perfect time to approach him."

Leaving Doug and Meg to their assignments, I decided to kill some time before trying to speak with Mrs. Langsford. Lucinda was on my list, too, and she might be an easier target. I spotted her chatting with a small city mayor from the state. Lucinda always found the meetings with local officials tedious, so it would be a great chance for me to interrupt, save Lucinda from Mayor Whomever, and pump her for critical information. As I sauntered toward her, I snagged a few cucumber sandwiches, which were delicious. Sleuthing was hard work, and you shouldn't do it on an empty stomach.

Two steps away from my mark, Detective O'Halloran moseyed on up to me and smiled wryly. "Well, if it isn't my first and only suspect."

"Well, if it isn't my favorite Capitol Hill police detective." It was a smart aleck retort, but O'Halloran was screwing up my plan.

"Nicely put, Ms. Marshall. It's unfortunate we keep meeting under less than pleasant circumstances."

"I agree, Detective. If we were no longer acquainted, I would assume someone had managed to solve my boss's murder." I deliberately said "someone" instead of "you." He'd get the drift.

"That's true. I haven't yet identified the origins of the blond strand of hair, which remains our one physical clue in the case." O'Halloran grabbed a mushroom cap stuffed with crabmeat and crammed it into his mouth.

I tried to ignore the juice dribbling down the side of his chin. After all, who was I to judge?

"Can I infer you're not any closer to apprehending the killer?" Trying to appear as nonchalant as possible, I fiddled with my glass of mimosa and took another sip.

"If you're asking whether we're ready to make an arrest, the answer is no. When you can't find the person who committed the crime, it makes sense to work backward and eliminate those who couldn't have committed the crime first. That's our process. But it's time consuming." O'Halloran sighed, then in one swift move, nabbed the last grilled chicken skewer from a server who darted past us. If O'Halloran had been as quick on the uptake working the case as he was with scoring food, this murder mystery would have been sewn up days ago.

"That's an interesting perspective, Detective. Have you eliminated a number of suspects at this point in time?" Now it was my turn to seize the day. I lifted a fresh mimosa off a tray and took a long drink.

His eyes narrowed. My question was exceedingly obvious. The champagne, whatever brand it was, had emboldened me a little too much.

"A few, Ms. Marshall. One individual of interest was out of town, which makes it impossible for him to be the guilty party. Others appear to have substantiated alibis, but we're still in the process of verifying." He turned the tables on me. "I might ask you a similar question. Have you discovered anything?" I assumed O'Halloran didn't want to state outright that he knew we'd been investigating the case.

It was time to let O'Halloran know what I had unearthed thus far, though it wasn't much. It certainly hadn't led me to the killer, at least not yet. I sipped my second mimosa, took a deep breath, and looked around to see if anyone was listening. Just to be safe, I lowered my voice and leaned closer to O'Halloran.

"To tell you the truth, I haven't been able to figure out who killed Senator Langsford. My biggest hunch is it has something to do with Carter Power. Langsford was going to defund the company, and everyone who's a suspect wanted the deal to go through. But Senator Regan claims he has an alibi, and so does Jeff Prentice.

Even though I feel like Carter Power is the answer, I can't seem to connect it to the murder."

O'Halloran looked at me with sympathetic eyes. "Don't beat yourself up too much, kid. This is a nasty business, and it's up to the police to figure out who killed the senator. We've looked into the Carter Power angle, too, and it's a dead end. Everyone associated with it has an alibi." Dejectedly, he chomped into a mini quiche Lorraine. O'Halloran's incessant nibbling was contagious. I grabbed a bacon-wrapped scallop off the next tray that zipped past.

After chewing the scallop and swallowing, I mumbled a barely coherent "Delicious." Once I could speak clearly, I said, "I have this nagging feeling the answer is right in front of me, but I can't put my finger on it." I looked at O'Halloran directly. "It keeps coming back whenever I think hard about the case." I shrugged. "Maybe I'm crazy, and it means nothing." I took the final drink of my second mimosa and placed the empty glass on a tray.

O'Halloran was silent for a moment. When he spoke, his tone was deadly serious. "Listen, Ms. Marshall. I'm not sure what your brain is trying to tell you, but I've been in the police business for over twenty years. Ninety-nine percent of the time, when investigators get that type of strong feeling, they're this close," he held his index finger and thumb an inch apart, "to solving the crime. Now, let's face it. You're not a professional." He paused to give me a condescending smile. "I have no idea what the source of this feeling is. It might be nothing. But on the off chance it's something, as soon as your revelation surfaces, I want you to call me, pronto. Do you understand that?"

I said I did. O'Halloran gave me his card, even though he'd provided one earlier in the week. "You take an extra card, just in case. I'm not holding out great hope here. I don't need to remind you that if you put the pieces of the puzzle together and the wrong person finds out about it, you could be in a whole lot of danger."

He couldn't know about the phone call I'd received last night. Should I come clean about the threat? I bit my tongue; it was best to stick to the plan and see if more clues emerged. If I told the detective about the anonymous warning, he'd either forbid me from further investigating or he might think I was lying to cast suspicion on someone else. Either scenario was no good.

I thanked Detective O'Halloran profusely for his time and concern and reassured him that if the little voice in my head started to speak to me, I'd call him right away. I put his card in the zippered compartment of my purse so I wouldn't lose it.

The timing with O'Halloran was perfect, since fewer people were now surrounding Lucinda. Despite O'Halloran's conclusion, the Carter Power deal was still our best lead. How many people were aware of Senator Langsford's impending decision? Matt had sworn me to secrecy. I almost always did what I was told, so I'd let no one know, even Meg. However, I doubted Lucinda had followed the same strict guidelines.

Lucinda had no drink in hand, but she looked like she needed one. After I asked if she'd like a mimosa, her face brightened considerably. That was a "yes." I dashed off and secured a glass for her in seconds. I also found a bottle of Perrier for myself, which would provide necessary hydration. Lapses in judgment due to alcohol consumption happened every day in D.C. I wondered if Meg was right and the drinks were really made with Dom Perignon. Whatever the vintner, those who had poured the cocktails hadn't been stingy with the champagne. It was still shy of noon. A teetotaler I was not, yet I did have my standards. And I had a job to do.

That said, this conversation would go much better if Lucinda loosened up. I placed my hand gently on her arm. "How are you holding up? You must have been under tremendous strain these past few days."

After taking an extended sip, Lucinda replied, "Why, thank you, Kit. It's kind of you to say." She dabbed her eyes with a handkerchief. "It's been a difficult time. Of course, I knew Lyndon for many years, so I'm mourning the loss of a friend. And then there's everything tied to the Senate office and the necessity to keep it running while the governor selects a successor. It's been almost too much to bear." She took another generous chug of her mimosa.

Lucinda had steered the conversation exactly in the right direction. "The pressures at work are just the icing on the cake, aren't they?" I said. "For example, I'm trying to wrap up the senator's commitments on committees, and there's this nagging issue of Carter Power. It's so hard to know who I can talk to about it—besides you and Matt, of course."

Lucinda straightened her glasses, eager to return to her role of supervising policy strategy. "To tell you the truth, Kit, I wouldn't be too worried about whom you discuss Senator Langsford's position on Carter Power with."

This wasn't a big surprise to me, but I deliberately plastered an astonished expression on my face. "Really? I'm confused. When Senator Langsford was still alive,

Matt told me his decision concerning Carter Power should be kept strictly under wraps, that I couldn't tell any staffer in the office or colleagues in the Senate."

Lucinda took another big drink of the mimosa. Most likely, she hadn't had too much to eat today. That champagne was going right to her head. I'd make sure she had water and food right after we finished our conversation.

"Well, that's true. We didn't want the decision leaking all over town. Just like anything in Washington, though, I had to make exceptions."

I looked at Lucinda directly. "Just how many exceptions did you make, Lucinda?" I didn't want to sound accusatory, but I needed Lucinda to 'fess up about the names of those who were aware of Langsford's leanings.

If my tone was overly emphatic, Lucinda didn't appear to pick up on it. Maybe the mimosa had taken the edge off. Either way, she answered without reservation, "Oh, I can't remember exactly. I did tell that handsome lobbyist for Carter Power. What's his name again?" Jeff had tipped us off that Lucinda had been his source, but it was still shocking to hear it from the horse's mouth.

"You told Jeff Prentice?"

She nodded. "I had to give Jeff a heads up. It wouldn't have been very nice to drop this on Carter Power at the hearing."

I turned my head away so Lucinda wouldn't see the anguish on my face. Senator Langsford had wanted to do exactly that; he had planned for his vote at the committee mark-up session to serve as a surprise so he wouldn't have to answer questions about his position beforehand.

"But Lucinda, I thought the senator didn't want his position made public prior to the hearing?" I didn't want to sound whiny, although I clearly didn't understand her political calculus.

Lucinda didn't hesitate. "That's true. But going public with his decision is different than telling a few close friends. Senator Regan was one of Lyndon's closest friends in the Senate. He couldn't just drop that bombshell on him. It was up to me to keep everything under wraps while informing a select group of people."

That explanation was helpful, but something still didn't make sense. Why hadn't she told Regan directly, rather than Jeff Prentice? How big was this "need to know" group?

"This select group of people, just who are they? You already said Senator Regan and Jeff Prentice. Anyone else?"

Lucinda put her finger up to her chin, seemingly deep in thought. After a few seconds, she said, "That sounds about right. Oh, but of course, Vivian knew, and so did Mandy Lippman. And you and Matt, as well. I think that's it."

I scratched my head. "Why Mandy Lippman? And why Vivian?"

"Mandy was our press person. We had to inform her so she could devise a plan to roll out the decision after he went public. It was going to be controversial, as you know. We needed an entire press strategy to combat the potentially negative coverage. Mandy deplored the decision because it was going to be a big headache for her."

Lucinda took another sip. "Vivian had been keeping close tabs on the senator regarding his decision. Between you and me," Lucinda leaned in closer, "the senator hadn't been very forthcoming to his wife."

I leaned in closer, practically whispering the question, "Why, Lucinda?"

She pulled back and looked at me. "Don't be so naïve, Kit. Do you see this beautiful house we're in right now? Mrs. Langsford brought all the money into the marriage. After Senator Langsford got elected to the Senate, Mrs. Langsford kept complete financial control. Nothing was signed over to Senator Langsford. That way, she could continue to monitor her investments in any manner she chose. Those assets weren't jointly owned." She put down her empty drink and instantly scored another from a passing waiter.

Lucinda hadn't finished her diatribe. "Vivian might seem like a bubblehead, but appearances are deceiving. Yes, she inherited money from her family. But she's retained that wealth her entire life and added to it. She's done that by keeping a close eye on the stocks she's owned over the years. Carter Power has been a significant part of her investment portfolio for decades. Senator Langsford, of course, knew this and kept as much information as possible from his wife. He felt that, ethically, he should stay tight-lipped on this matter."

I pulled away from Lucinda. "But you didn't feel the same? That you had to stay silent about Carter Power to Vivian?" My harsh question seemed to annoy Lucinda.

"Kit, this is a complicated matter. You may not know it, but I was friends with Vivian before she married Lyndon Langsford. My loyalties run deep with the Langsfords, and they run deepest with Vivian. Giving her a quick 'heads up' before the committee's action was the least I could do. She was the one who suggested me for Lyndon's chief of staff position in the first place. I had to let her know which way her husband was leaning."

Lucinda's reasoning sounded unethical, but I didn't have the time to conduct a full-scale moral inquiry into the supposed long-term relationship between Vivian Langsford and Lucinda. I remembered the phone call Trevor had talked about days ago. It must have been Lucinda warning Vivian that Senator Langsford had made his decision concerning Carter Power.

After ending our conversation on a more congenial note, I left Lucinda and headed down the hallway to the powder room. It was the only place I could get some privacy and sort through what I had just learned.

Luckily, the bathroom was unoccupied. I looked into the mirror and congratulated myself that my makeup still looked fresh. After reapplying lipstick, I rested on the settee. More people had known about Langsford's pending Carter Power decision than I'd thought. As far as I could tell, only two people actually supported the senator's position on Carter Power, and that was Matt and myself. Everyone else wanted Langsford to change his mind. I still thought our murderer came from that group. Someone had detested Senator Langsford's decision enough—or had enough to lose—that he or she felt it was worth killing for.

Lucinda had given me another tidbit that increased my interest in Mrs. Langsford. If she was so heavily invested in Carter Power that her husband's actions could have bankrupted her, she might have decided murder was the only option. Due to strict regulations and onerous reporting requirements, selling her shares was out of the question, unless she wanted to end up in federal prison like Martha Stewart.

Speaking with Vivian was my top priority.

I unlocked the door and peeked out. I headed back

into the dining room, where the reception was still going strong, and spotted Mrs. Langsford. She had managed to break free from the hordes of mourners and was speeding toward Senator Langsford's study. This might be my only opportunity to catch her alone.

I had begun to walk across the room when one of Senator Langsford's longtime friends recognized me. At the senator's request, I helped him several years ago when he was trying to increase federal funding for a rare disease his daughter had contracted. For the life of me, I couldn't remember what that disease was. There had been too many funding requests over the years for the eradication of terrible afflictions. After we locked eyes, I couldn't avoid him. Sure enough, he flagged me down, and I stopped to chat with him. I was terse with him while trying not to sound rude, all the while aware that I was missing my opportunity to talk to Vivian.

Finally, I was able to shake free by telling him I recognized a constituent I needed to speak with. I headed over to Senator Langsford's study and opened the door. This was the second time this week I had burst into a room unannounced. I certainly hadn't been prepared to find the body of Lyndon Langsford, and I couldn't believe what I saw this time, either.

TWENTY-THREE

IN THE CORNER of the study, Mrs. Vivian Langsford was locked in a torrid embrace with a man. When I opened the door, they moved apart. Her lover was a much younger fellow I did not recognize. He was dressed—oddly enough considering this was a wake—in jogging shorts and a tank top. At that precise moment, I realized I had no excuse for barging into Senator Langsford's study. There were flabbergasted glares all around. Vivian stifled a small scream but recovered almost instantly.

"Quickly, Kit, come in and shut the door before anyone else can see! Don't be a fool," she hissed.

I immediately did as I was told, stammering unintelligibly. Senator Langsford's impressive book collection gave me an idea. "I'm s-so sorry, Mrs. Langsford. I didn't know anyone was in here. I wanted to see if Senator Langsford had brought my boyfriend Doug's latest book home with him. He told me he was planning to read it, and I wanted to know if he had managed to look at it before he died."

It must have been a good enough lie, because Vivian didn't challenge me. "Yes, of course, dear. He mentioned a short time ago that he'd read Doug's book. Kit, I'd like you to meet my personal trainer, Henrik. He's originally from Estonia." She seemed proud to tell me

Henrik's origins. She let her hand linger on his naked left bicep as she introduced us.

Call me old fashioned, but something bothered me about having a social conversation with my dead boss's widow and her beefcake trainer boyfriend. Her interest in Henrik was self-explanatory. He was about six feet tall with wavy dark hair, muscular and ruggedly handsome. Mrs. Langsford was about two decades his senior, although I had to admit she was looking darn good. Maybe Henrik was an unusually talented personal trainer. It didn't matter since I doubted he was taking on new clients.

"Pleased to meet you, Henrik," I mumbled.

Vivian must have sensed my obvious discomfort with the situation. She addressed me with a knowing look. "Now, Kit. Let's be adults here. My affair with Henrik may not have been common knowledge, but it was far from the equivalent of a state secret. Lyndon knew Henrik and I had a relationship that went beyond trainer and client."

I swallowed hard. "You mean Senator Langsford was aware of your affair?"

Mrs. Langsford laughed as she walked next to me and put her arm around my shoulders. "Of course. Don't get so upset about it. How long have you been with Doug, dear?"

I told her just over five years.

She tittered at my response. "Let's talk again when you're going on twenty years together and your lover is married to his job. Don't get me wrong. Lyndon wasn't thrilled with my extracurricular activities. Still, he understood." She gave Henrik a long, lascivious look.

Suddenly, I remembered why I wanted to talk to Vivian in the first place. It couldn't hurt to go for broke.

"Were you with Henrik the morning of Senator Langsford's murder? That's what I heard from the police. Is it true?" I directed my question toward Henrik, who might get rattled and prove the weaker link if the alibi was indeed a lie. Facing Henrik, I added, "It's not too late to come clean."

My attempt to catch him off guard failed. Henrik, in a noticeable eastern European accent that only added to his overall sexiness, said, "No, no, no. Vivian and I were together that morning. We had our regular appointment scheduled, and there's proof that what we say is true."

"Proof that you were together that morning?"

Henrik answered hastily, "Yes, of course. We run a four-mile course on Tuesday mornings in the neighborhood." He looked at me skeptically. "Are you a runner?"

"Yes, I run when I have time. I have a demanding job."

Henrik scoffed lightly at my feeble excuse. "Then you know if you run with a GPS watch, it records your run and uploads it to your computer so you can keep track of your training time. That morning, we logged a run at the same time of the murder." He gave me a self-satisfied look. Alibi by exercise.

Vivian interrupted, "Henrik is right, Kit. We told this to Detective O'Halloran, who's been kind enough to assure us the specifics of our whereabouts wouldn't be released to the press. He and the rest of the police seemed satisfied when Henrik showed him evidence of our run that morning. In addition to the computer log, several people in the neighborhood saw us. If you remember, it was a gorgeous morning, and there were a number of people exercising or tending to their lawns."

I remembered how pristine the Capitol had appeared when I emerged from Union Station. Looking back, I didn't have a care in the world. How rapidly life can change—literally in an instant.

Snapping back to reality, I said, "Yes, Mrs. Langsford. It was a magnificent day that morning, until I found Senator Langsford dead. I'm sorry I interrupted you. It was nice to meet you, Henrik."

Mrs. Langsford grabbed my arm. "Kit, you always served my husband well. He told me several times about your work. You might think I'm a terrible person, but I did care for him and his work in the Senate. He trusted your judgment on important matters." She paused to gather her thoughts. "This might be a lot to ask, but can you keep the details of my affair with Henrik quiet for now? At a certain point in time, I'm sure we'll go public."

She looked briefly at Henrik, who was checking out his calf muscles in the full-length mirror mounted in the corner of the study. "For now, we need discretion. At least until Lyndon's killer is caught, the new appointment for the Senate seat is settled, and the affairs of the estate are finalized. Can I count on you?"

I wavered. Unlike Lucinda, my loyalties to the Langsfords ran through Senator Langsford, not Vivian. But her imploring face inspired a measure of sympathy. She wasn't a moral person by any stretch of the imagination, and if the press found out she had cheated on the senator, it would be ugly. Nonetheless, I believed her when she said she cared for Senator Langsford and his work as a politician. She'd been with him at every campaign stop during the last election; I saw it myself. I wasn't a reporter or a blogger hell-bent on uncovering the next political scandal. Would I want to be remembered as the staffer who had sullied the Langsford name?

I pulled my arm away from Mrs. Langsford and placed my hand on hers. "You don't have to worry about me, Mrs. Langsford. I'm not telling anyone in the press about what I saw today. I wish you the best of luck. I liked your husband, and I loved working for him. I have a lot of respect for what he accomplished, and I would never want his record diminished in any way."

Mrs. Langsford smiled broadly at me. "Thank you so much, Kit. Lyndon spoke highly of you, and now I know why. If you ever need my help, you'll know where to find me."

I withdrew my hand and gave Mrs. Langsford and Henrik a small wave. I closed the door to Senator Langsford's office behind me. Although my methods had been highly unorthodox and I'd learned more than I'd bargained for, my goal was achieved. Mrs. Langsford's alibi was confirmed, and we could strike her off the list of suspects, even though her list of motives, which now included adultery, was a mile long.

Halfway down the hallway toward the reception, I spotted Trevor. It was no surprise Trevor was standing alone; he wasn't the most popular person and consequently had few friends to socialize with at office functions. The visual of Trevor standing by himself at a party struck a familiar chord in my mind, and I got that funny feeling again. Without a firm motive, Trevor probably hadn't killed Senator Langsford, so I shook off the now familiar irksome sensation and headed in his direction.

Trevor saw me and nodded politely. He was drinking a mixed alcoholic beverage, likely a gin or vodka tonic with a lime twist.

"It's a bit early to be hitting the hard stuff, isn't it?"

He gave me a signature Trevor smirk. "Since I haven't consumed my fair share of alcohol at these events over the years, and it's not every day you attend your murdered boss's wake, I decided to loosen up."

Trevor's repartee was growing on me. It was unfortunate he had only shared his dry wit now that our time as colleagues was almost up.

I returned the smirk and clinked my glass with his. "It sounds like a perfectly reasonable justification to me. You certainly didn't take full advantage of the open bars at other office celebrations."

Trevor sighed and loosened his tie. "I have a few regrets, I'll admit. Now that I'm faced with the prospect of employment in the private sector, I wonder whether I should have enjoyed more of the social benefits of working on Capitol Hill, including the happy hours and office soirees." Trevor stared at his drink remorsefully and shifted his gaze toward Mandy and Kara, who were chatting amiably in the corner.

It was uncharacteristic of Trevor to rattle on, but he kept going. "Other people seem to have made lasting friendships in the Senate. You hit it off with Meg, even though I'm not envious of her company. Friendships developed from time spent outside the office. I didn't appreciate those opportunities, and even scorned them. My greatest connection to the office was Senator Langsford, and now he's dead. So after this wake, I won't see many of these people again."

I listened politely to Trevor's short speech. In four years of working next to him, I doubt he'd uttered as many uninterrupted syllables to me as he had just spoken. Trevor had a serious case of the blues. His expression was a dejected scowl, his clothes were rumpled, and his shoulders were hunched over. This was nothing like the confident, composed image Trevor normally projected. Empathy got the best of me. It was time to cheer him up.

"Oh, come on, Trevor. The grass is always greener on the other side. Everyone knows you're going to get a killer job making the big bucks on K Street. And you know the reason why you're going to be so successful?"

I didn't give him a chance to respond. "You weren't like the rest of us, who were obsessed with the Capitol Hill social scene. While we were out having a good time at happy hour, you were glued to your computer, doing more work for Senator Langsford and coming up with great ideas for the next hearing he was going to attend." This was a slight twist of the facts. We all logged long hours. Trevor simply had no other life, so he filled every waking hour with work.

Motioning toward Meg and Kara, I gave a small shrug in their direction. "Other people might have been the life of the party, but there's a downside to that. You took the high road and did the hard work, and I'm sure you'll get rewarded for it."

Trevor appeared to listen intently to my overstated motivational speech. He rubbed his chin thoughtfully. I waited for him to launch into another lament about how money wouldn't buy him happiness and he'd only had one chance to live the exciting existence of a young staffer on Capitol Hill. However, this was Trevor. I shouldn't have been surprised at his reaction.

"Thank you, Kit. You're exactly right. Here I was, feeling sorry for myself because I don't have a best buddy to commiserate with. I almost lost sight of the big picture. Of course those stupid parties meant nothing in the long run. They were tawdry affairs, resulting in most people drinking way too much and making comments they regretted the next day."

After taking a deep breath, he finished emphatically, "I never got caught up in any of that, and I'm better for it. I'm glad I didn't waste one more minute feeling sorry for myself."

Setting down his drink, he grabbed my shoulders with both hands, gave me a small shake, and marched off with renewed purpose, probably to seal the deal on some six-figure job with a lucrative lobbying firm. I shook my head in disbelief. Trevor had a unique perspective on life and his place in the world. There was something oddly admirable about his masculine self-confidence. At the same time, the silence that had existed between us for so long had been a blessing in disguise.

A glance at my watch confirmed it was past noon. Time to find Doug and Meg. The wake would be wrapping up soon, and lingering was inappropriate, especially after the encounter with Vivian. I spotted Meg near the makeshift bar the caterers had assembled. She was talking to a cute guy in a waiter's outfit. Leave it to Meg to find her next date at a memorial service. She wouldn't dash off as long as she was basking in male attention, so that left Doug. He wasn't visible in the dining room, so he had to be on the veranda.

I exited through the ornate French doors leading to the spacious patio and pool area. The guests were thinning out, making it easy to find Doug. He was deep in conversation with Senator Regan. It was awkward to stand there without joining them, so I headed in their direction.

Doug spotted me straightaway and gave a little wave to motion me over. I took that as a signal that he'd already completed his assigned task to investigate the validity of Regan's alibi.

I wondered how Regan would treat me, since our last interaction had been less than cordial. Politicians never forget anything, but they rarely hold grudges. Yesterday's enemy could be today's friend. Senator Regan greeted me warmly with a smile and a courteous embrace.

"So glad to see you, Kit. I've had a delightful conversation with your significant other, who I've learned is quite the expert in American history." Leave it to Doug to use his academic discipline to ingratiate himself.

I returned the cordial welcome and asked, "Has Doug told you about his next book?" Regan then launched into a story about a recent vacation to New England in which he walked the Freedom Trail in Boston with Senator Langsford. The story highlighted the closeness between the two men, further convincing me that Langsford's retreat on Carter Power must have been a bitter pill for Senator Regan to swallow.

Doug must have sensed my strong desire to know whether Regan's story had checked out. "Kit, before you joined us, Senator Regan was telling me how he heard about Senator Langsford's death. He was finishing up a long phone call with his chief of staff, and his wife had to interrupt to tell him what had happened because she heard the news on their other line." Doug raised his eyebrows. The message was clear: Regan was a dead end.

I managed to conceal my disappointment as Regan continued with the story. If Regan had been on an extended phone call at the time of the murder, he didn't just have one witness to corroborate his alibi. The chief of staff could verify the timing and the interruption in their conversation. Just like Jordan Jessop, Regan's whereabouts at the time of the murder were easy to confirm. No wonder Detective O'Halloran hadn't spent much time on him. Regan could not have been in two places at once.

Our task complete, Doug and I found a convenient point in the conversation to excuse ourselves. We headed back inside to collect Meg, who was, as I suspected, standing in exactly the same spot where I had last seen her, although she was sipping a fresh mimosa and appearing even more animated by the conversation with her new beau. It wasn't a great idea to start the day with multiple mimosas, even if they were made with Dom Perignon. Getting sucked into a vapid conversation with hot catering boy didn't seem appealing to me, so I texted Meg and told her to meet us at the front door in five minutes. I pinged her and watched as her BlackBerry buzzed and she read the message. She nodded tersely.

Doug asked, "Are we interrupting Meg's next conquest?"

I gently punched his arm. "There's no need for sarcasm. She'll be ready to go soon. Let's head for the exit." While we were waiting, I complimented Doug on his ability to elicit information from Senator Regan. Perhaps I had underestimated Doug's ability as a sleuth. After all, he was an accomplished historical researcher. He understood how to poke around and find the evidence he needed.

I briefly recounted the unexpected meeting with Vivian and Henrik. When I described Henrik to him, emphasizing his youth, Doug's eyes widened in disbelief. The Mrs. Robinson scenario must have shocked Doug's blue-blood sensibilities. No matter what the sordid details of the relationship, the facts were unassailable. Henrik gave Vivian an extra motive for wanting her husband dead, but he also provided her with a credible alibi for the time of the murder.

Meg rushed over to us. "Sorry to keep you waiting. I couldn't get away from Jack. He was fascinated by the fact that I work in a Senate office!"

I couldn't resist saying, "What a surprise. Meeting someone at a senator's wake who works in a Senate office!"

Meg shot me a dirty look. "Don't be so snarky, Kit. He only moved to D.C. a few months ago. He's working as a caterer, but he really wants to become an actor. Don't you think he has the looks for acting?"

Doug ignored her question and asked the obvious, "Wouldn't the better city for acting be New York rather than Washington?"

Obviously annoyed, Meg piped back, "Maybe ten years ago, Doug. These days, struggling actors move to other big cities first to gain experience. Then, after they have some credentials, they head to New York or Hollywood." She glared at both of us. "I can tell you're not impressed with Jack. I'll be sure to leave you off the invite list to the Oscars when he makes it!" With dramatic flair, she flounced off toward the row of cars.

Doug laughed, and so did I. He said, "She won't get far, since you have the valet ticket!" I fished through my purse for it and handed it over to the attendant. By the time our car had been brought around, Meg had realized the error of her ways and joined us again. Without saying a word, she got into the backseat and slammed the car door shut. Doug drove off, and I gave her a few minutes to calm down. I had been through this enough times with Meg. Her flashes of anger were always transitory. After she cooled off, she'd act like nothing happened.

I waited until we were halfway home before I gingerly asked Meg if she'd been able to speak to Jeff Prentice. Sure enough, Meg answered as if the recent outburst had never happened.

"Of course I talked to Jeff. He practically fell all over me when I flagged him down." She lowered her voice. "Much to Mandy's dismay, I might add."

Meg couldn't resist implying that even though Jeff was supposedly dating Mandy, he was eager for the opportunity to flirt with her at the wake.

She went on, "I didn't ask him point blank about Carter Power. I had to warm him up a bit. The small talk annoyed Mandy enough that she walked off, leaving us alone." Meg smiled, pleased with herself. "When she left, I had my opening." She paused for dramatic effect.

I appreciate a good story as much as anyone, but we were getting close to our condo and Doug needed to drop us off at the subway entrance so we could head into work. Meg needed a nudge. "Did Jeff tell you anything we didn't know already?"

Meg looked annoyed by my question. She pursed her lips and scowled. "Aren't you impatient today? I was getting to it."

I put my hands up in protest. "I apologize. Please continue." Doug looked straight ahead at the road, most likely thankful he was responsible for driving and therefore could steer clear of Meg's mercurial temperament, which reared its ugly head occasionally.

"Your hunch about a connection between Carter Power, Regan, and Jessop was right," Meg said. "We already knew Regan was Carter Power's strongest supporter, since thousands of jobs in California are at stake if the contract isn't renewed. But when Regan determined that Senator Langsford might end up voting to end Carter Power's sweetheart deal with the military, he needed a back-up plan to put pressure on our boss."

She took a deep breath before finishing her story. "He decided to approach Representative Jessop, knowing full well Jessop resented Senator Langsford after losing to him. Regan thought if he could convince Jessop to support Carter Power publicly, it would make Senator Langsford's position seem foolish. It would also give Jessop a reason to attack Langsford in the media. Jessop wanted to run against Senator Langsford again in a rematch, and Langsford's failure to support securing necessary supplies for the military could have provided material for a perfect campaign ad two years down the road." Meg sat back in her seat with a self-satisfied expression.

I turned around to face Meg as Doug pulled close to the Metro station. I was half-astonished Meg had managed to procure that much information from Jeff Prentice in such a delicate environment. Given the several instances in which Meg had proven resourceful during the past week, I shouldn't have been so surprised. "And Jeff offered you all these revelations?"

Meg shrugged. "It wasn't hard to get Jeff to divulge. We're barking up the same tree as Detective O'Halloran. Apparently, he asked Jeff similar questions yesterday. Once Jeff told the police the background on the connections, he didn't feel as though there was much to hide."

So Detective O'Halloran and I were running down parallel paths, focusing on a similar group of suspects with comparable motives. This news was both gratifying and disappointing. On the one hand, we were likely on the right track. On the other hand, none of us had cracked the case. Despite fishing in the same pond, we weren't closer to reeling in the big catch.

Doug put the car into park, interrupting my thoughts. He turned to us. "Have a great afternoon at work!" That was our cue to get out of the car so he could return to his peaceful communion with his history books and Clarence. After I gave him a quick kiss, we headed to the subway entrance.

Meg and I chatted the entire ride to Union Station about what we had learned and our list of suspects. We might have reached a dead end. Our best leads had been investigated, and each suspect had an airtight alibi. Maybe the killer didn't know Senator Langsford at all. Could it have been a murder for hire? Although that didn't explain why my memo to the senator had ended up in the recycling bin. Had that been a mere coincidence, unrelated to the crime? Also, wouldn't a contract killer come with his own murder weapon of choice? I didn't think too many professional killers actually improvised at the crime scene.

By the time we made our way to the office, it was already mid-afternoon. I doubted too much would get accomplished today. I flipped on my computer and saw that, even today, Mandy had issued a video blog. It had to be one of her last. She was moving to Senator Regan's office next week, according to the gossip. I minimized her face as soon as it appeared on my screen, wondering who in the office, if anyone, still bothered to listen to her stupid blogs.

I answered what emails I could and returned phone calls to constituents who needed help or assistance. I had nothing left to do for the remainder of the day, but I couldn't go home because of the 7 p.m. vigil for Langsford in the Capitol. Staffers in our office were expected to show up, and I wanted to attend. Senator Langsford had his enemies, but for the most part, he'd been well respected by his colleagues. The tributes tonight would be poignant.

Since considerable time remained between now and then, I had a perfect opportunity to start packing my belongings. The small size of my cubicle hadn't prevented me from accumulating quite a bit of stuff over the years. Photos of memorable events were thumb-tacked to the walls surrounding my computer and desk. As I looked one last time at my haphazard handiwork, I realized it could serve as a chronicle of the past four years.

It took several hours to sort through official papers and other belongings. Many of these records would be boxed and archived, which was required federal procedure. I carefully placed my files into neat stacks on the shelf of my workplace. Whenever the last day in the office came, presumably right after the governor appointed a new senator, I didn't want to spend my final hours combing through paperwork. I had also kept some of the smaller mementos lobbyists or representatives from various associations gave out. Ethics rules prohibited gifts of any significant value, but that didn't stop the distribution of inexpensive items, like buttons, miniature stuffed animals, pens, and pins. As I packed the paraphernalia into a box, I examined each item and tried to remember who gave it to me and what program or issue they had asked the senator to support.

I looked at my watch. The vigil was scheduled to start in about thirty minutes. Meg sent me an Instant Message on my computer: "Want to head over in 5?" My cubicle was now efficiently organized in "garbage" and "archive" and "take home" piles. The only task left was dismantling my photo wall. If I was really going to accept the reality about moving on, I needed to take down my photos, too. It would be a lot easier to leave on the last day if these reminders had already been removed.

I wrote back to Meg, "Go ahead without me. Cleaning up. C U there." She sent me a smiley face icon. I shut down my computer and decided to finish up with the photos.

Just like the trinkets, each of the photographs I had hung on my cubicle walls captured a particular memory. Senator Langsford had admired my photos when he came back to talk to me at my desk. A few times he'd asked the identity of specific people in the photos, and I had told him about family members and friends from college. Although I'll never know whether he genuinely enjoyed my stories or was simply feigning interest, he always listened politely and offered kind remarks.

I started to remove photos from a section on the wall displaying pictures from various Senate office functions. There were several shots from previous parties at the Langsford home, including an older photo from the senator's swearing-in party after he won reelection four years ago. It was a great shot of Meg, Doug, and me, decked out in party attire and drinking champagne. I thought about the wake and immediately felt depressed about the contrast. Even though champagne had been served, there had been no celebratory photos.

After removing the snapshots, I shuffled through them quickly. When I came to the picture of the Halloween party the office had thrown last year, I stopped. I had glanced at this photo a few days ago. Meg and I grinned at the camera. I had painted whiskers on my cheeks and put on cute cat ears to create a makeshift costume. Meg had dusted off an old witch costume she'd found at home and was clasping a small broom in her right hand. In the background corner, I noticed someone else who had been captured in the photo. I squinted to make out the image, since it was slightly out of focus. In one instant, everything clicked.

The person in the corner of the photo was Mandy Lippman, and she was sporting a long, blond wig.

TWENTY-FOUR

THE OFFICE WAS perfectly quiet. I got up from my cubicle and looked around. No one was here. I checked my watch. The vigil was scheduled to begin in fifteen minutes. Everyone had already left for the Capitol.

The gears in my mind started to crank. Didn't Mandy have an alibi for the morning of the senator's death? She'd claimed to be busy posting the video blog from home, which she did every morning right around the time the senator had been murdered. Mandy always complained she had to get up early to film her blog on her home computer, then upload it so it would be available for staff by the time they arrived at the office. After reading the morning news and notices, she summarized the major headlines and outlined the senator's schedule for the day.

In an instant, it hit me what had been bothering me. I sat at my desk, powered up my computer, navigated to our office's internal home page, and brought up the website with Mandy's video blogs. She was so enamored of her damn videos, she kept links to the last ten entries readily available. I found the one she had issued on Tuesday morning and clicked to watch it.

Something wasn't right about this blog, and it had been nagging at me. Until I saw the photo of the Halloween party, I hadn't been able to put my finger on what it was. Mandy's face appeared on the screen, and she gave a brief summary of the news. Typical for a Tuesday video, she talked about the legislative docket for the week issued by the Majority Leader. She then spoke about the senator's schedule for the day. I listened to her description of his appointments. In a flash, I knew what was wrong. She said the senator was scheduled to attend an Appropriations hearing later that day at three in the afternoon, but the committee had emailed a notice late on Monday night announcing a postponement. On my way to work the morning of the murder, I had read the notice on my BlackBerry and was relieved because I wasn't fully prepared for the hearing. If Mandy had filmed the video blog on Tuesday morning as she claimed, she would have never missed the postponed hearing. In fact, she relished last-minute cancellations, frequently using those time slots to schedule a cable TV interview for the senator. I stared at the video. Mandy had missed this change because she hadn't filmed the video blog that morning. She had filmed it earlier, probably the day before, because she was planning to come to work early and kill Senator Langsford!

Along with the photo of Mandy wearing the blond wig, the blog mistake was enough to cast a heavy dose of suspicion on her. The other pieces of the puzzle fit nicely as well. Mandy would have known about the model helicopter, and if Carter Power really was the motive, Mandy would have known she had to ditch my memo so it wouldn't become evidence after his body was discovered. I didn't know the exact tie between Mandy and Carter Power yet, but given the fact she had landed a new job with Senator Regan and was sleeping with Jeff Prentice, there had to be a connection that made sense. The threatening voice on the phone had been well disguised, but the rhythm of her menacing words was similar to that of her normal voice.

I took a deep breath. I needed to get over to the vigil, but first I had a call to make. I fished around in my purse for Detective O'Halloran's business card and punched his number into my phone. No luck; voicemail picked up. I was pretty sure O'Halloran carried either a BlackBerry or an iPhone like the rest of Capitol Hill. I fired off a quick text: "Figured out my funny feeling. Need to talk to you ASAP." Then I sent the same message as an email, just in case. Maybe O'Halloran was attending the vigil. After all, he had come to the wake. Either he would get my text or my email or I'd see him at the Capitol.

I took the elevator outside our office down to the basement, where I hopped onto the Senate subway. It was a short three-minute ride in the small underground "people-mover" that carried passengers from the Hart and Dirksen Senate office buildings to the Capitol. Senators benefited from the mini-monorail system during floor votes; many of them waited until the last possible second to leave their offices for the Senate chamber in the Capitol. Staff and escorted visitors could also use the subway—a quasi-tourist attraction in the summer. With the final Senate votes of the day long recorded, the underground tunnel was deserted. I got off at the Capitol stop and headed up the escalators toward the elevator bank for the room where the vigil was being held. As I got onto the elevator, I checked my Black-Berry. No message from Detective O'Halloran.

I snuck quietly into the Mansfield Room on the second floor of the Capitol right as the service was starting. Located in the East Front of the Capitol, Mansfield was a wooden paneled, stately chamber, used chiefly for receptions. It was packed with attendees, and after surveying the scene, I spotted Meg in a corner. I squeezed past several people so I could stand next to her. The Senate chaplain had just begun to say a prayer as I sidled up beside Meg.

I whispered, "I think I figured out who killed Senator Langsford." I looked at her apprehensively.

She stared back at me with a baffled look and hissed, "What? I can't hear anything you're saying." Several people behind us were talking in hushed tones, most likely discussing business while paying their respects. Multitasking had no limits in Washington. Between their conversations, the chaplain's prayer, and the poor acoustics, it was impossible for Meg to understand my whisper.

I cleared my throat and said in a slightly louder voice, "I figured out who the murderer is." Meg shook her head at me and cupped her hand to her right ear. The dull buzz of conversations acted like a sound barrier.

I raised my voice a third time, using a decibel level I thought unwise, given the information I was relaying. "I know who did it."

That caught Meg's attention. She turned toward me with a shocked expression. After looking around to see if anyone had noticed us, she asked, "Are you going to just stand there, or are you going to tell me who?"

I leaned in close to her and whispered Mandy's name into her ear. Immediately, a grin broke out on Meg's face, and she covered her mouth in obvious surprise. She murmured, "Why didn't we suspect her all along?"

My BlackBerry was blinking. Detective O'Halloran had texted me back. I clicked on his message, which

read, "Headed to Senate now. Meet U at ur office?" I
thought for a second. That wasn't a bad idea. I could
give him the photo of Mandy at the Halloween party,
which might raise enough suspicion for him to get a
search warrant and look for the wig to see if it was a
match to the hair found in Langsford's office. I could
also show him the video blog and explain why Mandy's omission that morning was credible circumstantial
evidence her alibi was bogus. I texted back, "Leaving
Capitol now. C U in 10."

I leaned toward Meg. "I have to go. Detective
O'Halloran is going to meet me at the office in ten minutes. I'll explain everything to you after I talk to him."

She nodded in agreement. "Good luck!" She gave
me a half hug and squeezed my arm, then added, "You
did it, Kit!"

I smiled and took off quickly. I didn't have any
time to waste. It was already 7:30, and talking with
O'Halloran before I headed back to Arlington meant it
was going to be a late night. I texted Doug to let him
know I wouldn't be home soon. "Have lead. Need to
talk to police." I hated to be so vague, but I didn't have
time for a detailed phone call.

Retracing my steps, I walked out of the Capitol elevator and down the escalator to the subway platform. After
the Senate adjourned for the day, the subway cars oper-
ated less frequently. I thought about the calorie-laden
food I had eaten earlier, in addition to the two mimosas. There had been no time for exercise this morning.
Walking back to the Hart Senate Office Building rather
than riding the subway would burn off some of those
goodies. I glanced at my watch. If I hustled, I could be
there in ten minutes.

I started down the concrete walkway that ran adjacent to the subway path tunnel. After taking several long strides, I heard footsteps behind me.

I peeked over my right shoulder. About twenty feet away, I saw Mandy Lippman. She was headed straight toward me with a silver object in her right hand.

TWENTY-FIVE

ONE GLIMPSE OF Mandy confirmed the crazed glare in her eyes. I didn't wait for her to explain why she was barreling toward me at running-back speed. I took off down the pathway, sprinting as fast as I could. There was a fork ahead. A left turn would put me in the Russell Building. The right corridor led to the Dirksen and Hart. Instinctively, I veered toward my office in Hart.

I glanced behind me. Mandy was hard on my tail. These damn sandals were slowing me down. Hadn't Mandy worn stilettos today? How in the hell was she moving so fast? I kicked off my shoes and kept running in my bare feet. If I could make it to the entrance of the Dirksen Building, I might happen upon the Capitol Hill police officer usually stationed at the subway stop. I stared down the runway. It seemed like it went on forever, and Mandy was right behind me. The gleaming object in her hand was a pair of office scissors. Leave it to Mandy to improvise on a murder weapon. She'd obviously done it before.

I screamed "HELP" as loud as I could, but my shrieks went unanswered in this desolate strip of the underground Capitol. No subway car had passed me. I glanced at the wall, decorated with the seals of the fifty states. I had admired them many times in the past. The seals were arranged in ascending order, from the first state to enter the union, Delaware, to the last, Hawaii.

I glanced to my left as I sprinted past. West Virginia. I was getting closer to the subway stop. West Virginia had become a state during the Civil War.

I came into the final straightaway of the walkway, where I could see the entrance to the Dirksen Building ahead.

Mandy yelled, "I'm going to kill you, bitch! You can't get away from me!"

To my utter horror, the stand where Capitol Police typically resided was empty. Those budget cuts were going to be the death of me.

At the same instant, a subway car rounded the bend, headed back in the direction of the Capitol. I knew what I had to do. With perfect timing, I could jump into the subway car and ride back to the Capitol, where police officers were abundant. If I approached the car just as the door opened, maybe I'd have a chance to get out of this situation alive. My heart pounded in my chest. No wonder... There was a maniacal killer on my heels, and I'd been neglecting my cardio conditioning lately. I looked to my left. Wyoming. I had to be getting closer. Hadn't Wyoming been one of the first states to approve female suffrage? It was one of the few bits of information I recalled from my women's studies class.

It was all or nothing, and I summoned every ounce of physical strength left in my body to lengthen my stride so I'd arrive in time to jump into the subway train when the door opened. The car slowed to a stop about twenty feet ahead. I had only a few precious seconds before the doors would close automatically. With no driver on the Hart-Dirksen line, the subway cars ran automatically through a computerized control center.

To my relief, I saw Hawaii's seal over my left shoul-

der. I had made it to the end of the hallway and the subway doors were still open. With a final burst of speed,
I dove into the closest car. It was a beautiful acrobatic
move, except I wasn't as agile as I should have been. My
body cleared the threshold, but the lower part of my leg
and foot didn't quite make it. As the doors attempted
to close, they sensed my appendage in the way and
bounced open. I pulled my leg in, and in that moment,
Mandy appeared at the front of the car, brandishing a
pair of glimmering silver scissors, which I recognized
as the sharp oversized shears from the workstation next
to Kara's desk.

Mandy had taken advantage of the automated delay
in the subway train and hurled herself inside the car.
At exactly that moment, the doors closed shut with a
resounding thud. My grand plan had backfired. Instead
of riding safely back to the Capitol, I was now locked
inside a tiny, confined subway car with the woman who
had stabbed our boss to death days earlier.

As the car lurched forward, Mandy lost her footing.
While she tried to regain her balance, I scrambled to
my feet. The ride from Dirksen to the Capitol would be
over in less than a minute. All I had to do was dodge
her while we were moving; I could make a break for it
as soon as the doors opened at the Capitol.

I assumed a defensive posture and held my hands
out in front of my body. "Wait a second, Mandy. Don't
make another mistake. There's no way you're going to
get away with this."

She tossed her disheveled hair around in a circle.
Her present state was a far cry from the Little-Miss-
Perfect image I observed every day in the office. The
face she showed me now was simply that of a demented

murderer. Though normally attractive by conventional standards, Mandy the Murderer was downright ugly, her features contorted with violent rage.

Her whiny voice was now a menacing snarl. "Don't tell me what I can or can't get away with. I killed the dealmaker of the United States Senate this week, and the police have no idea it was me."

I kept backing away until I was in the corner, with nowhere else to go. "Slow down there, Mandy. I emailed Detective O'Halloran right before I came to the Capitol. He's expecting me any moment now at the office. When I don't arrive, he's going to put it together and come looking for me."

She took a swipe with the scissors, which came way too close to my arm. I dodged out of the way in the nick of time.

"Nice try, Kit. But O'Halloran thinks you're a fool. He'll conclude that you and your sidekick decided to blow him off for happy hour instead. He won't give a second thought to your disappearance tonight."

With that pronouncement, Mandy raised her arm high in the air and swung downward in an attempt to stab me in the chest. I ducked down low, and when she missed me and hit the subway seat cushion behind me, I seized my chance and barreled my head into her midsection. Mandy might have the strength of the insane, but I had the definite weight advantage here. For once, those pounds were put to good use. The sheer force of my body and the fact that I projected my head from a crouch was enough to knock Mandy all the way to the other end of the small car.

At that exact moment, the doors flung open at the Capitol stop. I hurled my body outside the car to escape and landed right at the feet of several Capitol Hill police officers, whose guns were pointed directly at Mandy Lippman. My attack had knocked her upside-down, and I was pleased to see her behind was in the air so that everyone could see her Spanx underwear. No wonder her butt was so perfect.

Without a second thought, I grabbed my BlackBerry out of my purse and took a picture. This time, it wasn't going to be my photo gracing the front pages of every newspaper in town.

TWENTY-SIX

MEG, KYLE, TREVOR, Detective O'Halloran, Matt, Doug, and I sat together in a circle. We had just enjoyed a splendid catered dinner at our condo, courtesy of a neighborhood establishment with the reputation for the best barbecue ribs, chicken, and baked beans in the Washington environs.

Clarence was curled up next to me, happy to be part of the evening's festivities and content with his canine portion of the feast.

Doug had just served after-dinner drinks, which included a selection of port, sherry, and cognac. He brought coffee for Detective O'Halloran, who insisted he must restrict his alcohol consumption due to important work assignments the next day. Meg sighed contentedly and put her hand on Kyle's knee. Evidently, things had gotten serious, or at least more serious than Meg's typical transitory affairs of the heart.

Several weeks had passed since Mandy had been apprehended. The whirlwind following a national media blitz focused on the full story of Senator Langsford's murder had recently subsided. Despite determined attempts to avoid the media, I had been thrust into the limelight, my face predictably appearing on every network, cable news, and newspaper across the country. The story had been analyzed in every possible way, and interest in it had diminished only a few days ago. Only then did Doug and I feel it was safe to invite those most closely involved to our condo for a dinner to celebrate the life and career of Senator Langsford, a man we all missed terribly. Our grief for Senator Langsford had intensified since we permanently closed the doors to his Senate office this past Friday. For the time being, the Langsford clan had joined the ranks of the unemployed.

As expected, the governor had appointed Representative Jessop to serve the remainder of the Senate term. Before relinquishing the Senate office to Jessop, Matt and I convinced Lucinda we should leak the memo I had written on Carter Power to the press. Lucinda didn't want to hurt Vivian, but decided it would be best in the long run to make Senator Langsford's last wishes public. With Senator Langsford's death hot on the media's mind, it was a breeze to get the major newspapers to run front-page stories on Carter Power and Langsford's final policy decision. For the time being, Jessop had no choice but to follow Senator Langsford's lead. Shortly after assuming office, he announced that he wouldn't support the immediate renewal of Carter Power's military contracts.

During dinner, we discussed the details of Senator Langsford's murder. When all the clues came together that night in the Senate office, I wasn't entirely certain about Mandy's motive, although I had a good hunch it was tied to Carter Power. Two pieces of circumstantial evidence pointed to Mandy's guilt, namely the Halloween wig and her error in the video blog. Of course, Mandy had left no doubt in anyone's mind of her culpability after she chased me down the corridors of the Senate subway. Apparently she'd been eavesdropping on my discussion with Meg at the senator's vigil.

It turned out Mandy was deeply interested in the outcome of the Carter Power decision. Months earlier, she had decided she wanted to leave Capitol Hill for greener pastures—that is, a job that paid the big bucks. With her sights set on lobbying and a generous salary on K Street, she started informal talks with Carter Power. Even though Carter Power wanted to hire her, they held back because of the uncertain future of the military contract. Mandy learned that Senator Langsford was leaning against a vote for Carter Power from Lucinda, who'd apparently told everyone with a pulse about Langsford's leanings. Armed with that information, Mandy tried to change the senator's mind, to no effect. My belief was that Senator Langsford thought Mandy was a smart press secretary but recognized her zealous defense of Carter Power as self-interested. Senator Langsford could see through smokescreens.

Somewhere along the way, Mandy took up with Jeff Prentice. He gave her more information about the inner workings of Carter Power and told her that if Langsford voted against Carter Power, the chances of landing her dream job were next to zero. Even if Carter Power ended up getting a renewal on the military contract, the company would never hire a staffer from a senator who had stabbed them in the back...in the proverbial sense. Mandy had started to panic. She wanted to leave Langsford's office to make more money, and her best job prospect seemed to be fading away. Jeff Prentice, who had tentatively accepted an offer to work in Senator Regan's office, was likewise under pressure. If Regan couldn't guarantee the contract renewal, his reelection prospects were slim to none, and Jeff would soon be out of a job as well.

Mandy turned to Vivian Langsford, who she learned owned investments in Carter Power. If she couldn't convince the senator about the error of his ways, perhaps she could persuade the rich wife who had bankrolled many of his successful campaigns for public office. Mandy did succeed in pleading her case to Vivian. In fact, Trevor had overheard Vivian talking on the phone with Mandy—not Lucinda, as we originally thought— about the Carter Power contract. Nonetheless, Vivian had no luck influencing Senator Langsford. Vivian's pleadings only convinced the senator further that Carter Power's long relationship with the government had become corrupt. He vowed to increase scrutiny on Carter Power's dealings and scolded Vivian for her selfishness. This blow-up had driven Vivian further into the arms of her hunky personal trainer, Henrik.

In the meantime, Mandy concluded that Senator Langsford would not listen to reason. In her twisted mind, the only remaining option was to silence him permanently. Mandy's window of opportunity was narrow. A United States Senator was rarely alone during the day. He was either in private meetings, raising campaign money, or discharging the official duties of the job. After cozying up to Kara, she discovered a small pocket of time on the senator's schedule in which he was alone. She decided to make her move then.

Knowing that security cameras covered every Senate office building entrance, she devised a disguise so she wouldn't be recognized on the video camera digital tapes, which the police would scrutinize after the murder. Mandy had done a decent job with her camouflage. Only after she was in custody did the police find her on the security footage, dressed as an overweight blond tourist in a Nike tracksuit. No one would ever suspect it was Mandy hidden under all that padding. Furthermore, she'd entered Hart the evening before the murder, guessing correctly the police would focus on the surveillance tapes from the morning of the murder rather than the previous day. She spent the night inside our office suite, waiting for Senator Langsford to arrive early for work on Tuesday so she could murder him.

Even though it was her video blog that eventually tripped her up, Mandy thought the blog would give her an ironclad alibi for the murder. She filmed it the day before, since there was no way she would have enough time to murder Senator Langsford and film the blog before showing up for work. After she killed Senator Langsford, using the sharp weapon of the helicopter model inside his office, she left the office suite through the upstairs "secret exit" and raced home to post the blog at the normal time so she would have an alibi for the murder. Mandy's careful escape explained why I hadn't seen her that morning. But she hadn't considered that the information she'd included in her blog the night before might now be incorrect.

Mandy had also managed to swipe my memo from Senator Langsford's desk in the midst of the confusion after his death. My early arrival at the office had thrown her for a loop. Minutes after I discovered the body, she "arrived" at the office, dressed in her regular work clothes. When she learned I had been inside the senator's office, she thought I might have been there to deliver my final memo concerning Carter Power and the upcoming hearing. Before Detective O'Halloran arrived, she surreptitiously removed the memo from the senator's desk and placed it in the recycling receptacle. Without written evidence, there would never be concrete proof Senator Langsford and his staff had wavered in support of Carter Power. That would pave the way for Mandy to secure her dream job and shore up Carter Power's long-term financial prospects.

When I started asking too many questions about Langsford's murder, Mandy became unnerved. She tried to throw me off the trail by making that intimidating phone call, hoping the threat would be enough to stymie our efforts to find the killer. That phone call had the opposite effect. Her threat indicated we were on the right track and strengthened my resolve to find the person responsible for Langsford's death.

There was still a big question left unanswered. Now that we were enjoying our after-dinner drinks, Meg and I wanted one last piece of information from Detective O'Halloran.

"Detective, Meg and I want to know about Jeff Prentice's involvement in Senator Langsford's murder. Did he help Mandy hatch her plan?" I sat back in our comfy loveseat and rubbed Clarence's neck, earning a soft growl of pleasure. Press accounts indicated Jeff had been brought in for police questioning several times, yet no charges had been filed officially against him. Meg and I believed Mandy needed help to pull the crime off, and Jeff likely provided key assistance. Mandy was conniving, but she wasn't the brightest bulb. Langsford's murder required the careful timing, strategic planning, and precise execution reminiscent of a military campaign. These facts implied Jeff had been involved. He'd also claimed Mandy as his alibi, which fell apart when she confessed.

Detective O'Halloran took a long sip of his coffee before saying, "I shouldn't be telling you this, but why the heck not? Without your help, we might still be trying to figure out who killed the senator. We're still determining what role Prentice played. Because Mandy almost made mincemeat of you that night on the Senate subway, we got her for attempted murder. It didn't take long before she sang like a canary about the senator's death. She contends Jeff Prentice came up with the whole idea and encouraged her to go through with it. According to Mandy, Jeff manipulated her and convinced her to kill Senator Langsford. Obviously, she wants to leverage a deal with the federal prosecutor. Jeff has an altogether different story. He contends that he had no involvement whatsoever in the murder, and he didn't know she was planning to kill Senator Langsford."

"So, it's her word against his?" Meg asked.

"For right now, that's the case. But we're investigating both stories. The truth is most likely somewhere in between. We're tracing emails, voice messages, Instant Messages, text messages, Facebook posts, tweets, or any other communication between the two of them to determine what Prentice knew. We have search warrants for their apartments, and if there's any physical evidence to tie them both to the murder, we'll find it."

I was happy to hear Detective O'Halloran and the rest of the police force were sparing no expense to determine whether Jeff Prentice had been an accomplice to murder. A shiver ran down my back as I recalled the evening Meg and I had spent with Jeff after the murder.

"If Jeff really did know Mandy killed Senator Langsford, it makes our happy hour with him even more remarkable, huh?" I chuckled uneasily.

"Quite frankly, Kit, it terrifies me that we spent

hours with a person who knew the killer or might have helped her."

Detective O'Halloran spoke up. "I need to leave soon since I have an early day tomorrow, but Meg's comment reminded me of something. I appreciate that both of you," he pointed at Meg and me, "cared so much about your former boss and wanted to find his killer. From now on, though, you need to stay out of police business. It's a dangerous game, and we can't always stop a mad-woman from stabbing someone in the dark recesses of the Senate basement. We were darn fortunate one of our officers was watching the live video feed and no-ticed the struggle."

Doug raised his glass and said, "Thank you for those words of wisdom, Detective O'Halloran. This has been an exciting few weeks, but I'm happy Kit's investigative days have come to an end. Let's toast to leaving police work to the police." Doug smiled broadly.

Meg and I both remained silent. Although neither of us wanted to admit it, we had both enjoyed our brief foray as sleuths. No need to ignite unnecessary tension between Doug and me by saying so.

I chose my words carefully. "I'd like to thank De-tective O'Halloran for his patience, and I'd like make a toast to never having another murder to investigate." Everyone heartily agreed, and we clinked our glasses. After all, even though we enjoyed sleuthing, we cer-tainly didn't want another person to die.

Detective O'Halloran gave Meg and me hearty bear hugs before leaving. Standing at our door, he said, "I know this might be impolite, but I hope we never have a reason to meet again." He saluted us with his two fin-gers and waved goodbye to the others.

Trevor cleared his throat. He'd been quiet this evening, yet it seemed as though he'd smiled more during the course of our dinner than the last four years combined. "To build on what Detective O'Halloran recently said, I want to thank our hosts for the evening." He offered a brief toast to Doug and me. "For the record, I know I was not the most sociable or friendly person to work with in Senator Langsford's office." Meg cleared her throat, and Matt Rocker rolled his eyes. Matt had received numerous complaints about Trevor's rudeness, which was how they'd interpreted his reticence.

Trevor went on, "Now I know I made a mistake during my time in the office. I should have accepted the occasional invitation for a happy hour." He looked pointedly at Meg, whose overtures he had rebuffed consistently. "I could have also been a more pleasant colleague in general." Trevor paused for a moment to take a sip of his drink. "However, that's all water under the bridge. Even though I wasn't Mister Congeniality, I did accomplish a great deal in my several years as a Senate employee. To this end, I'm happy to announce I've been named the new government relations liaison for Carter Power!"

Trevor looked at the crowd with a triumphant expression. Five blank faces stared back at him. For several seconds, no one said anything. Finally, Matt broke the silence. "I guess congratulations are in order, Trevor. I must say this announcement is quite shocking. I think I speak for all of us."

Meg looked at Trevor incredulously. "That's an understatement, Matt. Senator Langsford was murdered over a contract with Carter Power, and now you're going to work for them?"

Before giving Trevor a chance to reply, I said, "Did you take the job Mandy wanted?"

Trevor calmly looked at us and smoothed the crease on his pants before speaking. "I thought there might be some consternation over my decision to accept Carter Power's generous offer, so I decided to break my usual habit of declining invitations for evening events and accept Kit's offer for dinner to explain my decision to all of you. This might seem appalling, but you must consider the whole story. Yes, I'll be taking the job slated previously for Mandy, although I'll do a much better job than she. Furthermore, what better way to preserve Senator Langsford's legacy on defense appropriations matters," he motioned toward me since I covered that issue for the senator, "than to have one of his former aides working for Carter Power? I will ensure Senator Langsford's sacrifice isn't soon forgotten. I've already led preliminary discussions for Carter Power's eventual endowment of a generous scholarship fund at his alma mater in Boston. I have numerous ideas for how Carter Power can move forward as a successful company, even if they don't continue to receive the same level of government contracts as in the past. Lastly—and even though this is none of your business—Carter Power offered me a deal so lucrative, no rational person could refuse." He took another sip of his drink and sat back in his chair.

Trevor made a good case for Carter Power. He would do a better job than Mandy, and he would be in a powerful position to secure Senator Langsford's legacy through generous company donations. While it was unorthodox and altogether awkward for a former Langsford staffer to work for the company that indirectly caused our boss's demise, Trevor was well suited for the job. Before I could speak, Matt said, "Trevor, you've been a challenge to supervise. Yet your talent and work ethic are unparalleled. I wish you the best at Carter Power." He lifted his glass in an informal toast. Everyone followed suit.

The room was silent for a few moments. Meg cleared her throat. "I have an announcement concerning my future as well." Doug looked at me quizzically. I raised my eyebrows and silently shook my head.

Meg had told me she'd been aggressively searching for a new job ever since Senator Langsford's murder had been solved. Due to the flurry of media activity, we'd spent a considerable amount of time attempting to mollify Doug's father, who almost had a heart attack when he heard what had happened. All this craziness had prevented me from chatting with Meg about career possibilities.

I was also curious about why Meg had asked if Kyle could join the dinner party. Meg often blew hot or cold in the dating department. This was the "hot" phase. I wondered whether Meg had told Kyle the real reason behind our visit to Representative Jessop's office. I could only hope she'd kept her mouth shut.

Meg patted Kyle's knee before she started speaking. "You all know how much I enjoyed working in the Senate with everyone here." She gave a sideways glance in Trevor's direction, reminding us all—probably not intentionally—that other than Mandy, he'd been the exception. She continued, "For a while, I believed I would work in the Senate for the rest of my life. However, dealing with Senator Langsford's death and helping Kit solve the murder has given me a new perspective." She paused to take a sip of her sherry. "I always thought of working in the Senate as the highest calling for someone interested in solving the difficult political problems our nation faces. In the past several weeks, I've grown close to Kyle." She squeezed his arm for emphasis. "As many of you know, he'll be moving with his boss to the Senate and will be continuing as chief of staff. Kyle has given me more insight into how the other half of Congress works, and by that I mean the House of Representatives. I know those of us who worked in the Senate think of working in the House as a demotion. But Kyle has convinced me there's great work to be done in the House, since it's so much closer to the people we're paid to serve and help represent."

This was starting to sound a bit like *Mr. Smith Goes to Washington*. Everyone remained silent and let Meg continue her brief civics lesson. "I thought long and hard about what type of job I wanted to tackle next." She grinned at me. "Although I felt terrible about the senator's death, that week I spent investigating his murder with Kit was the most thrilling challenge I've tackled in a long time. When I reflected on it with Kyle, I decided I was a born investigator. Initially, I thought my career on Capitol Hill was over. But then Kyle had a great idea about how I could merge my passion for searching out the truth with continuing to serve Congress."

Now she definitely had everyone's attention. Was Meg planning to join the Capitol Hill police? I couldn't imagine her agreeing to wear a uniform to work each day. Would she be allowed to accessorize? How would she juggle a designer purse and a gun? Had O'Halloran pulled strings to get her a job?

Before I could ponder the answers to those questions,

Meg went on, "Kyle was nice enough to share many of his contacts on the other side of the aisle with me. Earlier today, I accepted a position as an investigator for the House Committee on Oversight and Government Reform. I start on Monday, and I can't wait to begin exposing corruption and holding all guilty parties accountable to the American taxpayer!"

She spoke the last sentence with so much zeal that we all smiled. Matt seemed particularly amused. Meg had always been a hardworking and productive member of the senator's staff; nevertheless, she had never expressed any interest in "exposing corruption" or holding "guilty parties accountable." Either solving the senator's murder had been a life-changing event for Meg, or Kyle had planted the investigative seed in her brain. Probably both. This was a monumental shift, even for her, although I admired her enthusiasm. She hadn't wasted any time getting back on the horse.

Thank goodness for Matt. He was always quick on his feet. As with Trevor, he took the lead. "This is tremendous news, Meg. The House of Representatives is lucky to have you as an employee." He narrowed his eyes. "Tell me, did your involvement in solving Senator Langsford's death help you land this job?"

It might have been an uncomfortable question, but Meg didn't treat it as such. She smiled broadly. "As a matter of fact, the staff director on the committee was extremely impressed. Most of my interview dealt with the steps we took to bring Mandy to justice. He loved hearing the details."

Matt nodded. I could tell he thought the whole thing was a bit farfetched and Meg might have profited from her ten minutes of fame. But Matt also wanted the staffers who worked for Senator Langsford to find good jobs. If Meg had landed a plum position, she was one fewer person he had to worry about. Yes, it was crazy a congressional committee would hire Meg because she had played a role in solving the murder of a senator. On the other hand, this was Washington, and the committee knew Meg's selection would make for a great press release and terrific headlines to follow.

"Meg," I said, "I know we haven't had a chance to catch up lately, so your announcement is news to me. I'm so happy for you, and I'm inspired to hear you've found a new calling. I'm also sad we won't be working together anymore. We've had great times, and I'll always cherish the experiences we've shared." Before I knew it, tears had welled up in my eyes. The wine was talking, but my words came straight from the heart.

Doug put his arm around me and gave me a squeeze as Kyle leaned forward in his seat. "What if you could still work with Meg?" My eyes brightened immediately at Kyle's question.

"I'd love that more than anything, but I have no contacts in the House of Representatives. It would be difficult for me to find a job there." I gave a small sigh.

"I have a lot of friends who work in the House, and I'm sure I could help you. Given your newfound fame, it might not be as hard as you think to find a suitable job there."

Matt said, "I know several chiefs of staff in the House, Kit. If that's where you want to work, I can serve as a strong reference."

Suddenly, the task of job hunting seemed much less daunting. "I'm lucky to have such great friends! Maybe it's time to work on the other side of the Capitol for a change."

Doug remarked, "It seems as though everyone is going to have new careers soon." He turned to Meg. "Your new job seems like a perfect way to satisfy your interest in investigating suspicious activity without putting yourself in harm's way."

"I don't know about that, Doug," I said. "Don't you ever follow congressional committee investigations? They can be downright deadly."

Meg grinned. "I'm counting on it."

I returned the smile. "Me, too."

* * * * *

ABOUT THE AUTHOR

COLLEEN J. SHOGAN is the deputy director of the Congressional Research Service (CRS) at the Library of Congress. She is a former Senate staffer who started reading mysteries at the age of six. A political scientist by training, Colleen has taught American government at George Mason University, Georgetown, and Penn. *Stabbing in the Senate* is her first novel.

Colleen is a native of Pittsburgh, Pennsylvania. She received her BA from Boston College and her doctorate from Yale. A member of Sisters in Crime, she lives in Arlington, Virginia, with her husband Rob Raffety and their rescue mutt, Conan.

For more information, please go to:
www.colleenshogan.com.

Get 4 FREE REWARDS!

We'll send you 2 FREE Books plus 2 FREE Mystery Gifts.

Harlequin® Intrigue books feature heroes and heroines that confront and survive danger while finding themselves irresistibly drawn to one another.

FREE Value Over **$20**

YES! Please send me 2 FREE Harlequin® Intrigue novels and my 2 FREE gifts (gifts are worth about $10 retail). After receiving them, if I don't wish to receive any more books, I can return the shipping statement marked "cancel." If I don't cancel, I will receive 6 brand-new novels every month and be billed just $4.99 each for the regular-print edition or $5.74 each for the larger-print edition in the U.S., or $5.74 each for the regular-print edition or $6.49 each for the larger-print edition in Canada. That's a savings of at least 12% off the cover price! It's quite a bargain! Shipping and handling is just 50¢ per book in the U.S. and 75¢ per book in Canada*. I understand that accepting the 2 free books and gifts places me under no obligation to buy anything. I can always return a shipment and cancel at any time. The free books and gifts are mine to keep no matter what I decide.

Choose one: ☐ **Harlequin® Intrigue**
Regular-Print
(182/382 HDN GMYW)

☐ **Harlequin® Intrigue**
Larger-Print
(199/399 HDN GMYW)

Name (please print)

Address   Apt. #

City   State/Province   Zip/Postal Code

Mail to the **Reader Service:**
IN U.S.A.: P.O. Box 1341, Buffalo, NY 14240-8531
IN CANADA: P.O. Box 603, Fort Erie, Ontario L2A 5X3

Want to try two free books from another series? Call 1-800-873-8635 or visit www.ReaderService.com.

Get 4 FREE REWARDS!

We'll send you 2 FREE Books plus 2 FREE Mystery Gifts.

FREE
Value Over
$20

Both the **Romance** and **Suspense** collections feature compelling novels written by many of today's best-selling authors.

Get 4 FREE REWARDS!

We'll send you 2 FREE Books plus 2 FREE Mystery Gifts.

Love Inspired® Suspense books feature Christian characters facing challenges to their faith... and lives.

FREE Value Over $20

LIS18

READERSERVICE.COM

Manage your account online!

- Review your order history
- Manage your payments
- Update your address

> **We've designed the Reader Service website just for you.**

Enjoy all the features!

- Discover new series available to you, and read excerpts from any series.
- Respond to mailings and special monthly offers.
- Browse the Bonus Bucks catalog and online-only exculsives.
- Share your feedback.

Visit us at:

ReaderService.com

RS16R